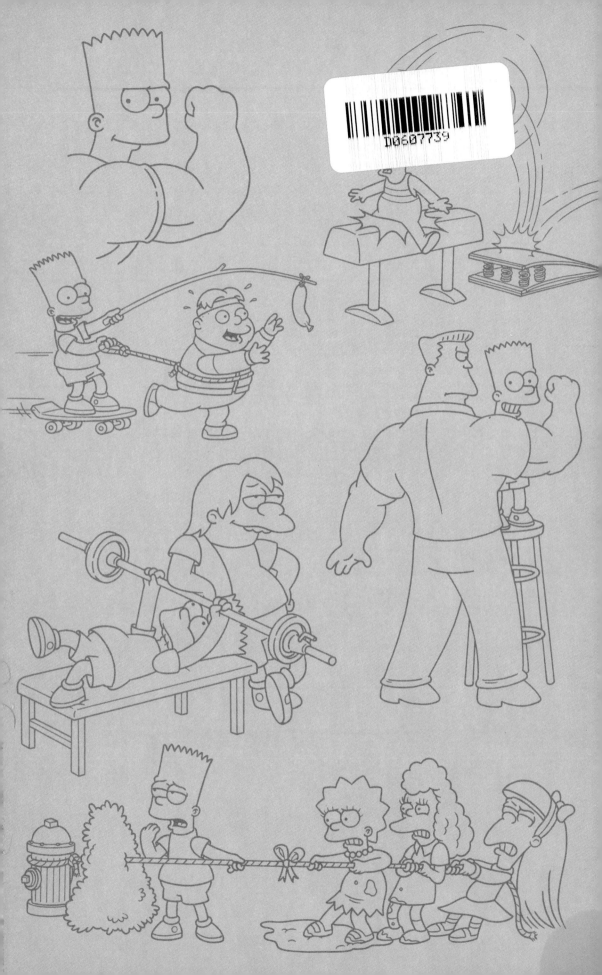

BIG BEEFY BOOK OF
BART SIMPSON

Perennial
Currents

An Imprint of HarperCollinsPublishers

BIG BEEFY BOOK OF BART SIMPSON

HarperCollins books may be purchased for educational, business, or sales
promotional use. For information please write
Special Markets Department,
HarperCollins Publishers Inc.,
10 East 53rd Street, New York, NY 10022.

FIRST EDITION

ISBN 0-06-074819-2

05 06 07 08 09 QWM 10 9 8 7 6 5 4 3 2 1

Publisher: MATT GROENING
Creative Director: BILL MORRISON
Managing Editor: TERRY DELEGEANE
Director of Operations: ROBERT ZAUGH
Art Director: NATHAN KANE
Art Director Special Projects: SERBAN CRISTESCU
Production Manager: CHRISTOPHER UNGAR
Legal Guardian: SUSAN A. GRODE

Trade Paperback Concepts and Design: SERBAN CRISTESCU

Contributing Artists:
KAREN BATES, JOHN COSTANZA, LUIS ESCOBAR, TIM HARKINS, JASON HO,
BRIAN ILES, NATHAN KANE, JAMES LLOYD, ISTVAN MAJOROS, JOEY MASON,
BILL MORRISON, KEVIN M. NEWMAN, JOEY NILGES, PHYLLIS NOVIN, PHIL ORTIZ,
PATRICK OWSLEY, RICK REESE, RYAN RIVETTE, MIKE ROTE,
HOWARD SHUM, CHRIS UNGAR, ART VILLANUEVA, MIKE WORLEY

Contributing Writers:
JAMES BATES, TERRY DELEGEANE, ABBY DENSON, TONY DIGEROLAMO,
GEORGE GLADIR, EVAN GORE, EARL KRESS, AMANDA McCANN,
JESSE LEON McCANN, MICHAEL NOBORI, DAVID RAZOWSKY,
JEFF ROSENTHAL, ERIC ROGERS, GAIL SIMONE, BRYAN UHLENBROCK,
SERAN WILLIAMS, CHRIS YAMBAR

PRINTED IN CANADA

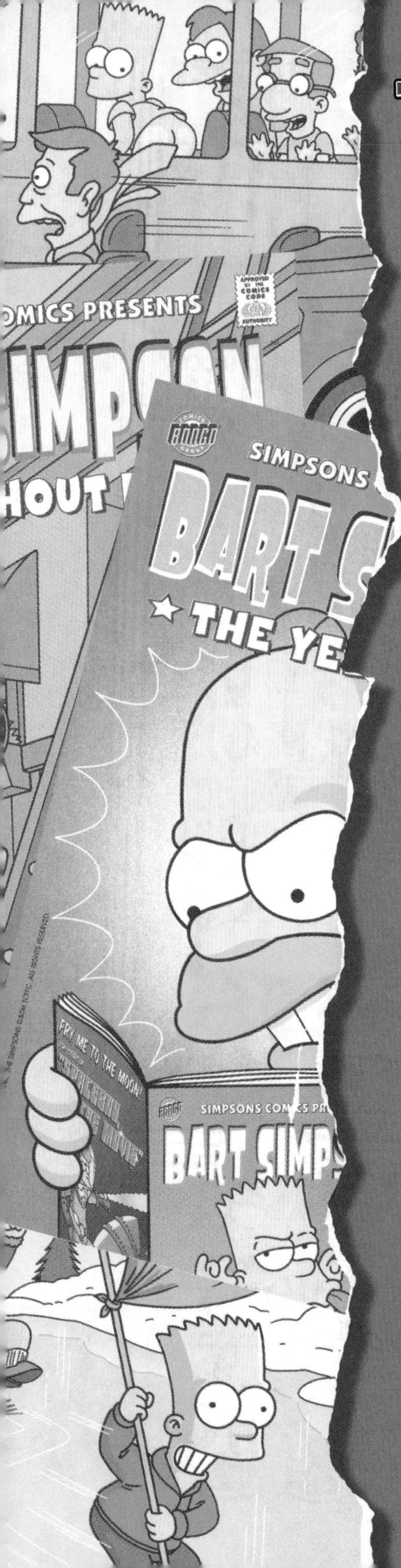
SIMPSONS
FRY ME TO THE MOON!

TABLE OF CONTENTS

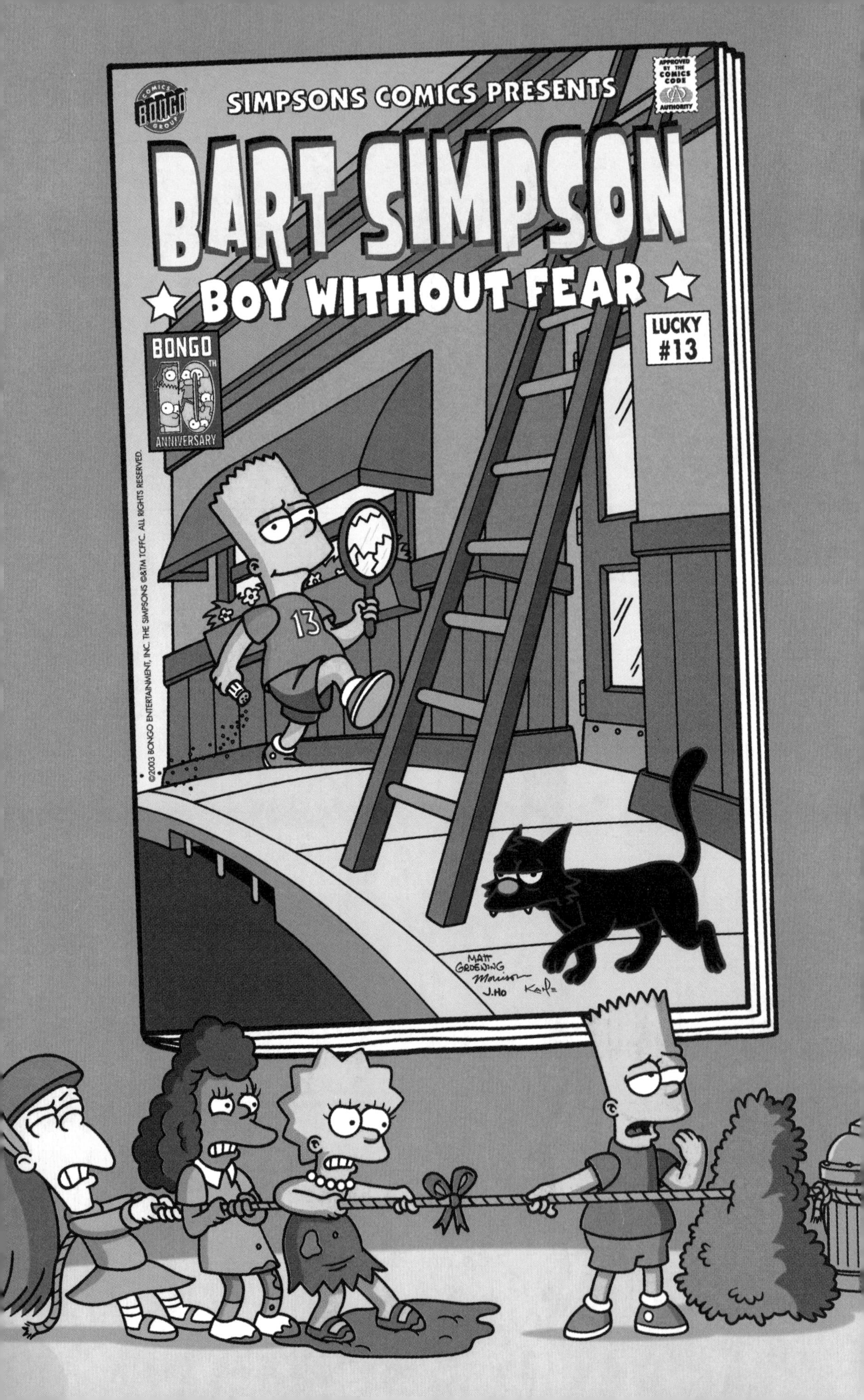

SIMPSONS COMICS PRESENTS
BART SIMPSON
BOY WITHOUT FEAR
LUCKY #13
APPROVED BY THE COMICS CODE AUTHORITY
BONGO 10TH ANNIVERSARY
©2003 BONGO ENTERTAINMENT, INC. THE SIMPSONS ©&TM TCFFC. ALL RIGHTS RESERVED.
13
MATT GROENING
J.HO

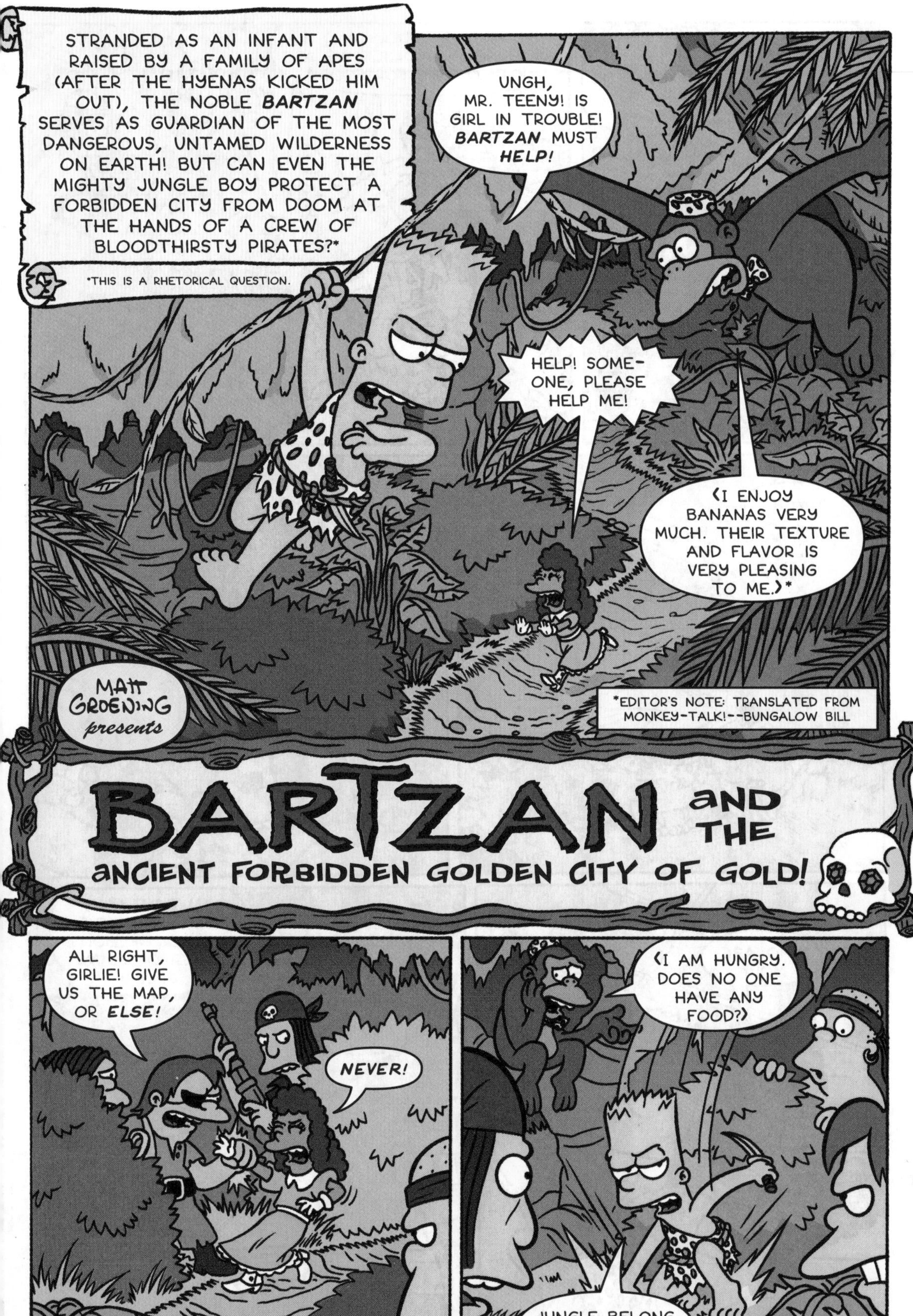
STRANDED AS AN INFANT AND RAISED BY A FAMILY OF APES (AFTER THE HYENAS KICKED HIM OUT), THE NOBLE BARTZAN SERVES AS GUARDIAN OF THE MOST DANGEROUS, UNTAMED WILDERNESS ON EARTH! BUT CAN EVEN THE MIGHTY JUNGLE BOY PROTECT A FORBIDDEN CITY FROM DOOM AT THE HANDS OF A CREW OF BLOODTHIRSTY PIRATES?*
*THIS IS A RHETORICAL QUESTION.
UNGH, MR. TEENY! IS GIRL IN TROUBLE! BARTZAN MUST HELP!
HELP! SOME-ONE, PLEASE HELP ME!
‹I ENJOY BANANAS VERY MUCH. THEIR TEXTURE AND FLAVOR IS VERY PLEASING TO ME.›*
*EDITOR'S NOTE: TRANSLATED FROM MONKEY-TALK!--BUNGALOW BILL
MATT GROENING presents
BARTZAN AND THE ANCIENT FORBIDDEN GOLDEN CITY OF GOLD!
ALL RIGHT, GIRLIE! GIVE US THE MAP, OR ELSE!
NEVER!
‹I AM HUNGRY. DOES NO ONE HAVE ANY FOOD?›
JUNGLE BELONG TO BARTZAN! LEAVE NOW!

GAIL SIMONE *SCRIPT* · **JASON HO** *PENCILS* · **HOWARD SHUM** *INKS* · **JOEY MASON** *COLORS* · **KAREN BATES** *LETTERS* · **BILL MORRISON** *EDITOR*

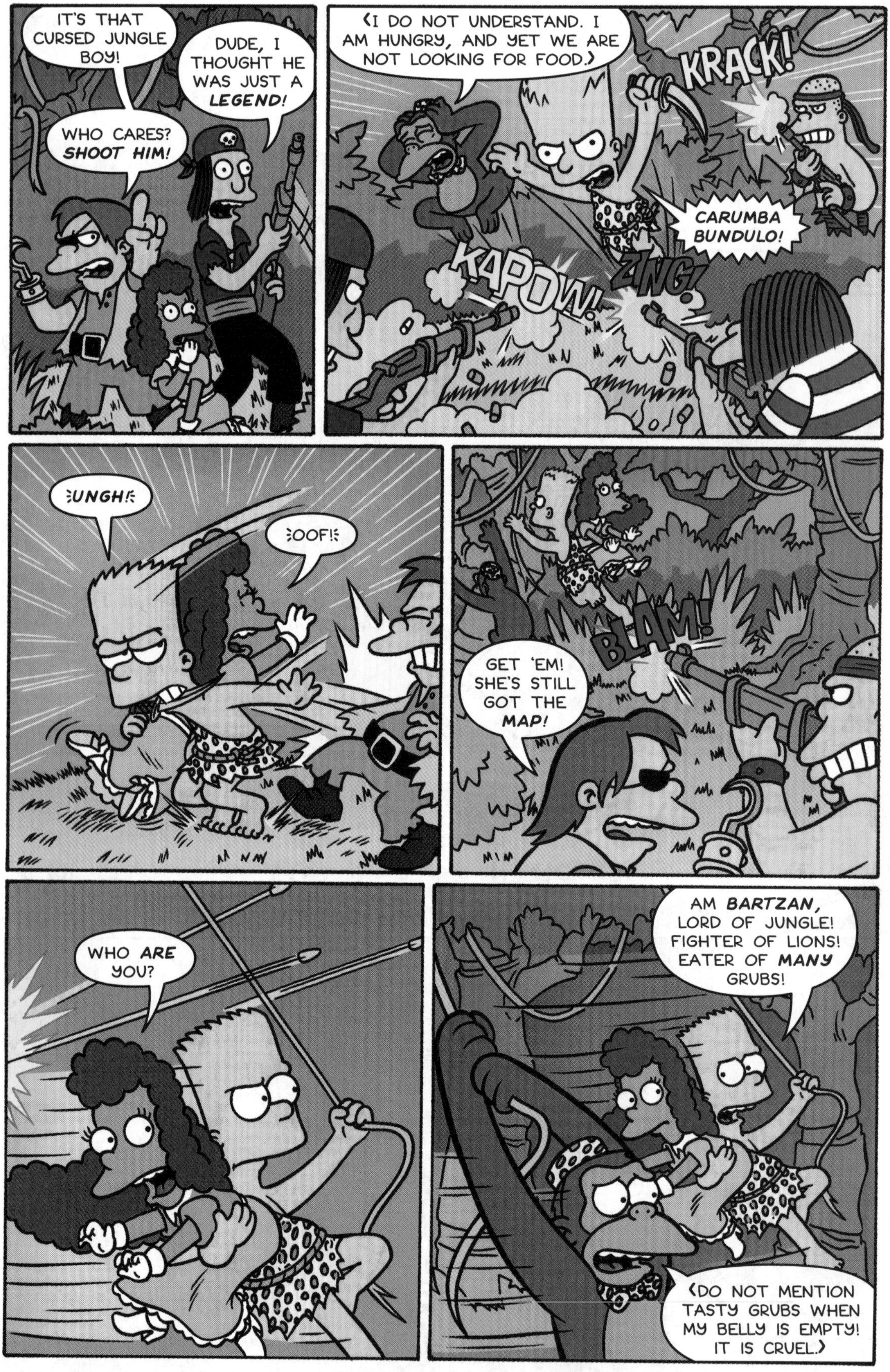
IT'S THAT CURSED JUNGLE BOY!
DUDE, I THOUGHT HE WAS JUST A LEGEND!
WHO CARES? SHOOT HIM!
‹I DO NOT UNDERSTAND. I AM HUNGRY, AND YET WE ARE NOT LOOKING FOR FOOD.›
KRACK!
CARUMBA BUNDULO!
KAPOW!
ZING!
UNGH!
OOF!
BLAM!
GET 'EM! SHE'S STILL GOT THE MAP!
WHO ARE YOU?
AM BARTZAN, LORD OF JUNGLE! FIGHTER OF LIONS! EATER OF MANY GRUBS!
‹DO NOT MENTION TASTY GRUBS WHEN MY BELLY IS EMPTY! IT IS CRUEL.›

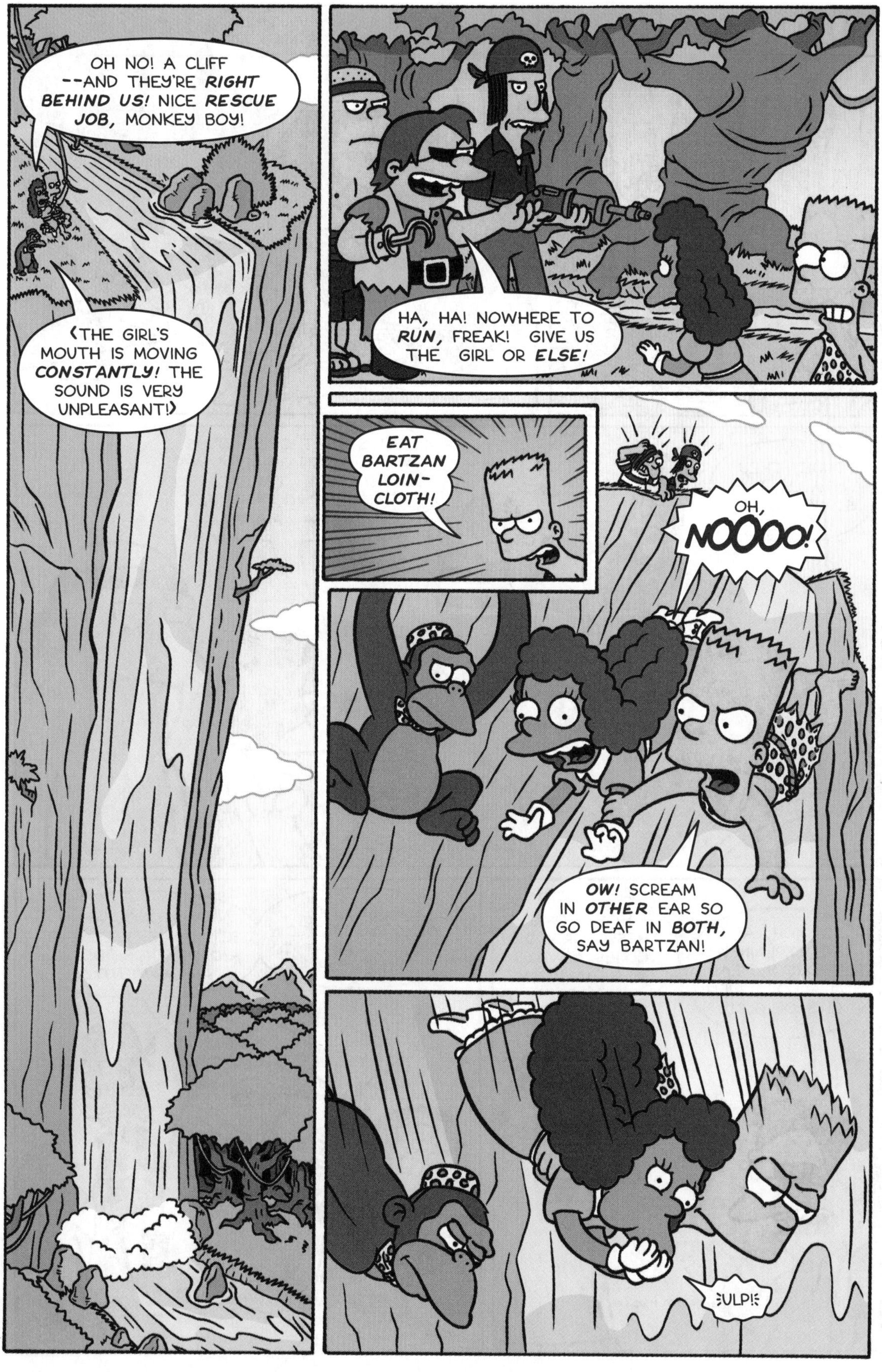
OH NO! A CLIFF --AND THEY'RE RIGHT BEHIND US! NICE RESCUE JOB, MONKEY BOY!
‹THE GIRL'S MOUTH IS MOVING CONSTANTLY! THE SOUND IS VERY UNPLEASANT!›
HA, HA! NOWHERE TO RUN, FREAK! GIVE US THE GIRL OR ELSE!
EAT BARTZAN LOIN-CLOTH!
OH, NOOOO!
OW! SCREAM IN OTHER EAR SO GO DEAF IN BOTH, SAY BARTZAN!
ULP!

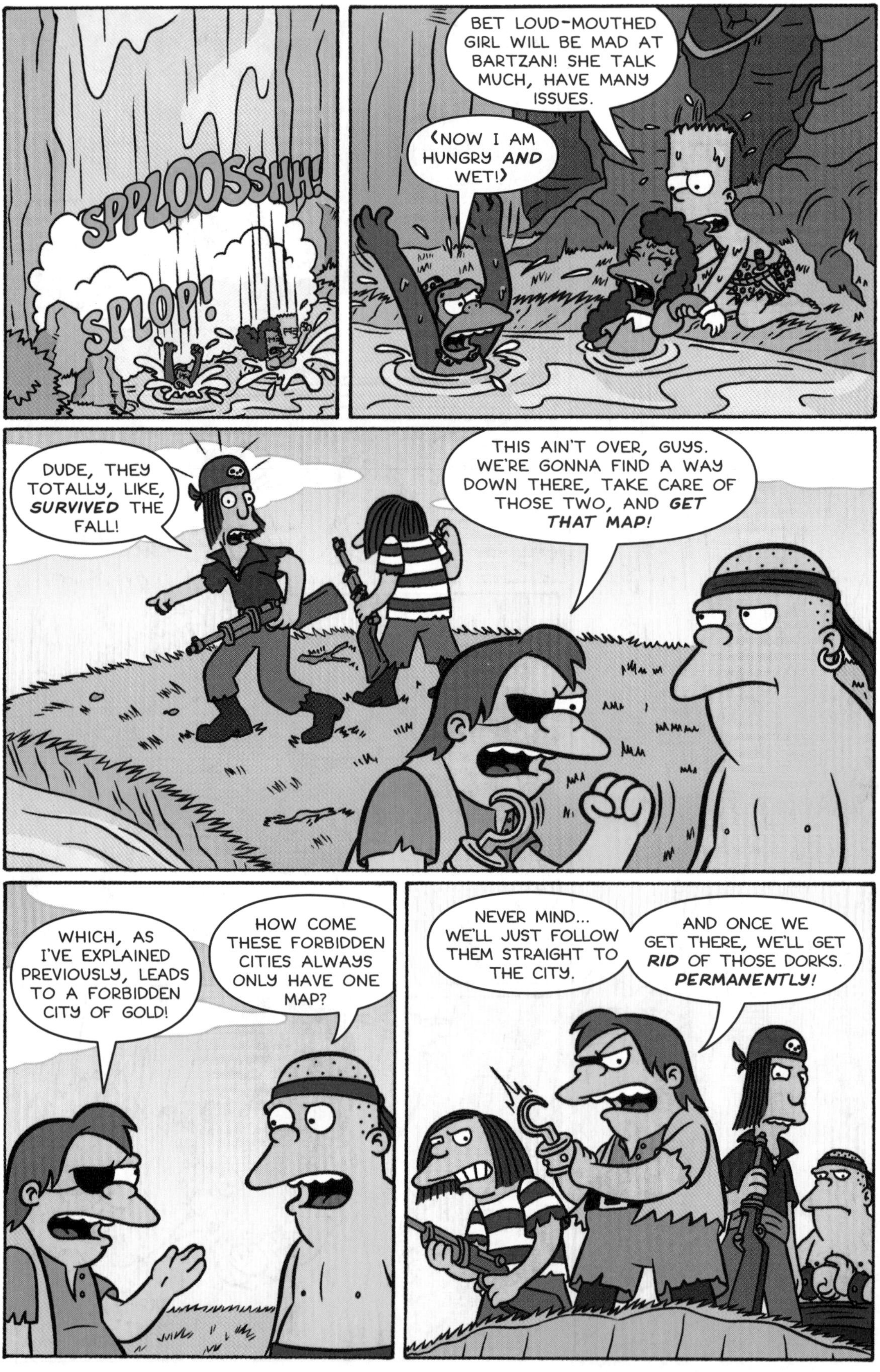
SPPLOOSSHH!
SPLOP!
BET LOUD-MOUTHED GIRL WILL BE MAD AT BARTZAN! SHE TALK MUCH, HAVE MANY ISSUES.
‹NOW I AM HUNGRY AND WET!›
DUDE, THEY TOTALLY, LIKE, SURVIVED THE FALL!
THIS AIN'T OVER, GUYS. WE'RE GONNA FIND A WAY DOWN THERE, TAKE CARE OF THOSE TWO, AND GET THAT MAP!
WHICH, AS I'VE EXPLAINED PREVIOUSLY, LEADS TO A FORBIDDEN CITY OF GOLD!
HOW COME THESE FORBIDDEN CITIES ALWAYS ONLY HAVE ONE MAP?
NEVER MIND... WE'LL JUST FOLLOW THEM STRAIGHT TO THE CITY.
AND ONCE WE GET THERE, WE'LL GET RID OF THOSE DORKS. PERMANENTLY!

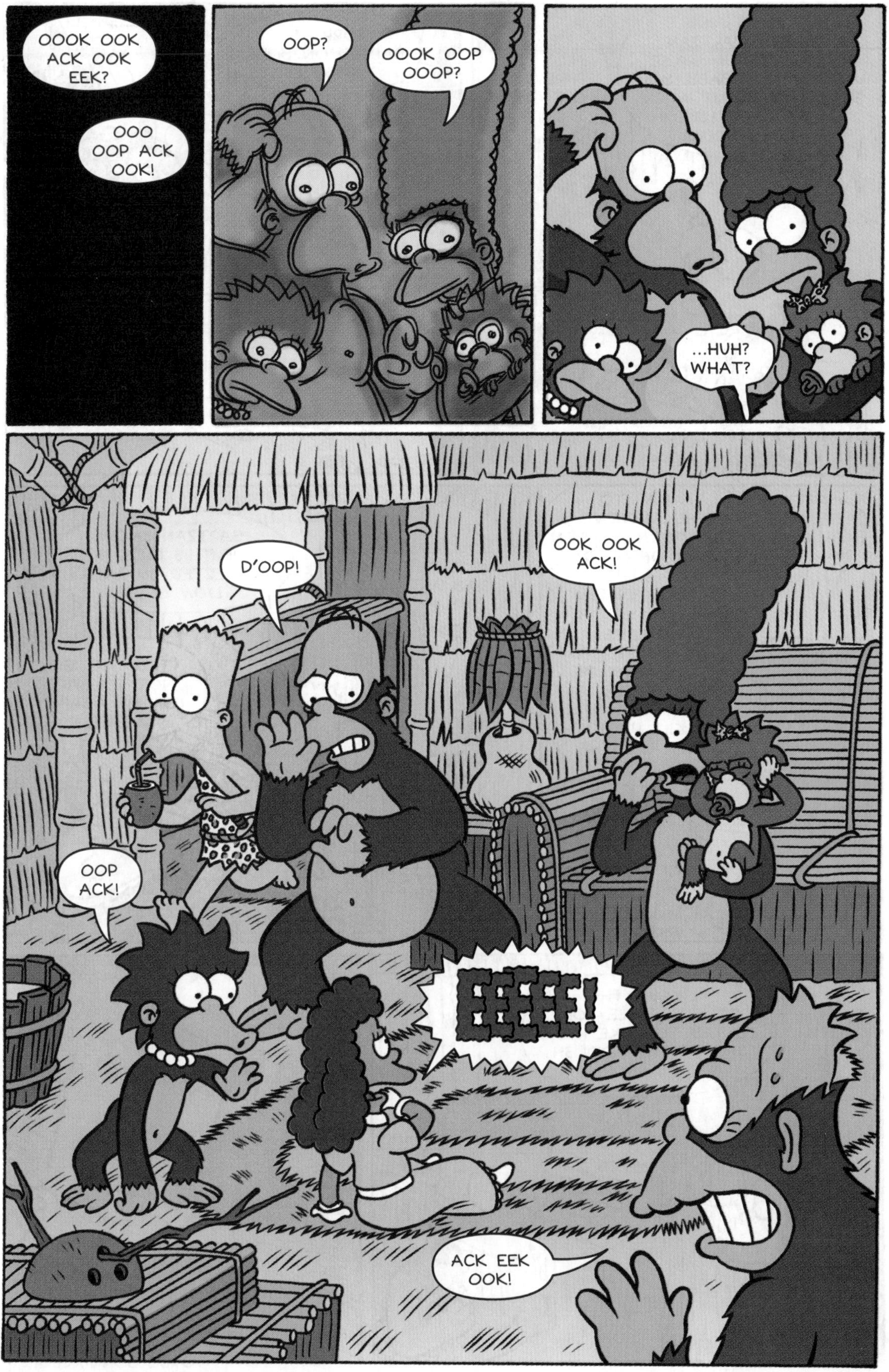
OOOK OOK ACK OOK EEK?
OOO OOP ACK OOK!
OOP?
OOOK OOP OOOP?
...HUH? WHAT?
D'OOP!
OOK OOK ACK!
OOP ACK!
EEEEE!
ACK EEK OOK!

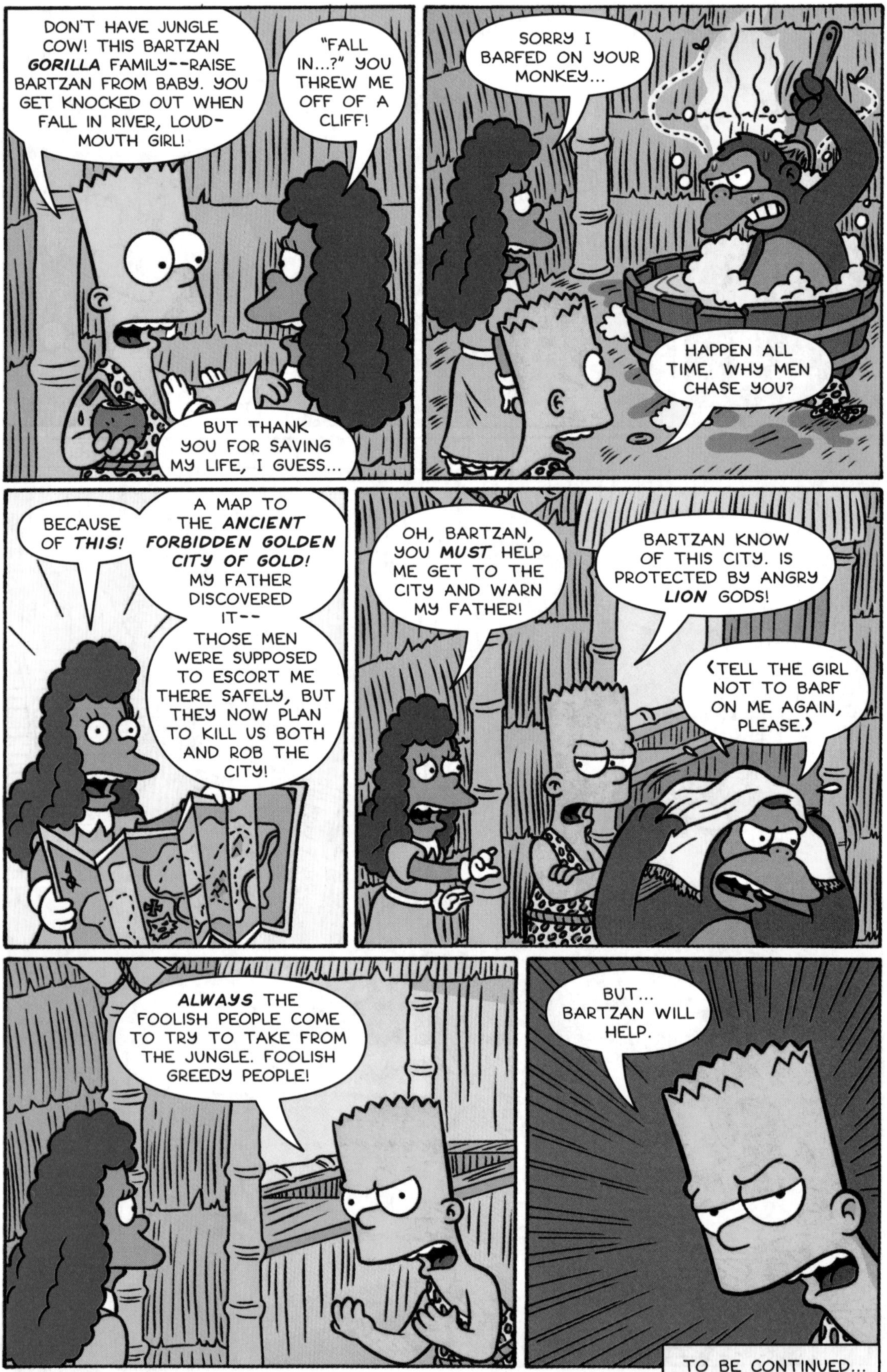
DON'T HAVE JUNGLE COW! THIS BARTZAN **GORILLA** FAMILY--RAISE BARTZAN FROM BABY. YOU GET KNOCKED OUT WHEN FALL IN RIVER, LOUD-MOUTH GIRL!
"FALL IN...?" YOU THREW ME OFF OF A CLIFF!
BUT THANK YOU FOR SAVING MY LIFE, I GUESS...
SORRY I BARFED ON YOUR MONKEY...
HAPPEN ALL TIME. WHY MEN CHASE YOU?
BECAUSE OF **THIS**!
A MAP TO THE ***ANCIENT FORBIDDEN GOLDEN CITY OF GOLD!*** MY FATHER DISCOVERED IT--
THOSE MEN WERE SUPPOSED TO ESCORT ME THERE SAFELY, BUT THEY NOW PLAN TO KILL US BOTH AND ROB THE CITY!
OH, BARTZAN, YOU ***MUST*** HELP ME GET TO THE CITY AND WARN MY FATHER!
BARTZAN KNOW OF THIS CITY. IS PROTECTED BY ANGRY ***LION*** GODS!
‹TELL THE GIRL NOT TO BARF ON ME AGAIN, PLEASE.›
ALWAYS THE FOOLISH PEOPLE COME TO TRY TO TAKE FROM THE JUNGLE. FOOLISH GREEDY PEOPLE!
BUT... BARTZAN WILL HELP.
TO BE CONTINUED...

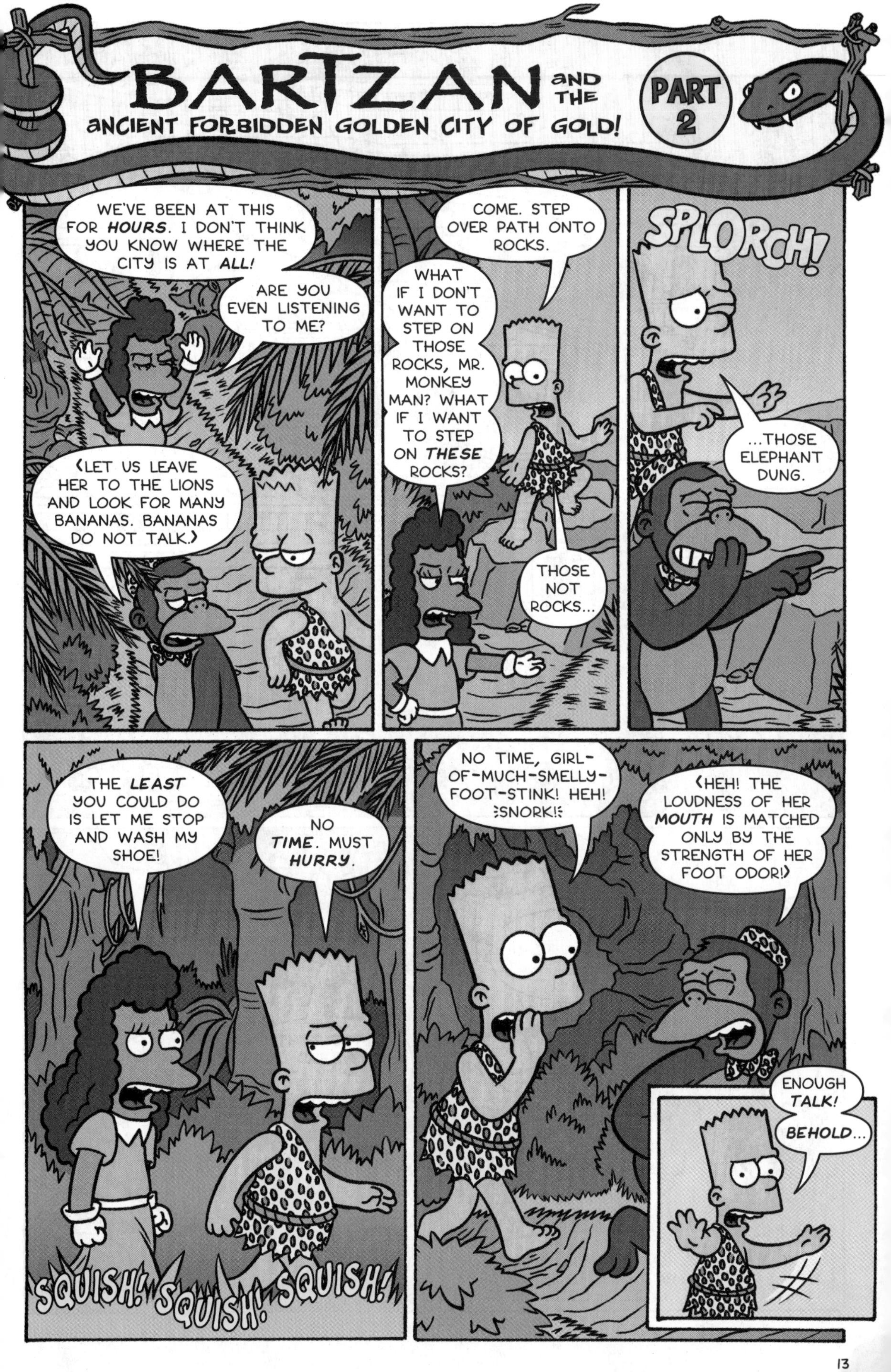
BARTZAN AND THE ANCIENT FORBIDDEN GOLDEN CITY OF GOLD!
PART 2
WE'VE BEEN AT THIS FOR HOURS. I DON'T THINK YOU KNOW WHERE THE CITY IS AT ALL!
ARE YOU EVEN LISTENING TO ME?
‹LET US LEAVE HER TO THE LIONS AND LOOK FOR MANY BANANAS. BANANAS DO NOT TALK.›
COME. STEP OVER PATH ONTO ROCKS.
WHAT IF I DON'T WANT TO STEP ON THOSE ROCKS, MR. MONKEY MAN? WHAT IF I WANT TO STEP ON THESE ROCKS?
THOSE NOT ROCKS...
SPLORCH!
...THOSE ELEPHANT DUNG.
THE LEAST YOU COULD DO IS LET ME STOP AND WASH MY SHOE!
NO TIME. MUST HURRY.
SQUISH! SQUISH! SQUISH!
NO TIME, GIRL-OF-MUCH-SMELLY-FOOT-STINK! HEH! SNORK!
‹HEH! THE LOUDNESS OF HER MOUTH IS MATCHED ONLY BY THE STRENGTH OF HER FOOT ODOR!›
ENOUGH TALK!
BEHOLD...

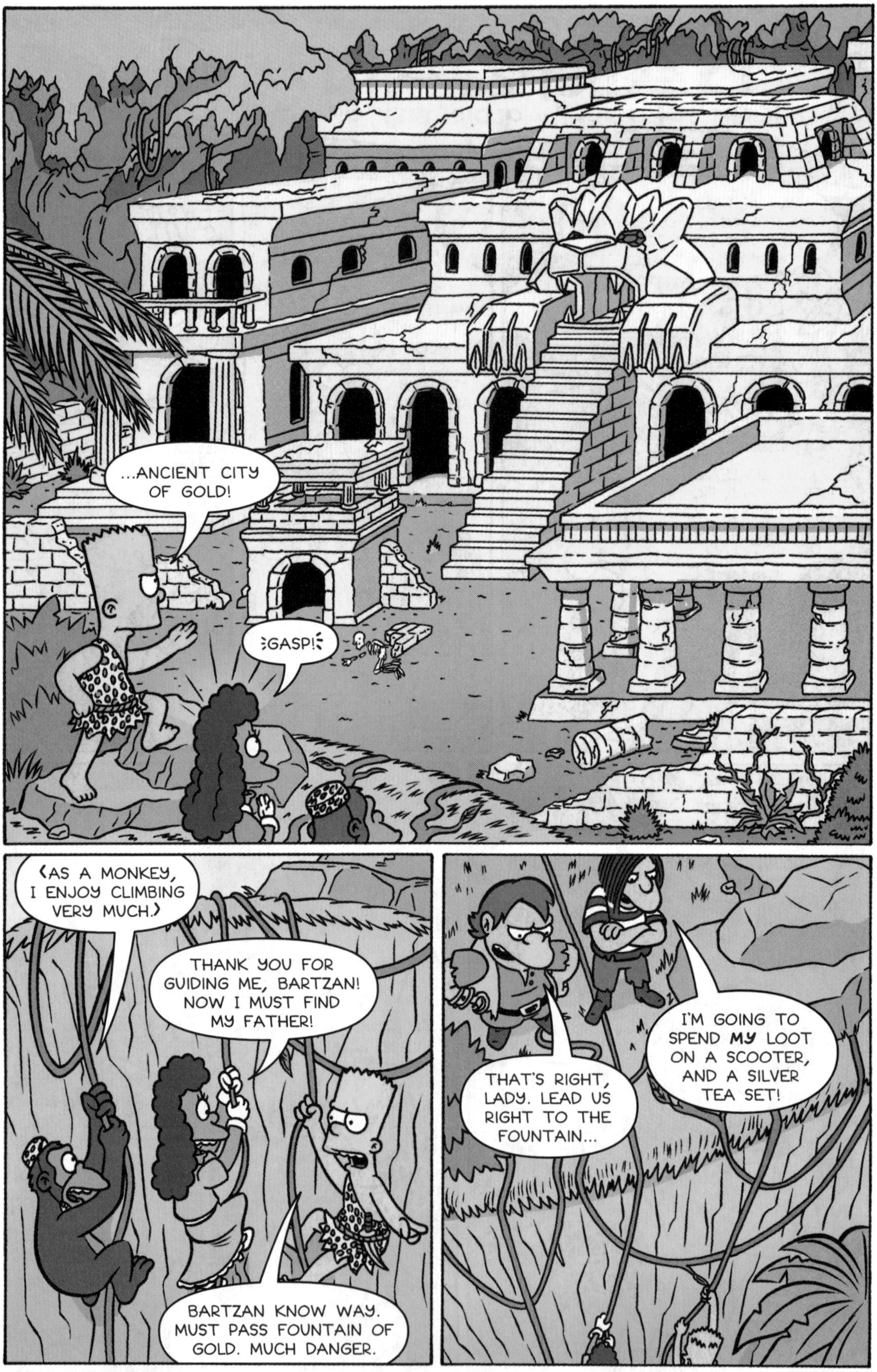

...ANCIENT CITY OF GOLD!
GASP!
‹AS A MONKEY, I ENJOY CLIMBING VERY MUCH.›
THANK YOU FOR GUIDING ME, BARTZAN! NOW I MUST FIND MY FATHER!
BARTZAN KNOW WAY. MUST PASS FOUNTAIN OF GOLD. MUCH DANGER.
THAT'S RIGHT, LADY. LEAD US RIGHT TO THE FOUNTAIN...
I'M GOING TO SPEND **MY** LOOT ON A SCOOTER, AND A SILVER TEA SET!

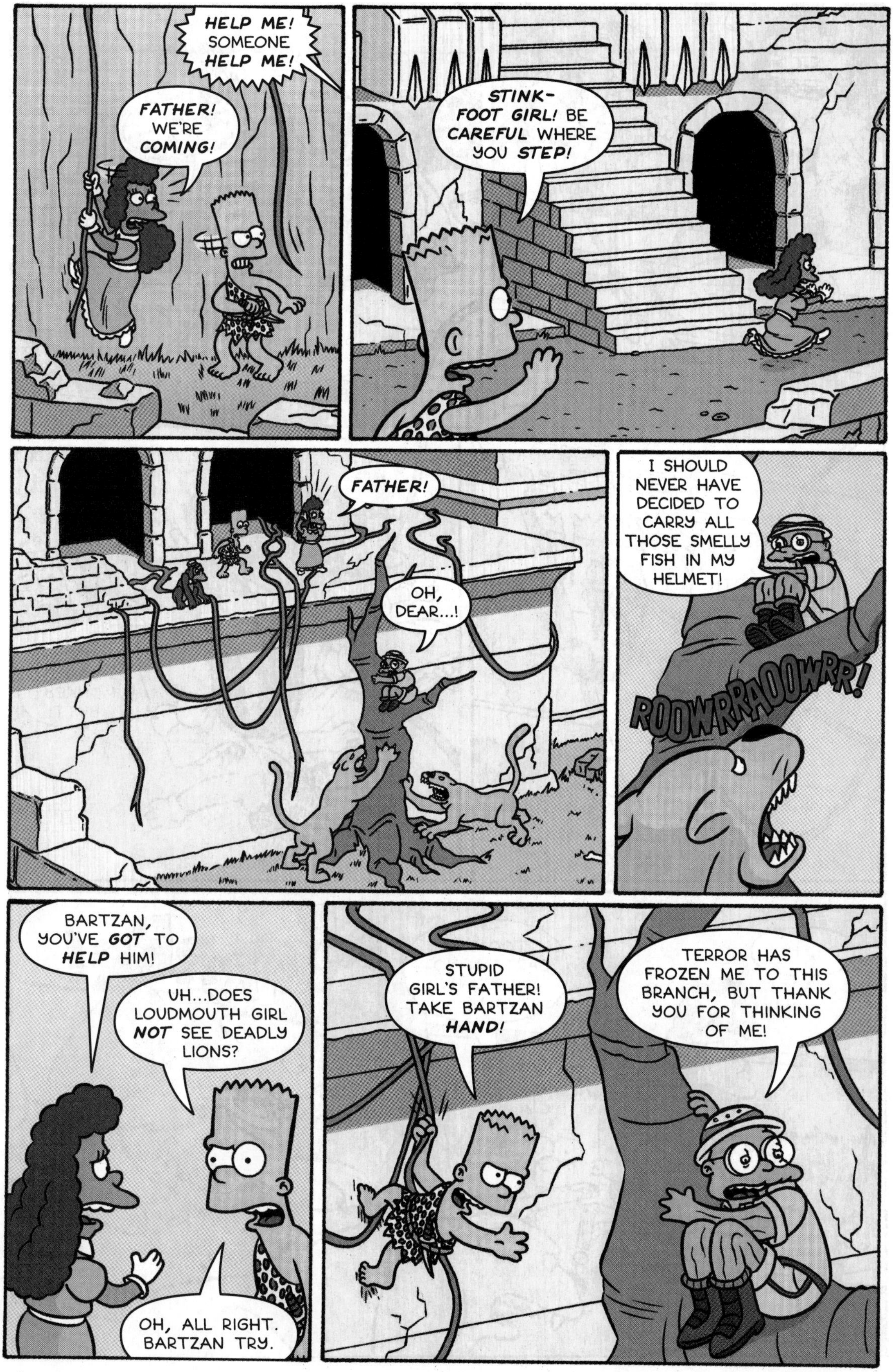
HELP ME! SOMEONE HELP ME!
FATHER! WE'RE COMING!
STINK-FOOT GIRL! BE CAREFUL WHERE YOU STEP!
FATHER!
OH, DEAR...!
I SHOULD NEVER HAVE DECIDED TO CARRY ALL THOSE SMELLY FISH IN MY HELMET!
ROOWRRAOOWRR!
BARTZAN, YOU'VE GOT TO HELP HIM!
UH...DOES LOUDMOUTH GIRL NOT SEE DEADLY LIONS?
OH, ALL RIGHT. BARTZAN TRY.
STUPID GIRL'S FATHER! TAKE BARTZAN HAND!
TERROR HAS FROZEN ME TO THIS BRANCH, BUT THANK YOU FOR THINKING OF ME!

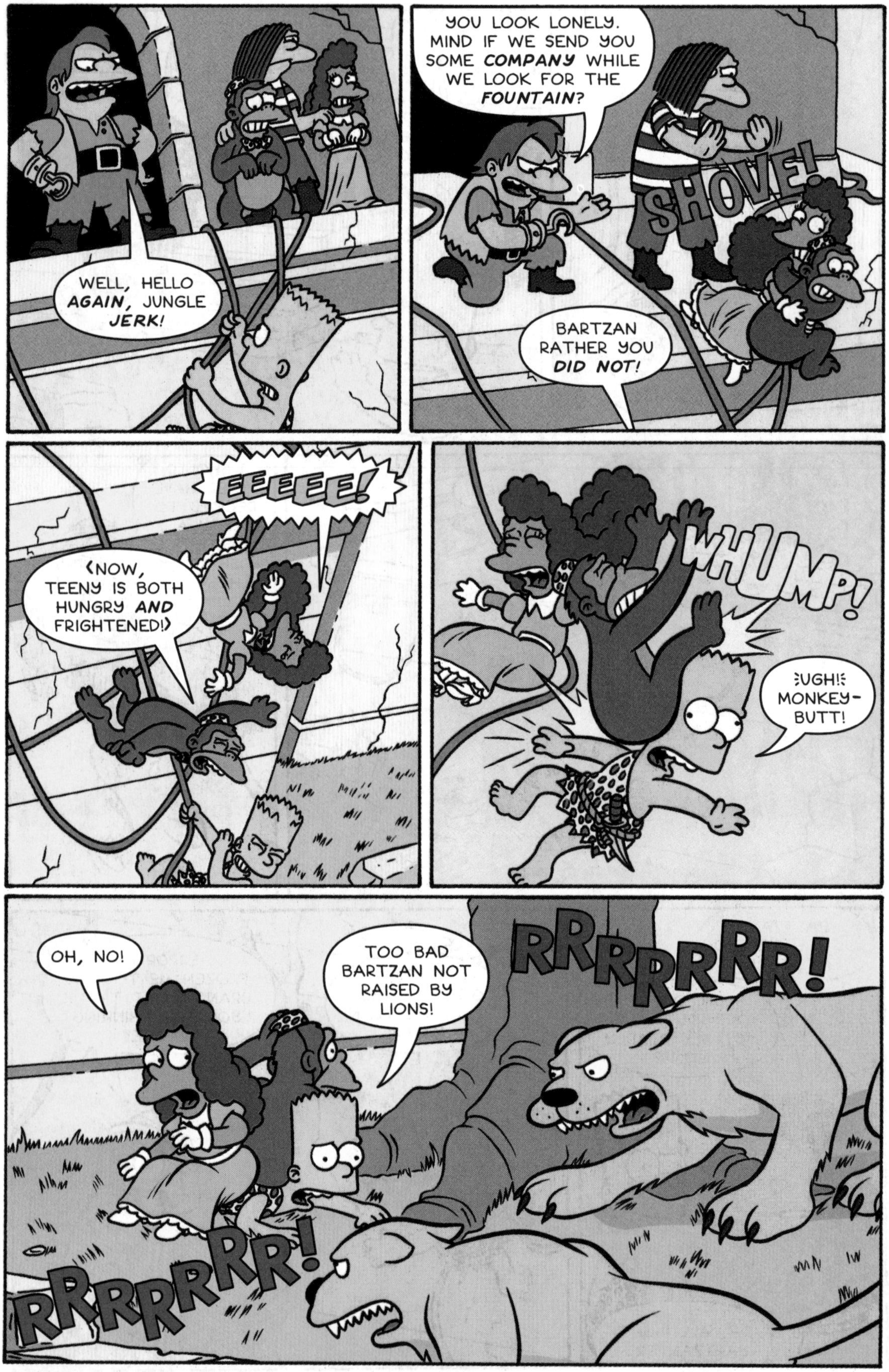
WELL, HELLO AGAIN, JUNGLE JERK!
YOU LOOK LONELY. MIND IF WE SEND YOU SOME COMPANY WHILE WE LOOK FOR THE FOUNTAIN?
SHOVE!
BARTZAN RATHER YOU DID NOT!
EEEEE!
‹NOW, TEENY IS BOTH HUNGRY AND FRIGHTENED!›
WHUMP!
UGH! MONKEY-BUTT!
OH, NO!
TOO BAD BARTZAN NOT RAISED BY LIONS!
RRRRRRRR!
RRRRRRRR!

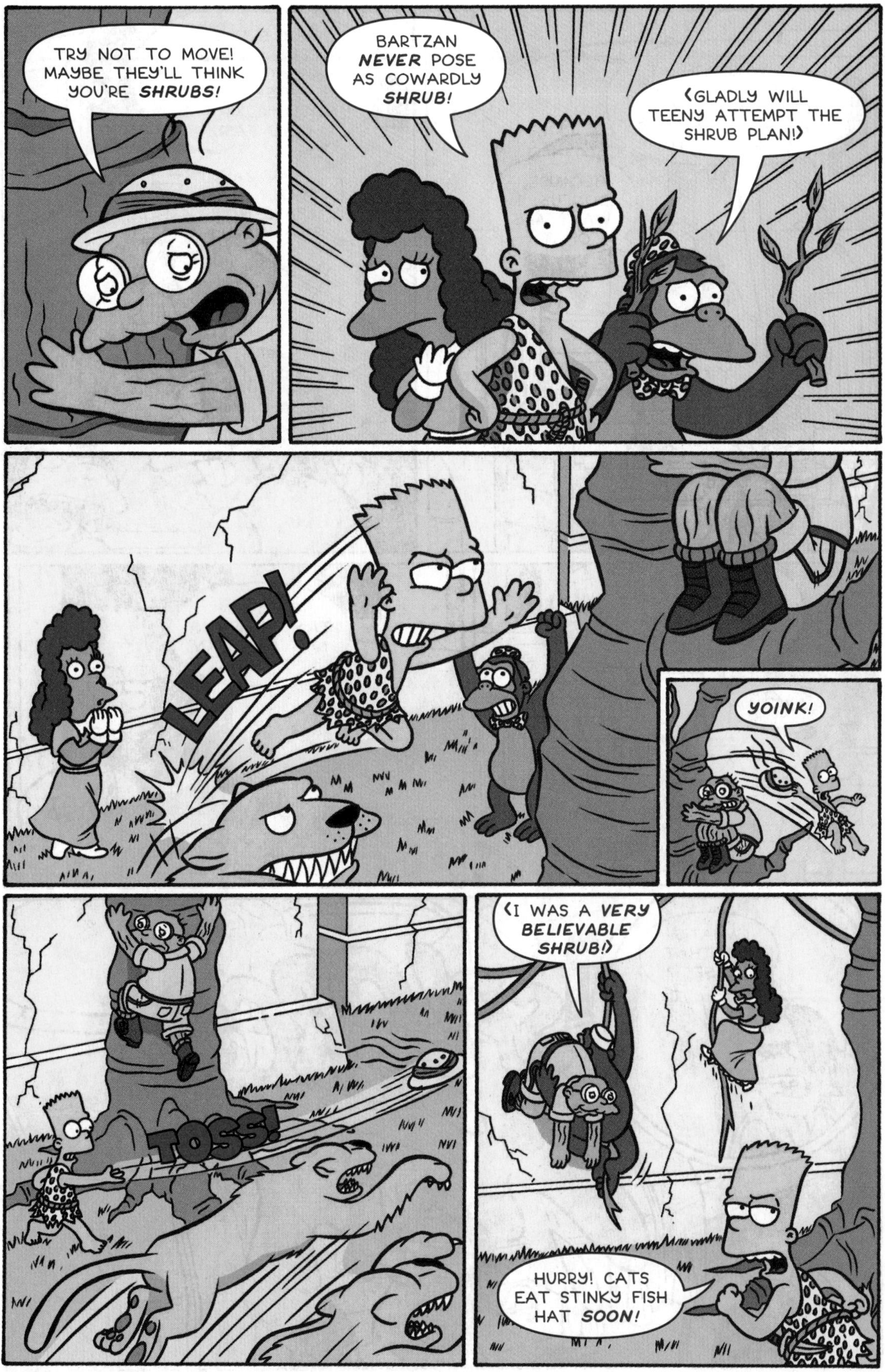
TRY NOT TO MOVE! MAYBE THEY'LL THINK YOU'RE *SHRUBS!*
BARTZAN *NEVER* POSE AS COWARDLY *SHRUB!*
‹GLADLY WILL TEENY ATTEMPT THE SHRUB PLAN!›
LEAP!
YOINK!
TOSS!
‹I WAS A *VERY BELIEVABLE SHRUB!*›
HURRY! CATS EAT STINKY FISH HAT *SOON!*

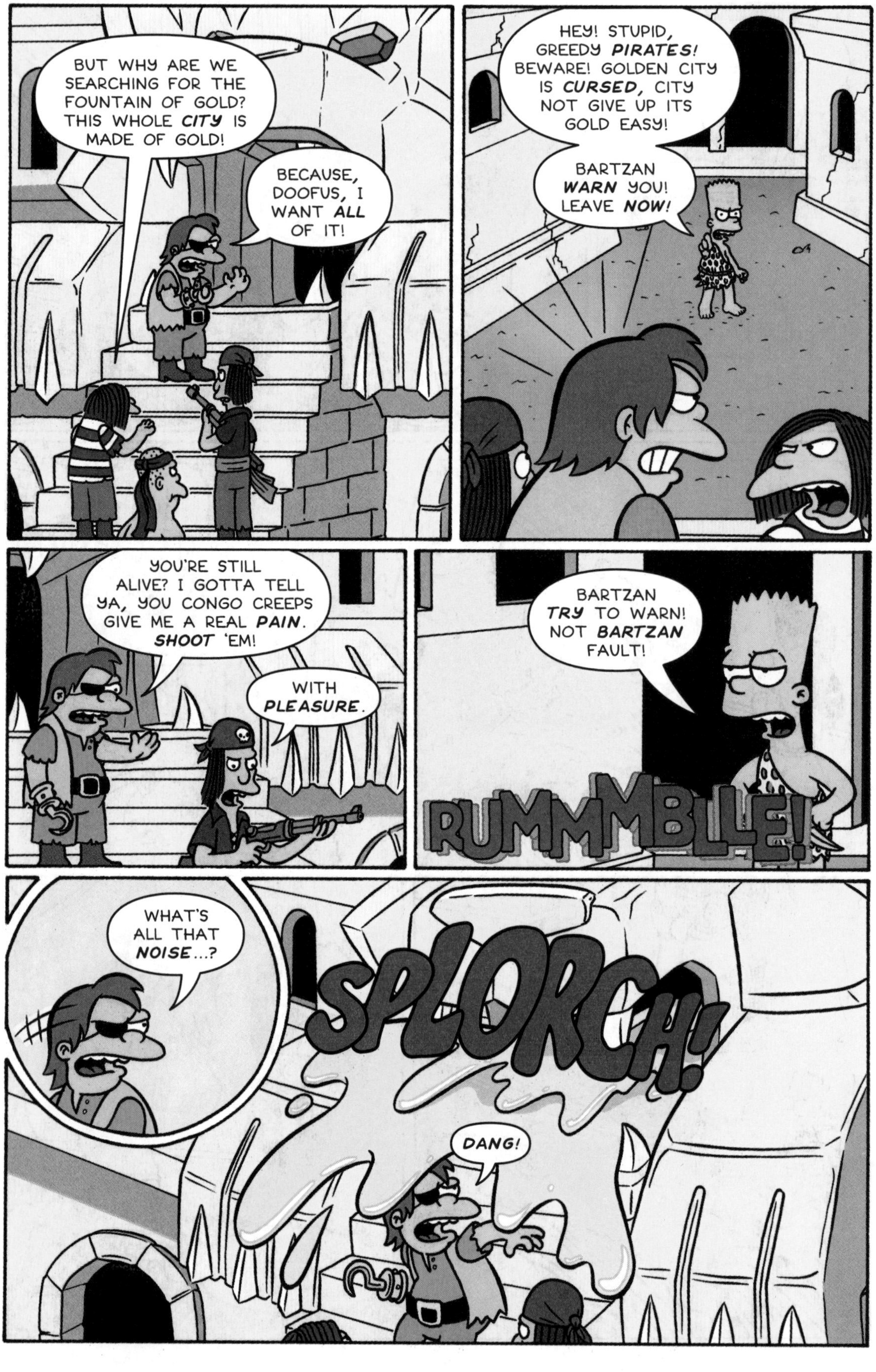
BUT WHY ARE WE SEARCHING FOR THE FOUNTAIN OF GOLD? THIS WHOLE CITY IS MADE OF GOLD!
BECAUSE, DOOFUS, I WANT ALL OF IT!
HEY! STUPID, GREEDY PIRATES! BEWARE! GOLDEN CITY IS CURSED, CITY NOT GIVE UP ITS GOLD EASY!
BARTZAN WARN YOU! LEAVE NOW!
YOU'RE STILL ALIVE? I GOTTA TELL YA, YOU CONGO CREEPS GIVE ME A REAL PAIN. SHOOT 'EM!
WITH PLEASURE.
BARTZAN TRY TO WARN! NOT BARTZAN FAULT!
RUMMMBLLE!
WHAT'S ALL THAT NOISE...?
SPLORCH!
DANG!

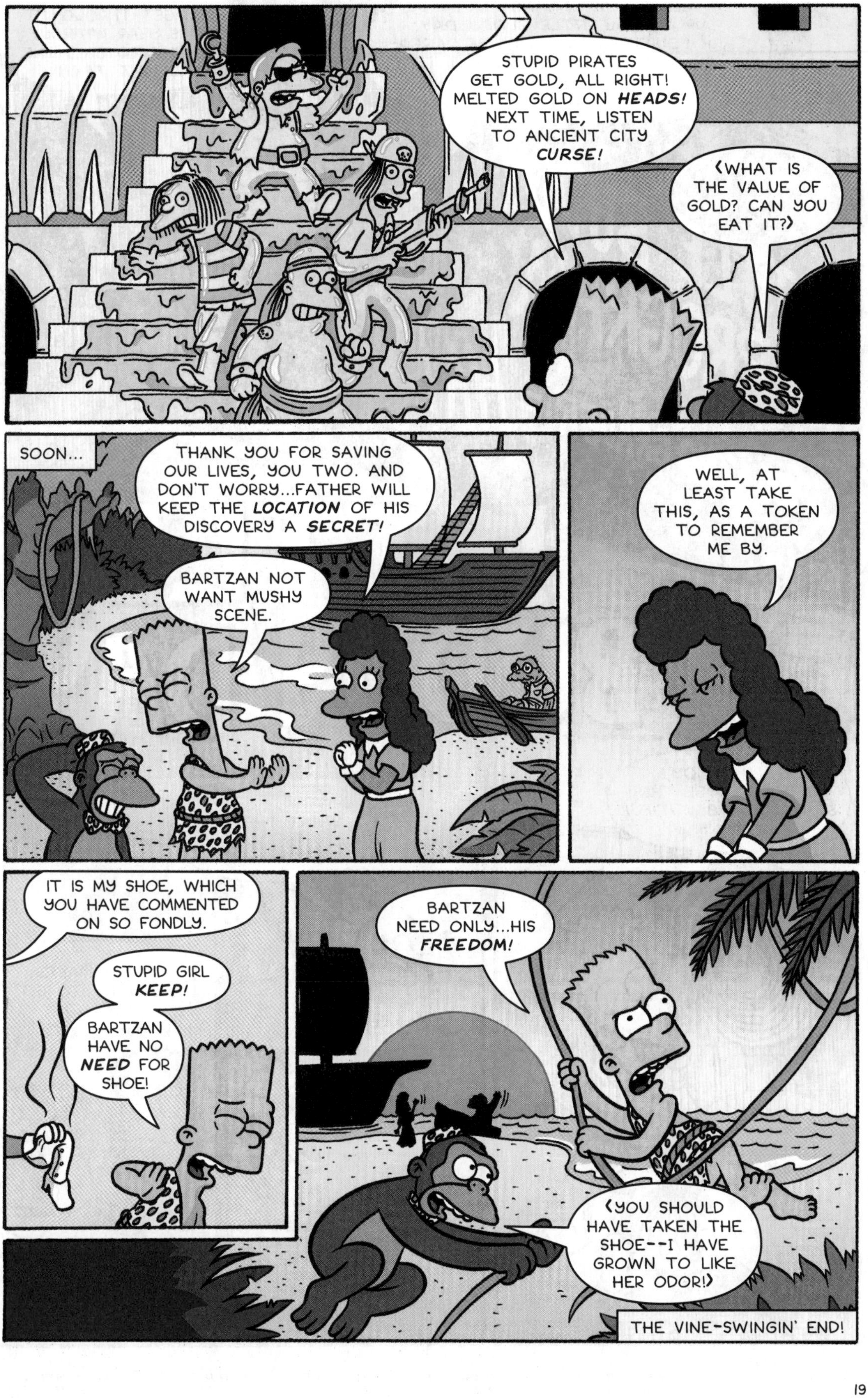
STUPID PIRATES GET GOLD, ALL RIGHT! MELTED GOLD ON **HEADS**! NEXT TIME, LISTEN TO ANCIENT CITY **CURSE**!
‹WHAT IS THE VALUE OF GOLD? CAN YOU EAT IT?›
SOON...
THANK YOU FOR SAVING OUR LIVES, YOU TWO. AND DON'T WORRY...FATHER WILL KEEP THE **LOCATION** OF HIS DISCOVERY A **SECRET**!
BARTZAN NOT WANT MUSHY SCENE.
WELL, AT LEAST TAKE THIS, AS A TOKEN TO REMEMBER ME BY.
IT IS MY SHOE, WHICH YOU HAVE COMMENTED ON SO FONDLY.
STUPID GIRL **KEEP**!
BARTZAN HAVE NO **NEED** FOR SHOE!
BARTZAN NEED ONLY...HIS **FREEDOM**!
‹YOU SHOULD HAVE TAKEN THE SHOE--I HAVE GROWN TO LIKE HER ODOR!›
THE VINE-SWINGIN' END!

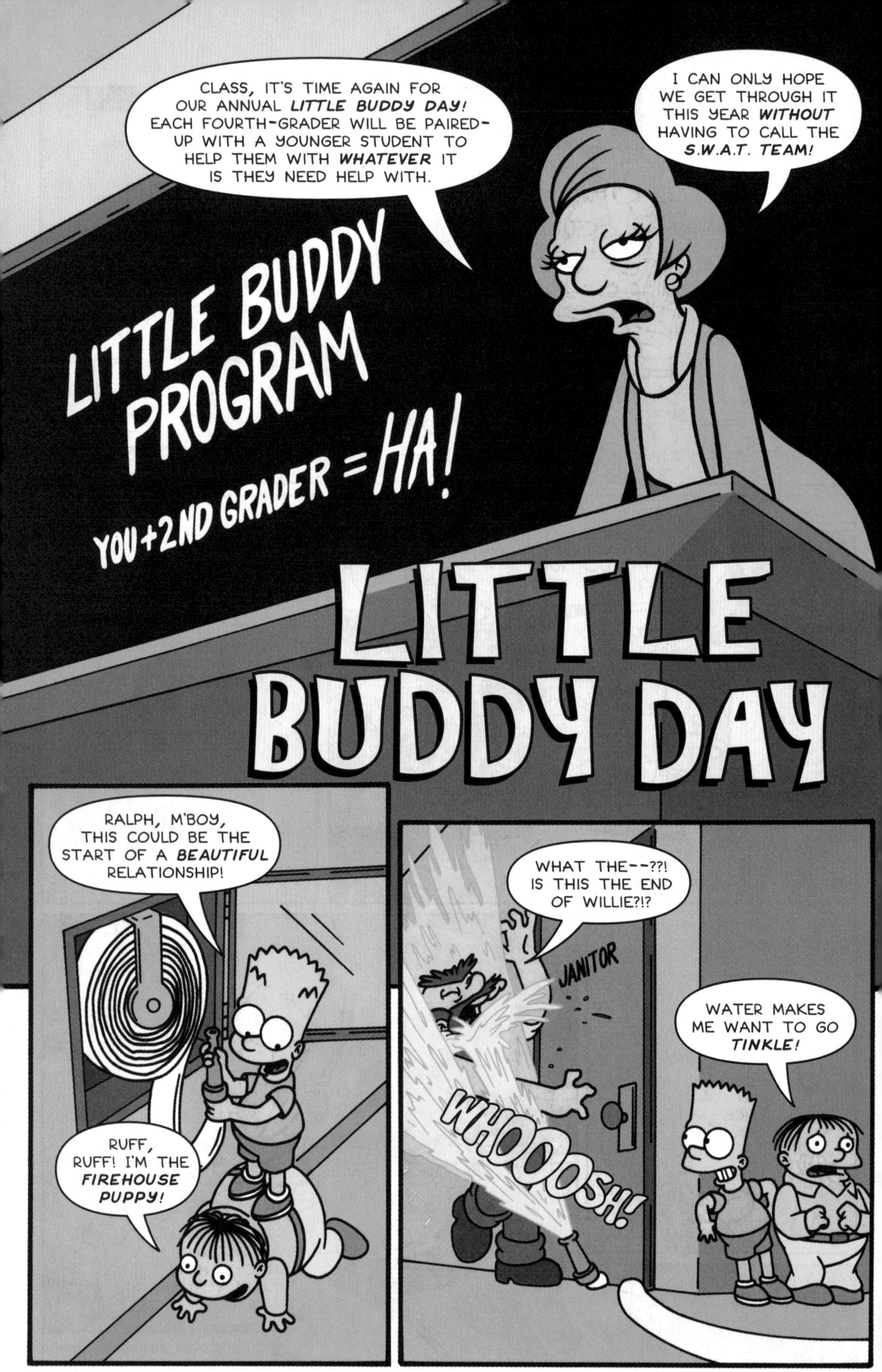
CLASS, IT'S TIME AGAIN FOR OUR ANNUAL LITTLE BUDDY DAY! EACH FOURTH-GRADER WILL BE PAIRED-UP WITH A YOUNGER STUDENT TO HELP THEM WITH WHATEVER IT IS THEY NEED HELP WITH.
I CAN ONLY HOPE WE GET THROUGH IT THIS YEAR WITHOUT HAVING TO CALL THE S.W.A.T. TEAM!
LITTLE BUDDY PROGRAM
YOU+2ND GRADER =HA!
LITTLE BUDDY DAY
RALPH, M'BOY, THIS COULD BE THE START OF A BEAUTIFUL RELATIONSHIP!
RUFF, RUFF! I'M THE FIREHOUSE PUPPY!
WHAT THE--??! IS THIS THE END OF WILLIE?!?
JANITOR
WHOOOOSH!
WATER MAKES ME WANT TO GO TINKLE!

JESSE MCCANN & AMANDA MCCANN SCRIPT | LUIS ESCOBAR PENCILS | PATRICK OWSLEY INKS | CHRIS UNGAR COLORS | KAREN BATES LETTERS | BILL MORRISON EDITOR

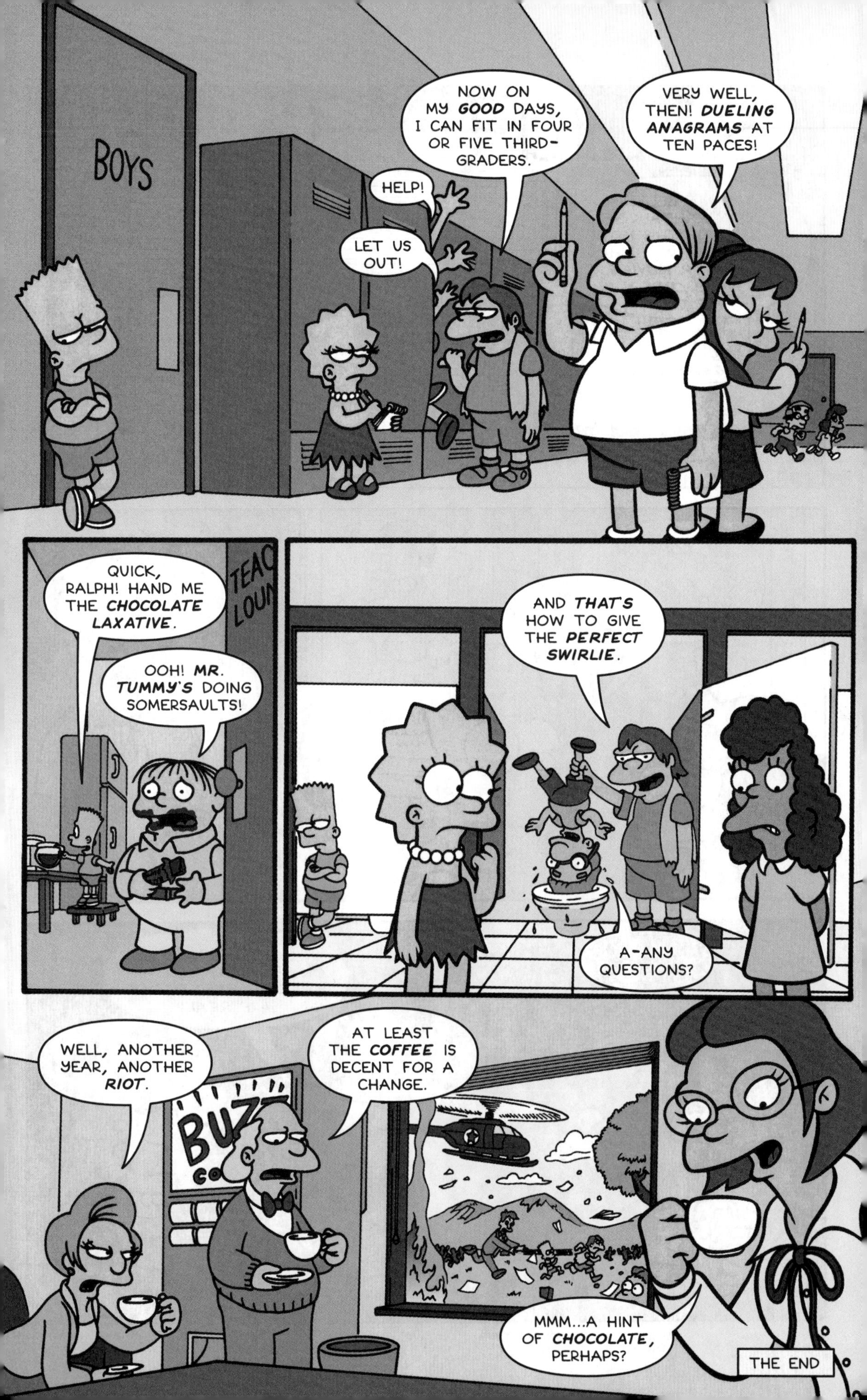
BOYS
HELP!
LET US OUT!
NOW ON MY GOOD DAYS, I CAN FIT IN FOUR OR FIVE THIRD-GRADERS.
VERY WELL, THEN! DUELING ANAGRAMS AT TEN PACES!
TEAC
LOUN
QUICK, RALPH! HAND ME THE CHOCOLATE LAXATIVE.
OOH! MR. TUMMY'S DOING SOMERSAULTS!
AND THAT'S HOW TO GIVE THE PERFECT SWIRLIE.
A-ANY QUESTIONS?
WELL, ANOTHER YEAR, ANOTHER RIOT.
AT LEAST THE COFFEE IS DECENT FOR A CHANGE.
MMM...A HINT OF CHOCOLATE, PERHAPS?
THE END

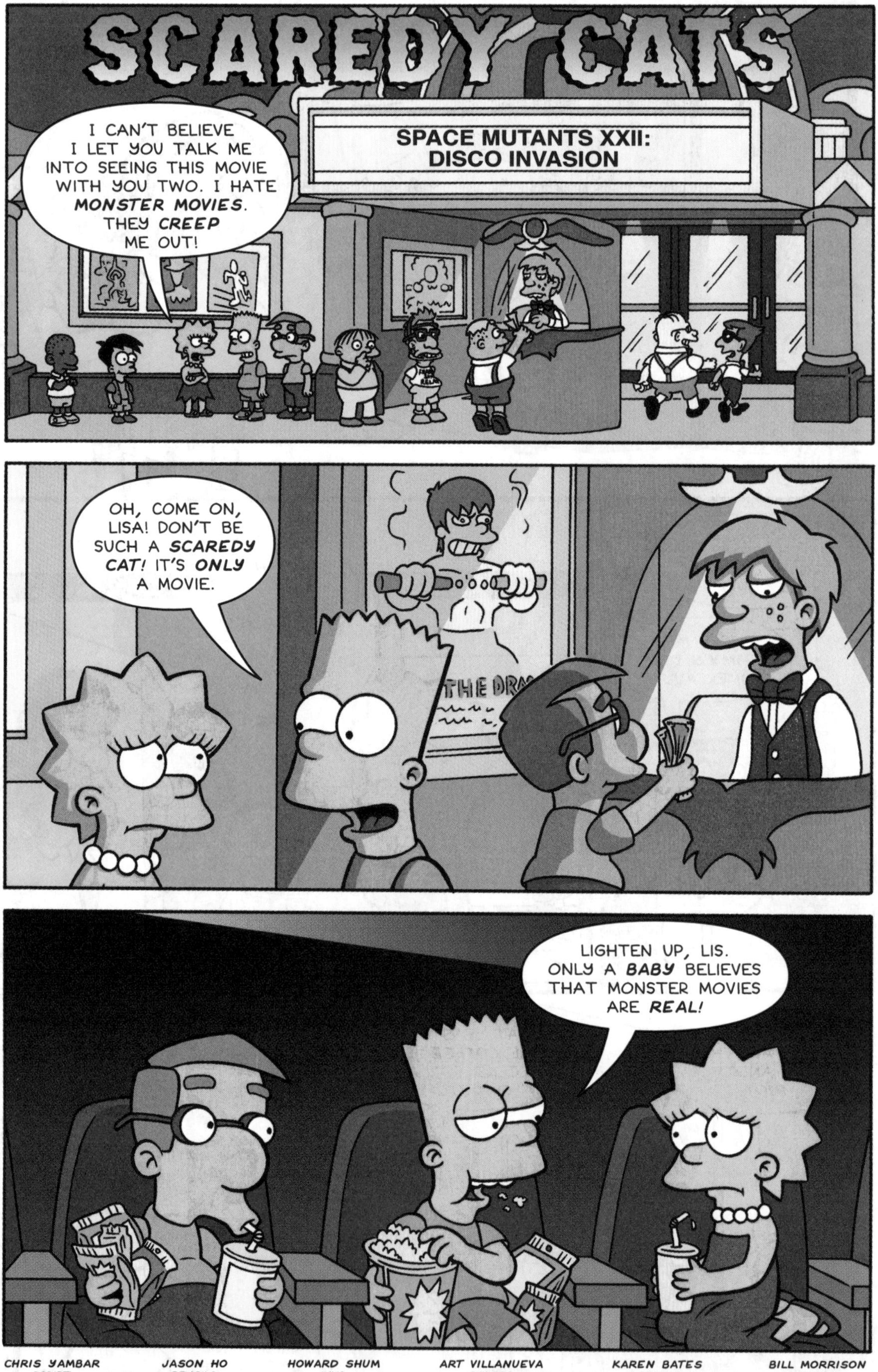
SCAREDY CATS
SPACE MUTANTS XXII: DISCO INVASION
I CAN'T BELIEVE I LET YOU TALK ME INTO SEEING THIS MOVIE WITH YOU TWO. I HATE MONSTER MOVIES. THEY CREEP ME OUT!
OH, COME ON, LISA! DON'T BE SUCH A SCAREDY CAT! IT'S ONLY A MOVIE.
LIGHTEN UP, LIS. ONLY A BABY BELIEVES THAT MONSTER MOVIES ARE REAL!

CHRIS YAMBAR SCRIPT | ***JASON HO*** PENCILS | ***HOWARD SHUM*** INKS | ***ART VILLANUEVA*** COLORS | ***KAREN BATES*** LETTERS | ***BILL MORRISON*** EDITOR

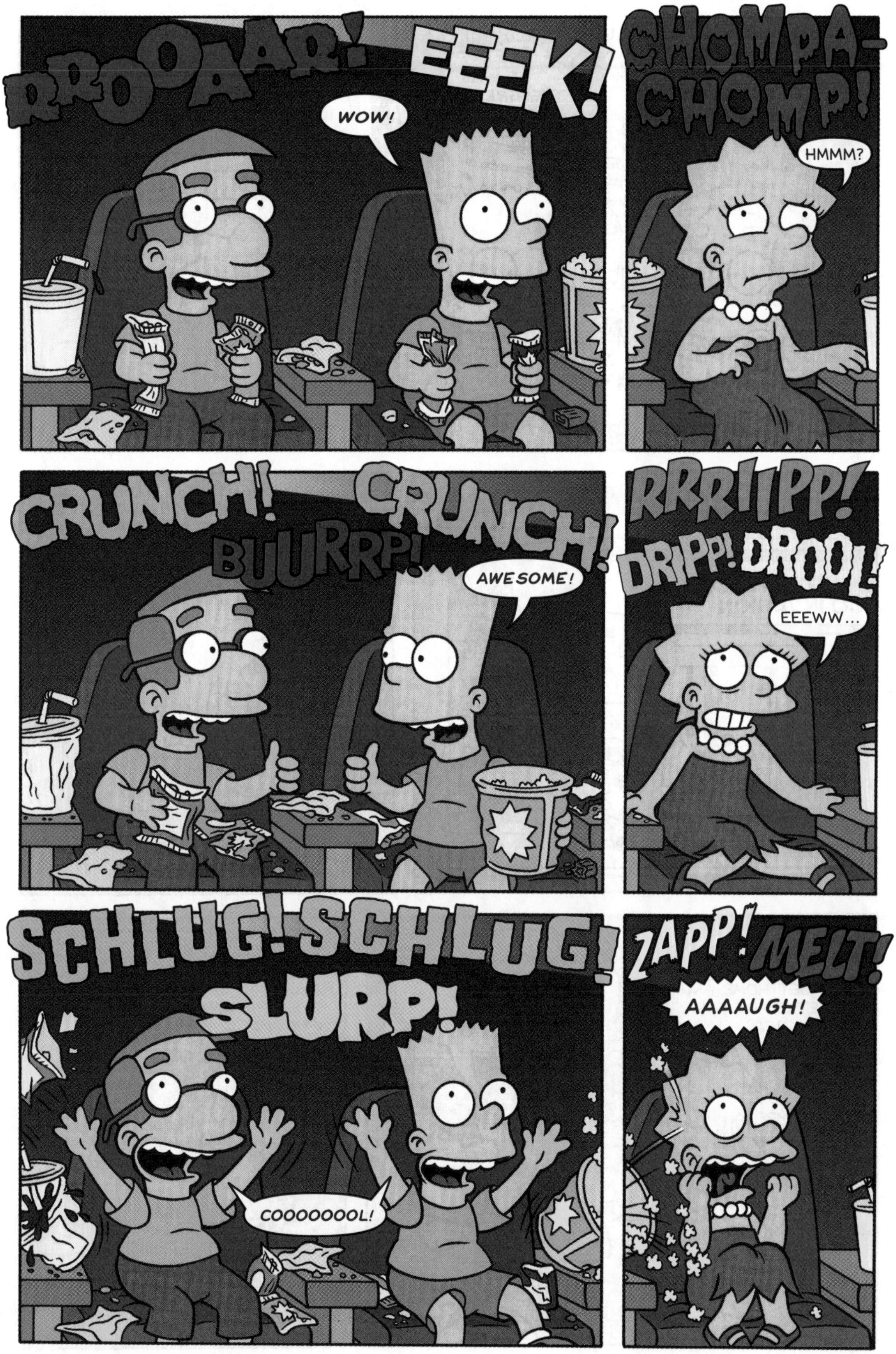
RROOAAR!
EEEK!
WOW!
CHOMPA-CHOMP!
HMMM?
CRUNCH! CRUNCH!
BUURRP!
AWESOME!
RRRIIPP!
DRIPP! DROOL!
EEEWW...
SCHLUG! SCHLUG!
SLURP!
COOOOOOOL!
ZAPP! MELT!
AAAAUGH!

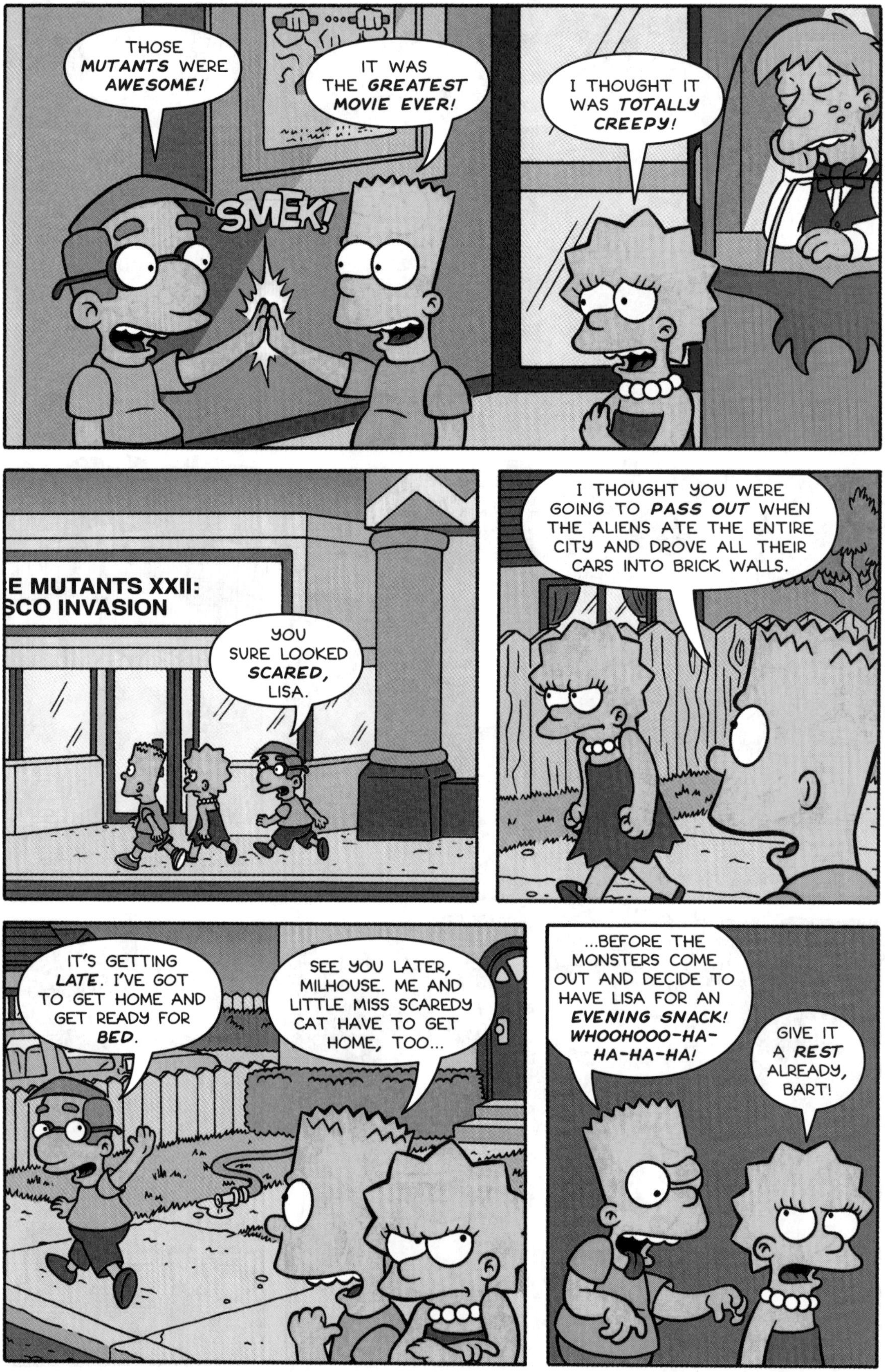
THOSE MUTANTS WERE AWESOME!
IT WAS THE GREATEST MOVIE EVER!
SMEK!
I THOUGHT IT WAS TOTALLY CREEPY!
E MUTANTS XXII:
SCO INVASION
YOU SURE LOOKED SCARED, LISA.
I THOUGHT YOU WERE GOING TO PASS OUT WHEN THE ALIENS ATE THE ENTIRE CITY AND DROVE ALL THEIR CARS INTO BRICK WALLS.
IT'S GETTING LATE. I'VE GOT TO GET HOME AND GET READY FOR BED.
SEE YOU LATER, MILHOUSE. ME AND LITTLE MISS SCAREDY CAT HAVE TO GET HOME, TOO...
...BEFORE THE MONSTERS COME OUT AND DECIDE TO HAVE LISA FOR AN EVENING SNACK! WHOOHOOO-HA-HA-HA-HA!
GIVE IT A REST ALREADY, BART!

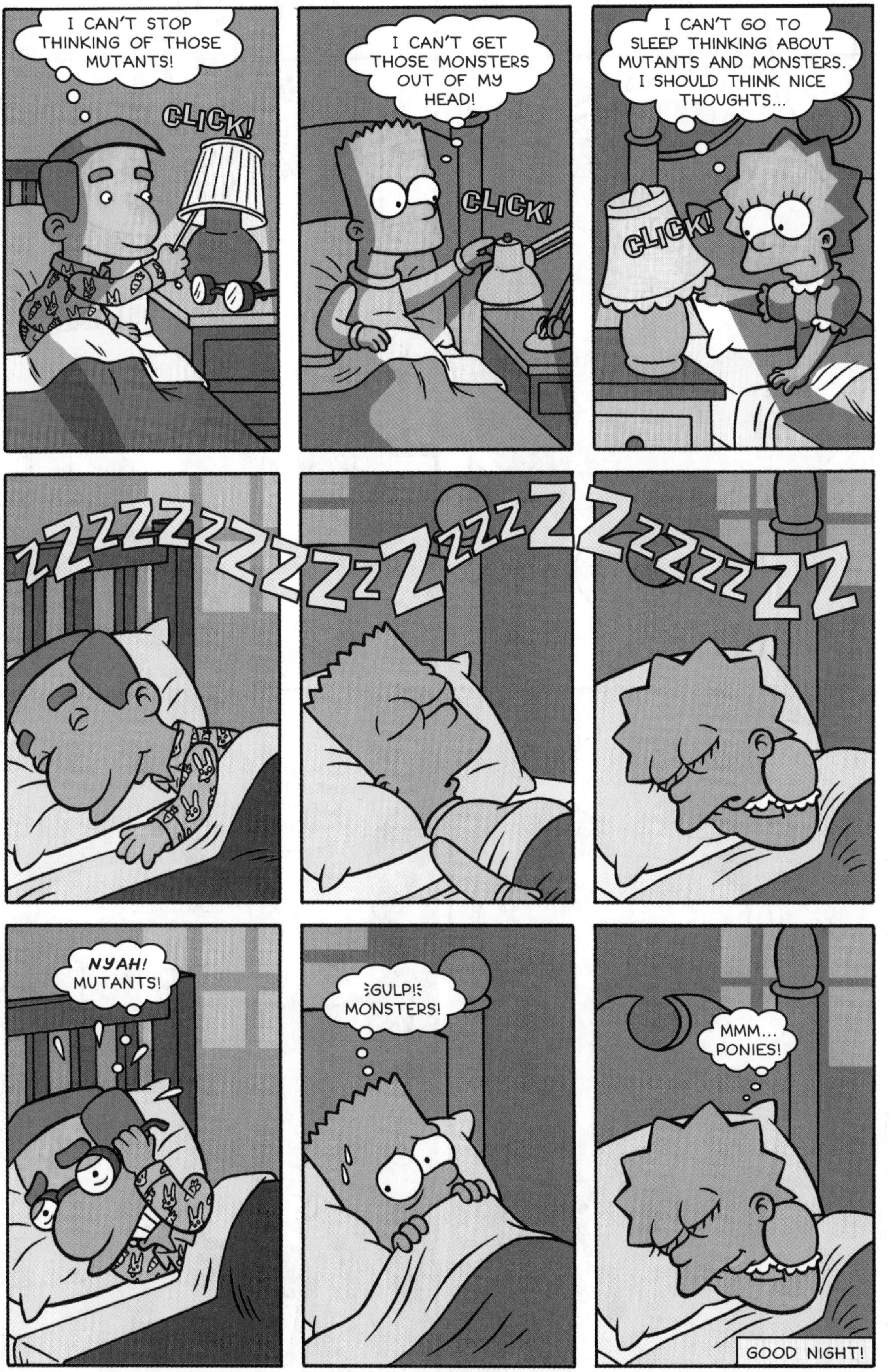
I CAN'T STOP THINKING OF THOSE MUTANTS!
CLICK!
I CAN'T GET THOSE MONSTERS OUT OF MY HEAD!
CLICK!
I CAN'T GO TO SLEEP THINKING ABOUT MUTANTS AND MONSTERS. I SHOULD THINK NICE THOUGHTS...
CLICK!
zZzZZzZZZZzZzzzZZZzzzzZZ
NYAH! MUTANTS!
GULP! MONSTERS!
MMM... PONIES!
GOOD NIGHT!

BART'S BIG SPILL

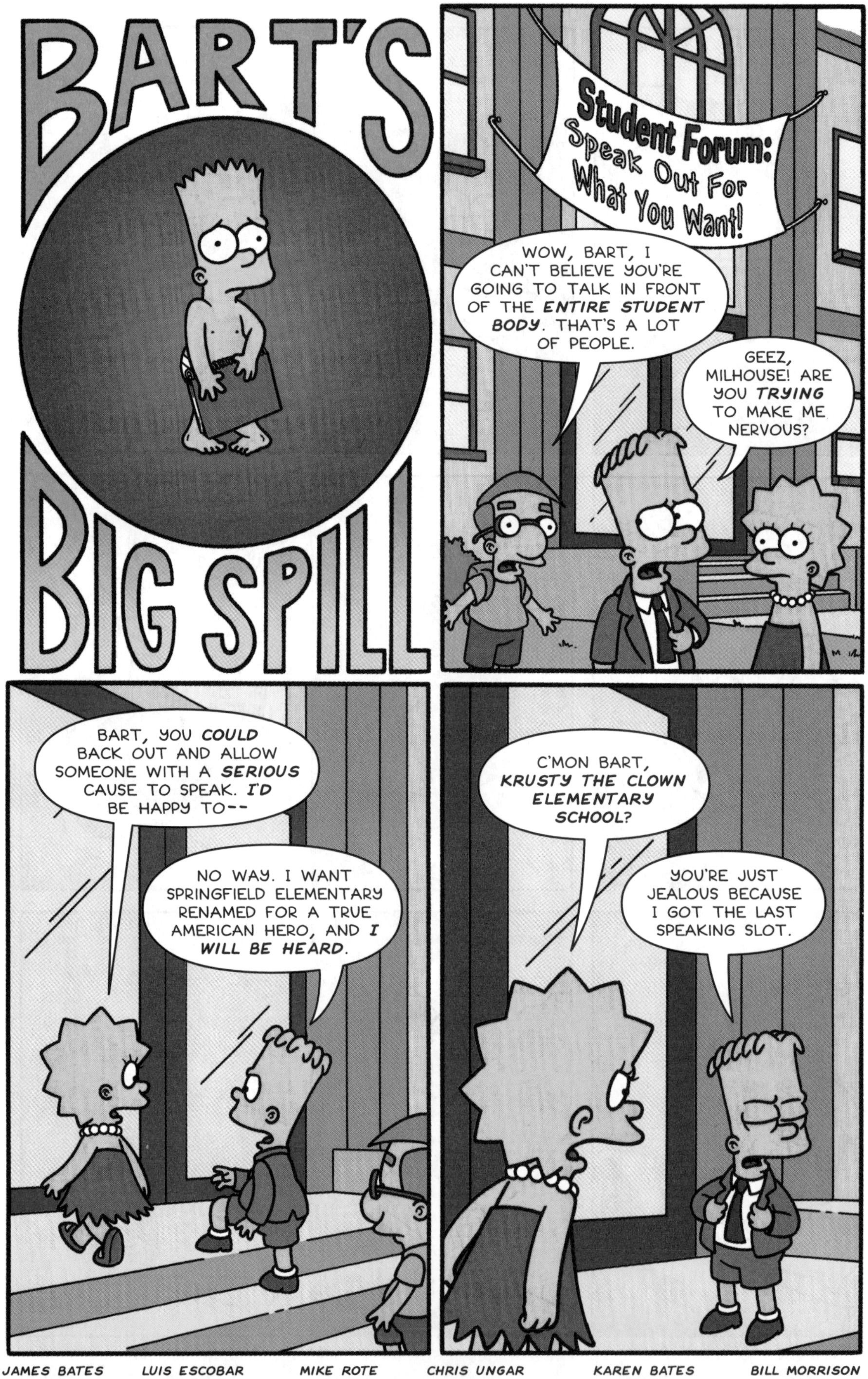

Student Forum: Speak Out For What You Want!
WOW, BART, I CAN'T BELIEVE YOU'RE GOING TO TALK IN FRONT OF THE *ENTIRE STUDENT BODY*. THAT'S A LOT OF PEOPLE.
GEEZ, MILHOUSE! ARE YOU *TRYING* TO MAKE ME NERVOUS?
BART, YOU *COULD* BACK OUT AND ALLOW SOMEONE WITH A *SERIOUS* CAUSE TO SPEAK. *I'D* BE HAPPY TO--
NO WAY. I WANT SPRINGFIELD ELEMENTARY RENAMED FOR A TRUE AMERICAN HERO, AND *I WILL BE HEARD*.
C'MON BART, *KRUSTY THE CLOWN ELEMENTARY SCHOOL?*
YOU'RE JUST JEALOUS BECAUSE I GOT THE LAST SPEAKING SLOT.

JAMES BATES SCRIPT | *LUIS ESCOBAR* PENCILS | *MIKE ROTE* INKS | *CHRIS UNGAR* COLORS | *KAREN BATES* LETTERS | *BILL MORRISON* EDITOR

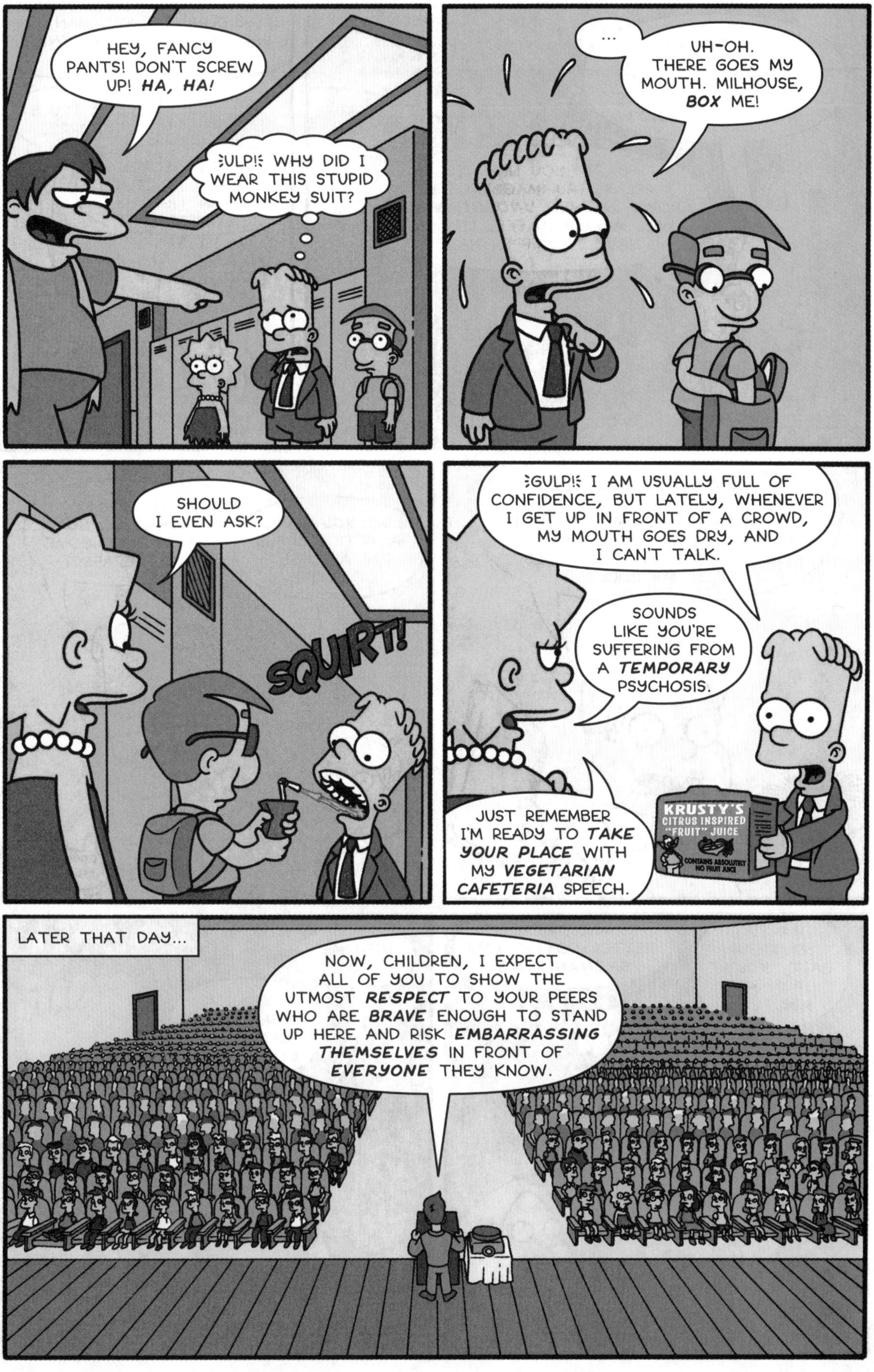
HEY, FANCY PANTS! DON'T SCREW UP! HA, HA!
ULP! WHY DID I WEAR THIS STUPID MONKEY SUIT?
...
UH-OH. THERE GOES MY MOUTH. MILHOUSE, BOX ME!
SHOULD I EVEN ASK?
SQUIRT!
GULP! I AM USUALLY FULL OF CONFIDENCE, BUT LATELY, WHENEVER I GET UP IN FRONT OF A CROWD, MY MOUTH GOES DRY, AND I CAN'T TALK.
SOUNDS LIKE YOU'RE SUFFERING FROM A TEMPORARY PSYCHOSIS.
JUST REMEMBER I'M READY TO TAKE YOUR PLACE WITH MY VEGETARIAN CAFETERIA SPEECH.
KRUSTY'S CITRUS INSPIRED "FRUIT" JUICE
CONTAINS ABSOLUTELY NO FRUIT JUICE
LATER THAT DAY...
NOW, CHILDREN, I EXPECT ALL OF YOU TO SHOW THE UTMOST RESPECT TO YOUR PEERS WHO ARE BRAVE ENOUGH TO STAND UP HERE AND RISK EMBARRASSING THEMSELVES IN FRONT OF EVERYONE THEY KNOW.

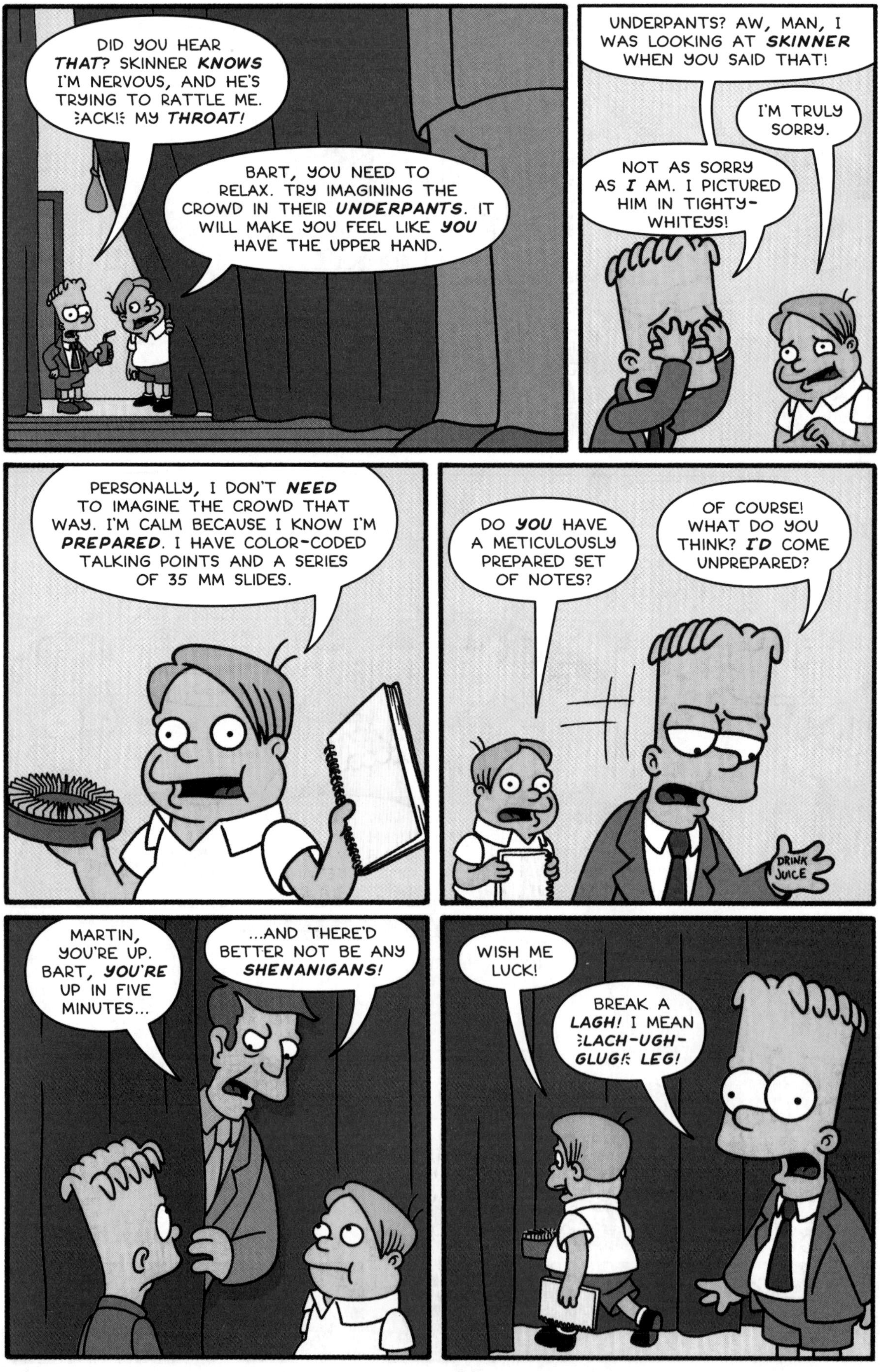
DID YOU HEAR THAT? SKINNER KNOWS I'M NERVOUS, AND HE'S TRYING TO RATTLE ME. ACK! MY THROAT!
BART, YOU NEED TO RELAX. TRY IMAGINING THE CROWD IN THEIR UNDERPANTS. IT WILL MAKE YOU FEEL LIKE YOU HAVE THE UPPER HAND.
UNDERPANTS? AW, MAN, I WAS LOOKING AT SKINNER WHEN YOU SAID THAT!
I'M TRULY SORRY.
NOT AS SORRY AS I AM. I PICTURED HIM IN TIGHTY-WHITEYS!
PERSONALLY, I DON'T NEED TO IMAGINE THE CROWD THAT WAY. I'M CALM BECAUSE I KNOW I'M PREPARED. I HAVE COLOR-CODED TALKING POINTS AND A SERIES OF 35 MM SLIDES.
DO YOU HAVE A METICULOUSLY PREPARED SET OF NOTES?
OF COURSE! WHAT DO YOU THINK? I'D COME UNPREPARED?
DRINK JUICE
MARTIN, YOU'RE UP. BART, YOU'RE UP IN FIVE MINUTES...
...AND THERE'D BETTER NOT BE ANY SHENANIGANS!
WISH ME LUCK!
BREAK A LAGH! I MEAN LACH-UGH-GLUG! LEG!

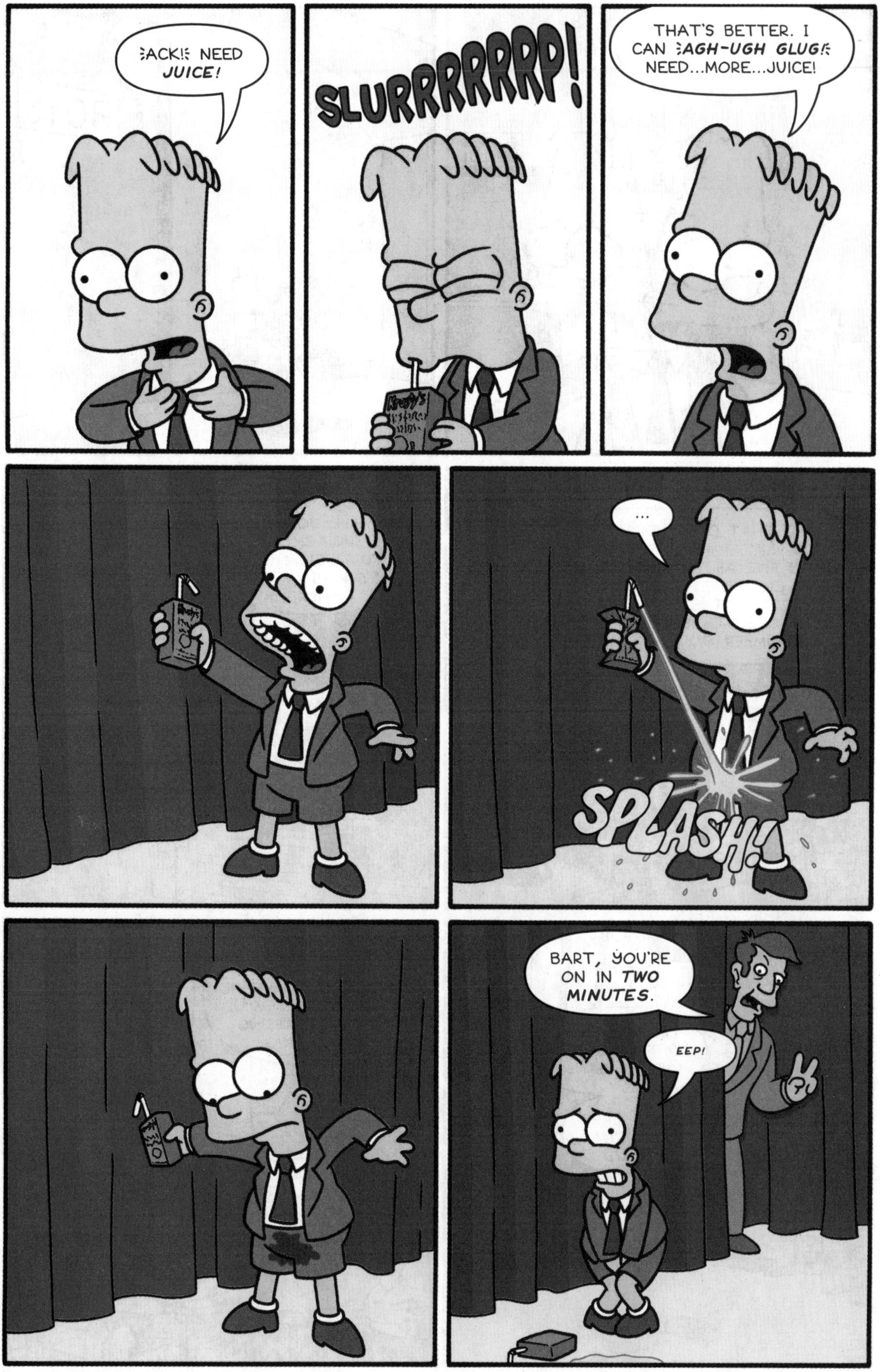

ACK! NEED JUICE!
SLURRRRRRP!
THAT'S BETTER. I CAN AGH-UGH GLUG! NEED...MORE...JUICE!
...
SPLASH!
BART, YOU'RE ON IN TWO MINUTES.
EEP!

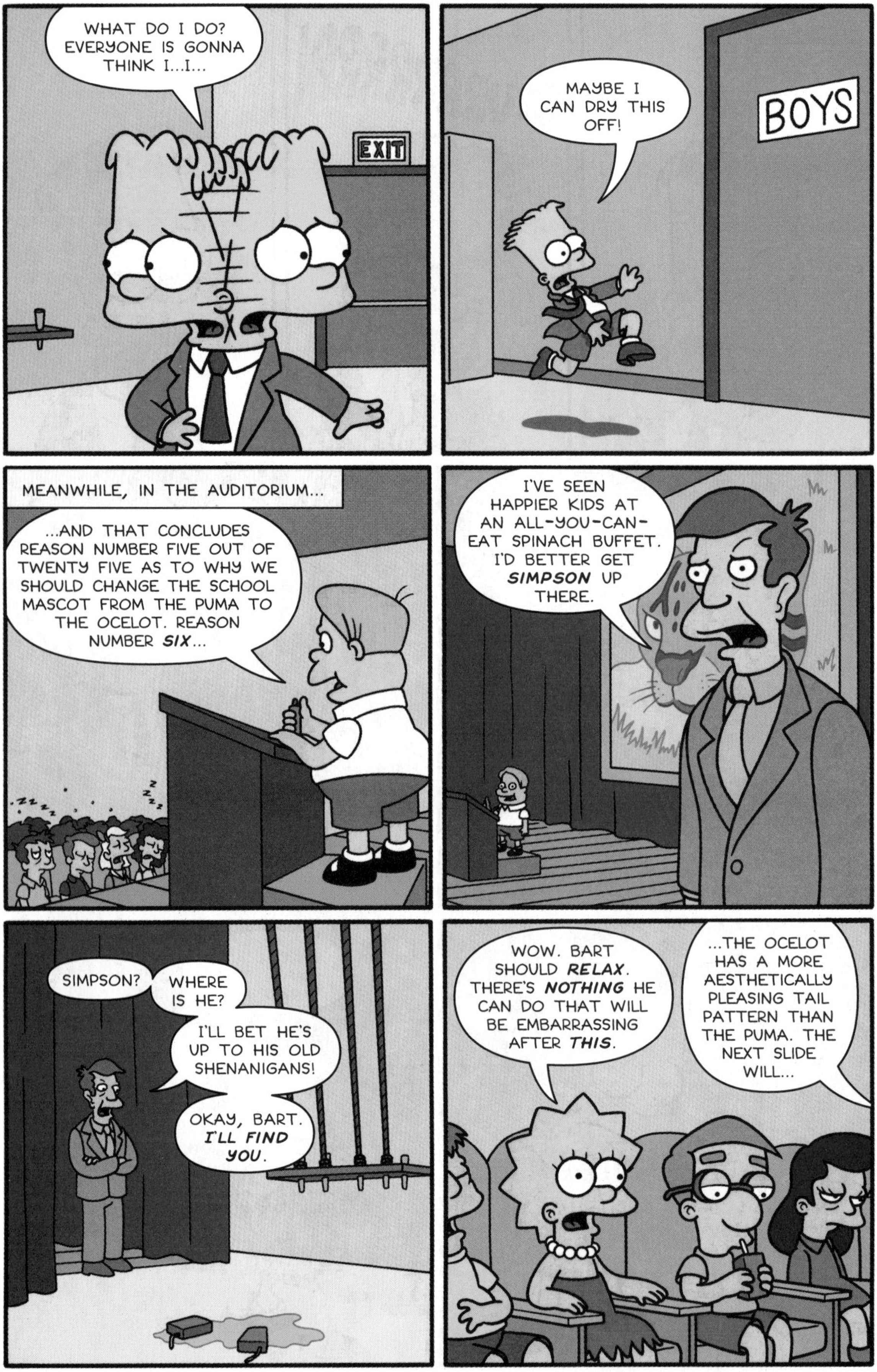
WHAT DO I DO? EVERYONE IS GONNA THINK I...I...
EXIT
MAYBE I CAN DRY THIS OFF!
BOYS
MEANWHILE, IN THE AUDITORIUM...
...AND THAT CONCLUDES REASON NUMBER FIVE OUT OF TWENTY FIVE AS TO WHY WE SHOULD CHANGE THE SCHOOL MASCOT FROM THE PUMA TO THE OCELOT. REASON NUMBER *SIX*...
I'VE SEEN HAPPIER KIDS AT AN ALL-YOU-CAN-EAT SPINACH BUFFET. I'D BETTER GET *SIMPSON* UP THERE.
SIMPSON?
WHERE IS HE?
I'LL BET HE'S UP TO HIS OLD SHENANIGANS!
OKAY, BART. *I'LL FIND YOU*.
WOW. BART SHOULD *RELAX*. THERE'S *NOTHING* HE CAN DO THAT WILL BE EMBARRASSING AFTER *THIS*.
...THE OCELOT HAS A MORE AESTHETICALLY PLEASING TAIL PATTERN THAN THE PUMA. THE NEXT SLIDE WILL...

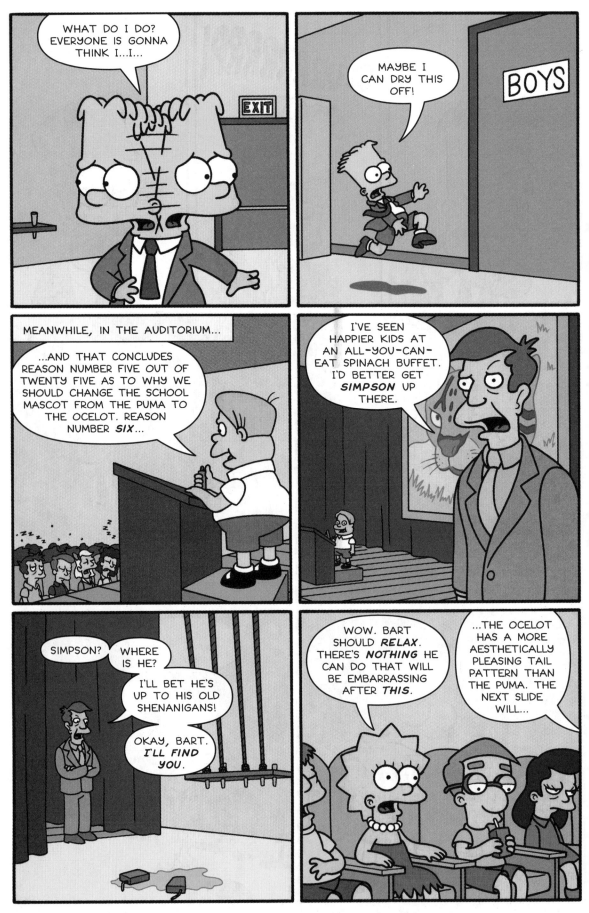

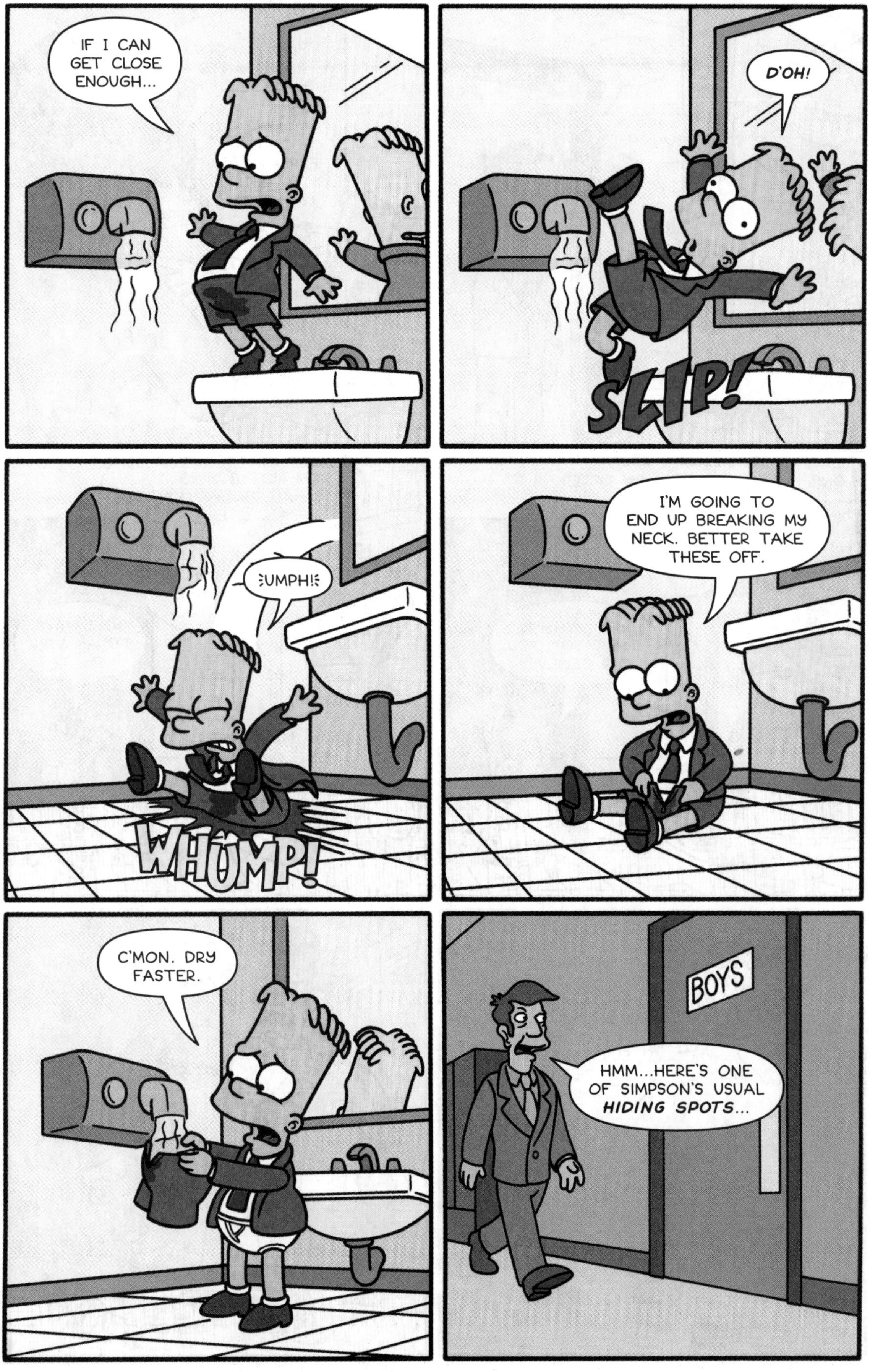
IF I CAN GET CLOSE ENOUGH...
D'OH!
SLIP!
UMPH!
WHUMP!
I'M GOING TO END UP BREAKING MY NECK. BETTER TAKE THESE OFF.
C'MON. DRY FASTER.
BOYS
HMM...HERE'S ONE OF SIMPSON'S USUAL *HIDING SPOTS*...

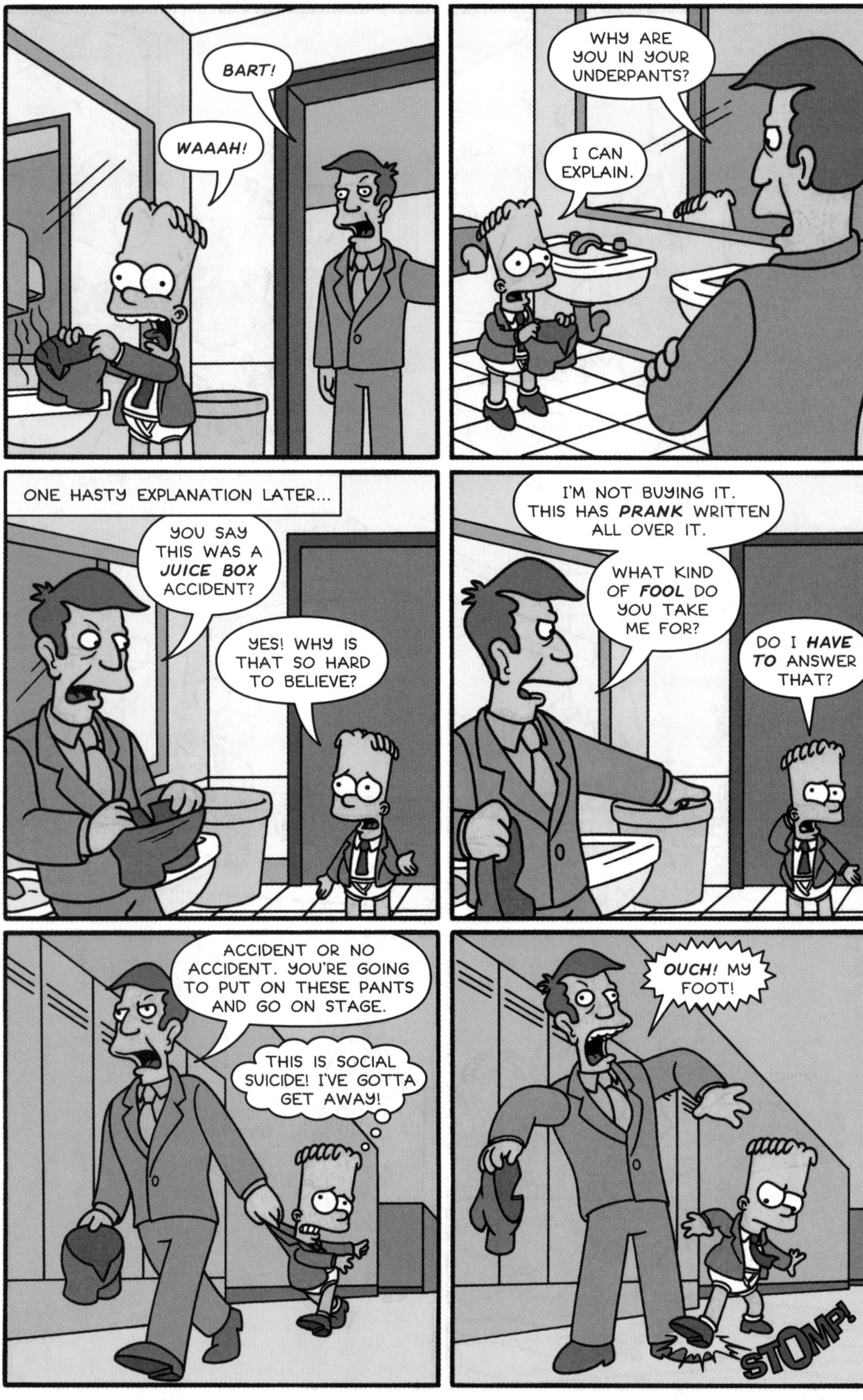
BART!
WAAAH!
WHY ARE YOU IN YOUR UNDERPANTS?
I CAN EXPLAIN.
ONE HASTY EXPLANATION LATER...
YOU SAY THIS WAS A *JUICE BOX* ACCIDENT?
YES! WHY IS THAT SO HARD TO BELIEVE?
I'M NOT BUYING IT. THIS HAS *PRANK* WRITTEN ALL OVER IT.
WHAT KIND OF *FOOL* DO YOU TAKE ME FOR?
DO I *HAVE TO* ANSWER THAT?
ACCIDENT OR NO ACCIDENT. YOU'RE GOING TO PUT ON THESE PANTS AND GO ON STAGE.
THIS IS SOCIAL SUICIDE! I'VE GOTTA GET AWAY!
OUCH! MY FOOT!
STOMP!

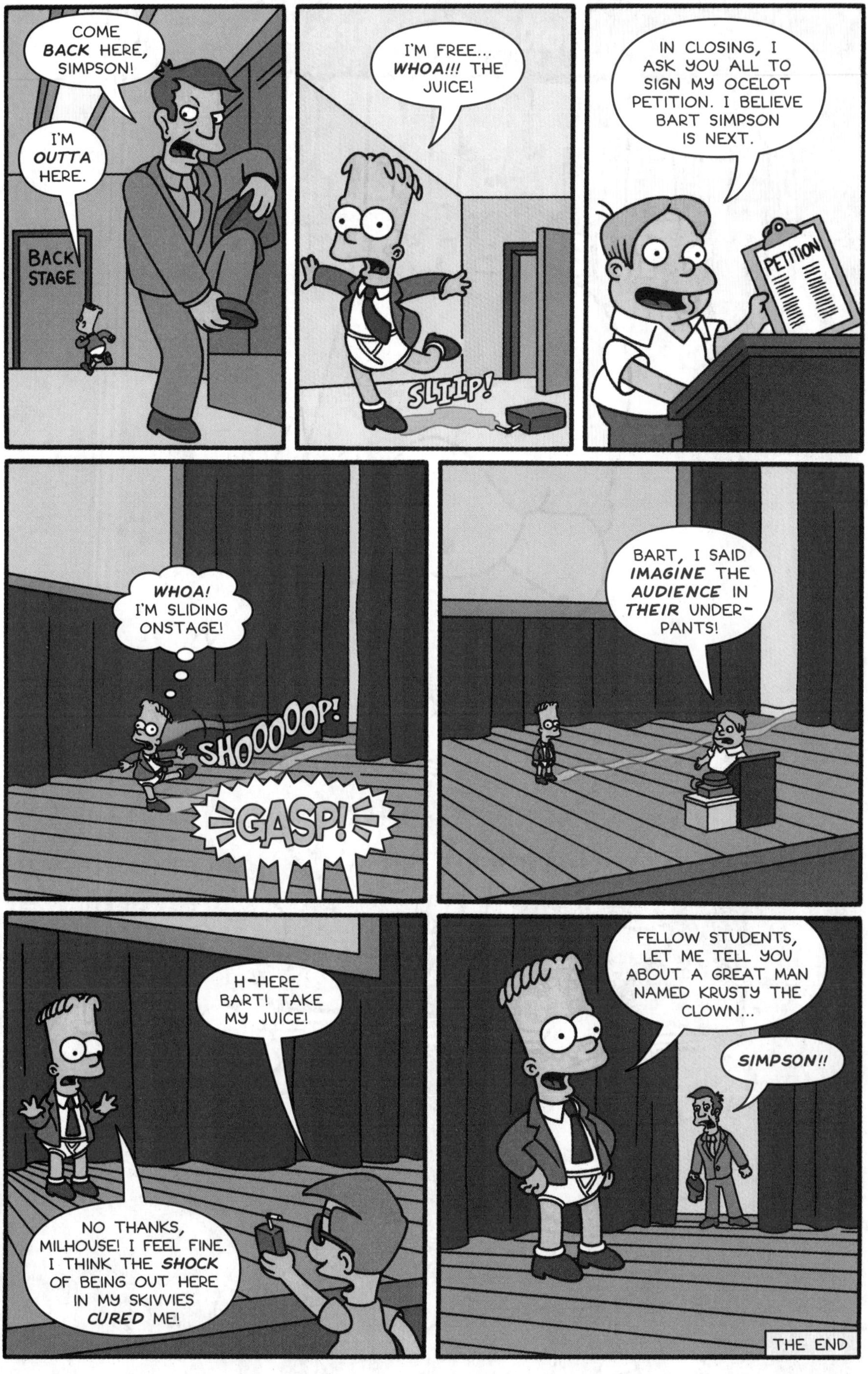
COME BACK HERE, SIMPSON!
I'M OUTTA HERE.
BACK STAGE
I'M FREE... WHOA!!! THE JUICE!
SLIIP!
IN CLOSING, I ASK YOU ALL TO SIGN MY OCELOT PETITION. I BELIEVE BART SIMPSON IS NEXT.
PETITION
WHOA! I'M SLIDING ONSTAGE!
SHOOOOOP!
GASP!
BART, I SAID IMAGINE THE AUDIENCE IN THEIR UNDER-PANTS!
H-HERE BART! TAKE MY JUICE!
NO THANKS, MILHOUSE! I FEEL FINE. I THINK THE SHOCK OF BEING OUT HERE IN MY SKIVVIES CURED ME!
FELLOW STUDENTS, LET ME TELL YOU ABOUT A GREAT MAN NAMED KRUSTY THE CLOWN...
SIMPSON!!
THE END

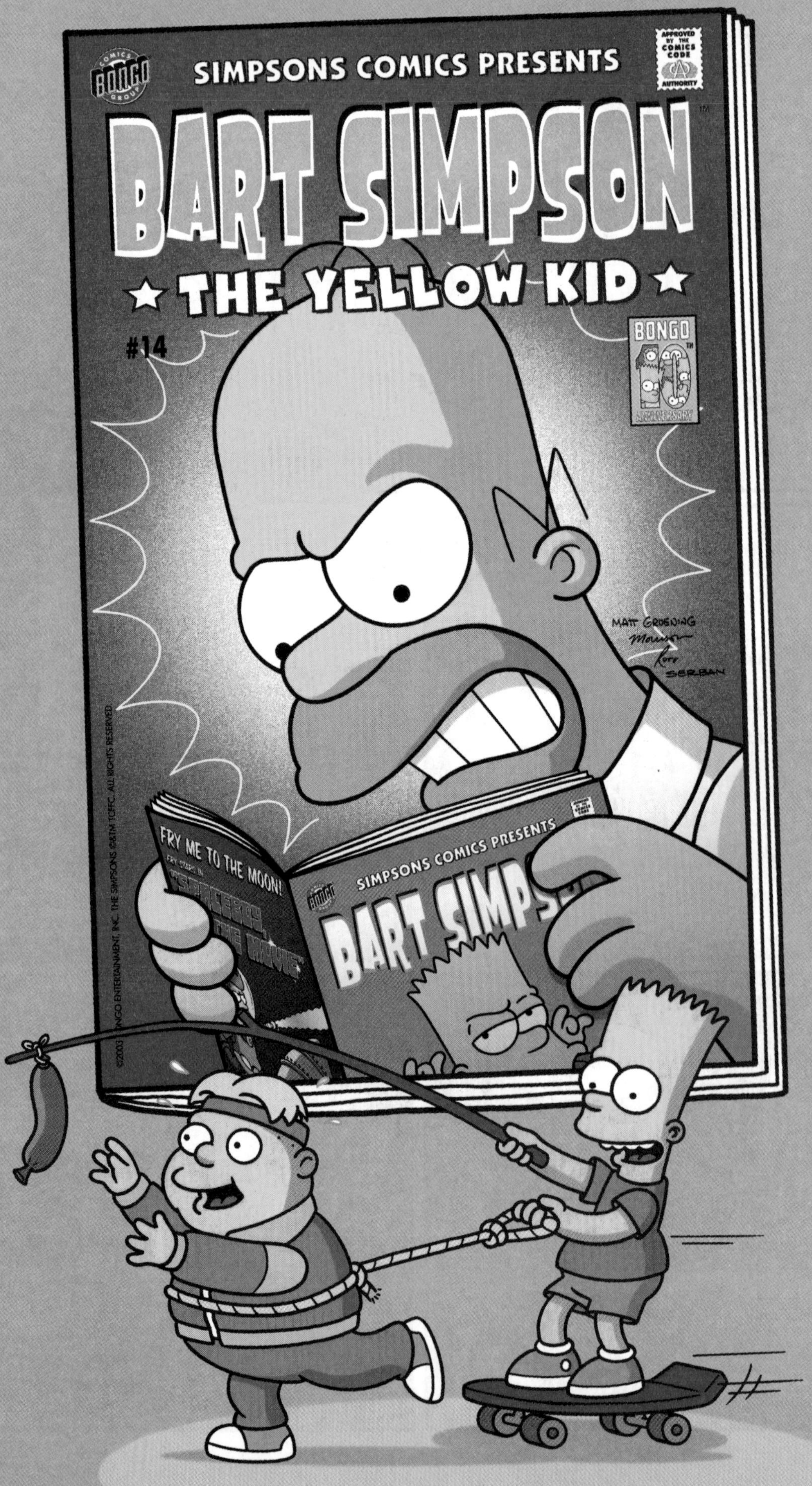
SIMPSONS COMICS PRESENTS
APPROVED BY THE COMICS CODE AUTHORITY
BART SIMPSON
THE YELLOW KID
#14
BONGO 10TH ANNIVERSARY
MATT GROENING
SERBAN
©2003 BONGO ENTERTAINMENT, INC. THE SIMPSONS ©&TM TCFFC. ALL RIGHTS RESERVED.
FRY ME TO THE MOON!
SIMPSONS COMICS PRESENTS
BART SIMPS

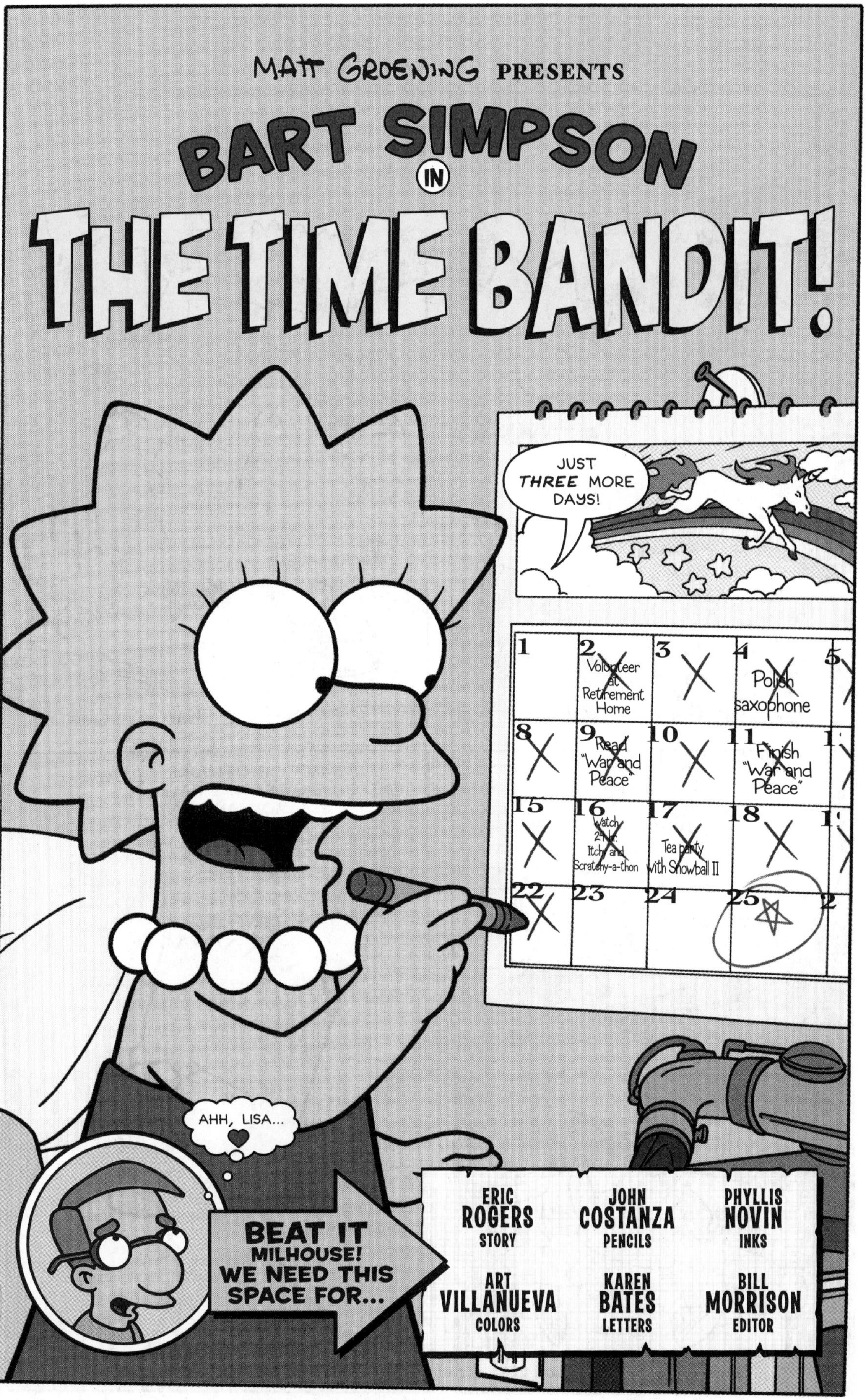

MATT GROENING PRESENTS
BART SIMPSON IN
THE TIME BANDIT!
JUST THREE MORE DAYS!
1
2 Volunteer at Retirement Home
3
4 Polish saxophone
5
8
9 Read "War and Peace"
10
11 Finish "War and Peace"
15
16 Watch 24 hr. Itchy and Scratchy-a-thon
17 Tea party with Snowball II
18
22
23
24
25
AHH, LISA...
BEAT IT MILHOUSE! WE NEED THIS SPACE FOR...
ERIC ROGERS STORY
JOHN COSTANZA PENCILS
PHYLLIS NOVIN INKS
ART VILLANUEVA COLORS
KAREN BATES LETTERS
BILL MORRISON EDITOR

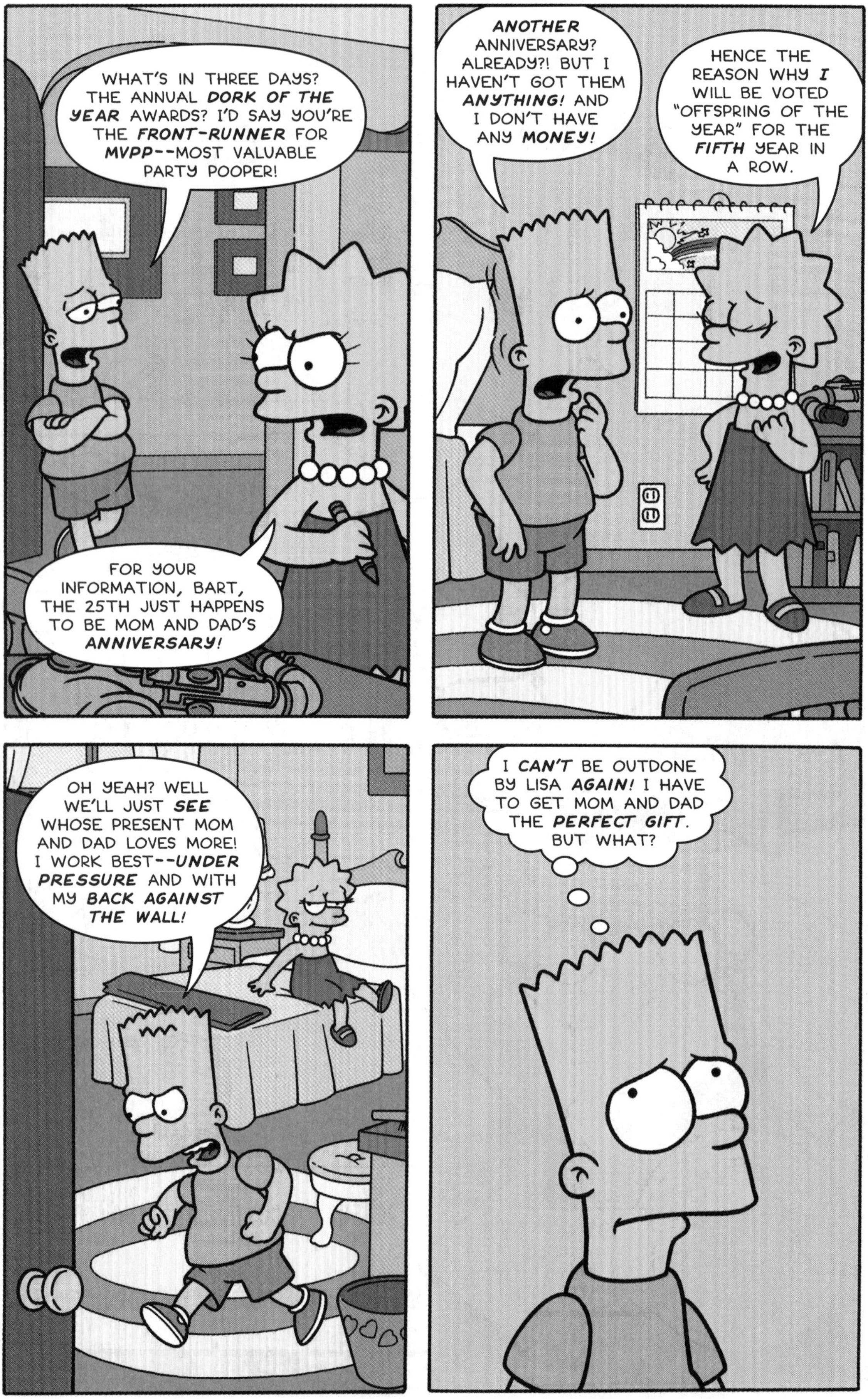
WHAT'S IN THREE DAYS? THE ANNUAL DORK OF THE YEAR AWARDS? I'D SAY YOU'RE THE FRONT-RUNNER FOR MVPP--MOST VALUABLE PARTY POOPER!
FOR YOUR INFORMATION, BART, THE 25TH JUST HAPPENS TO BE MOM AND DAD'S ANNIVERSARY!
ANOTHER ANNIVERSARY? ALREADY?! BUT I HAVEN'T GOT THEM ANYTHING! AND I DON'T HAVE ANY MONEY!
HENCE THE REASON WHY I WILL BE VOTED "OFFSPRING OF THE YEAR" FOR THE FIFTH YEAR IN A ROW.
OH YEAH? WELL WE'LL JUST SEE WHOSE PRESENT MOM AND DAD LOVES MORE! I WORK BEST--UNDER PRESSURE AND WITH MY BACK AGAINST THE WALL!
I CAN'T BE OUTDONE BY LISA AGAIN! I HAVE TO GET MOM AND DAD THE PERFECT GIFT. BUT WHAT?

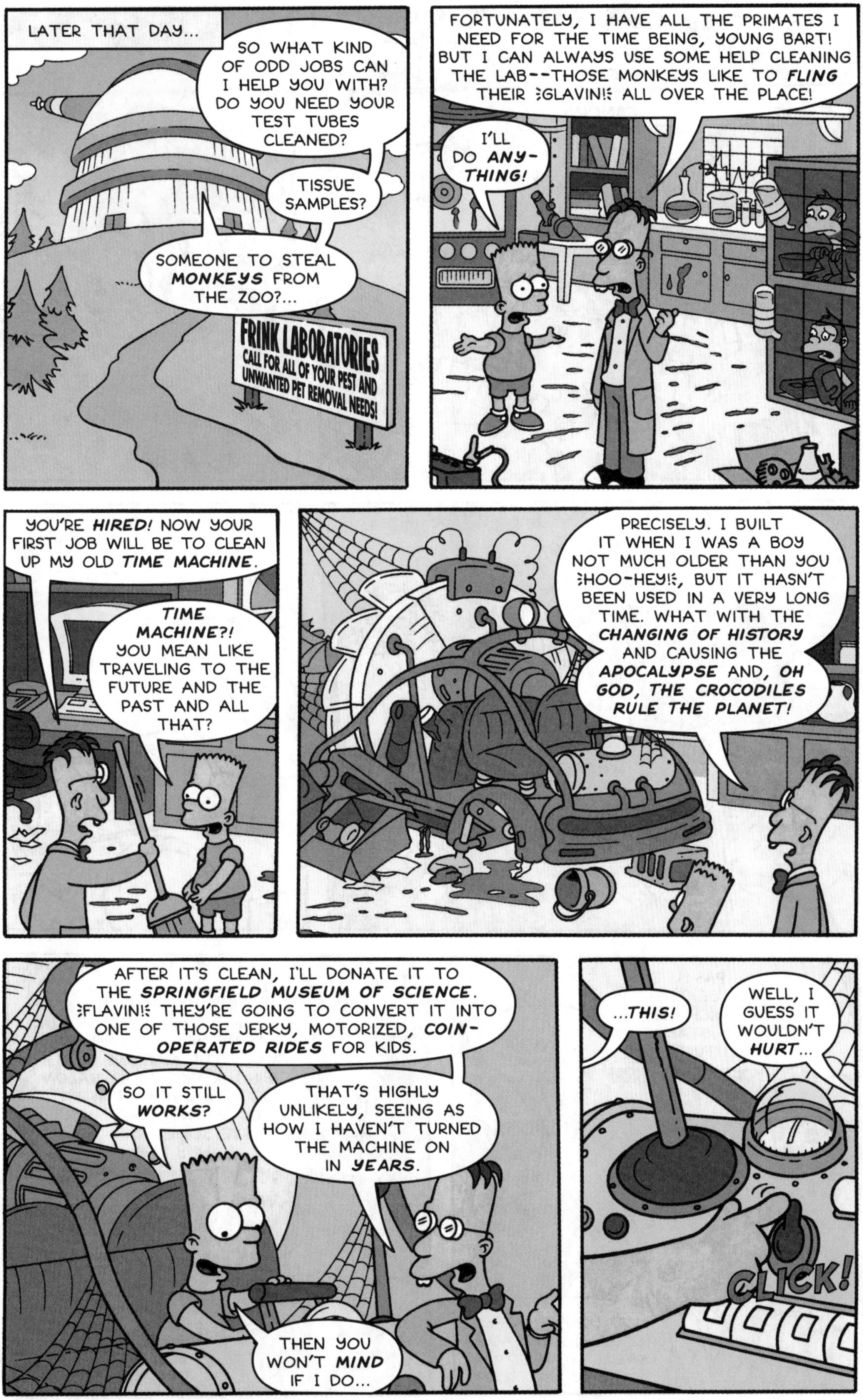
LATER THAT DAY...
SO WHAT KIND OF ODD JOBS CAN I HELP YOU WITH? DO YOU NEED YOUR TEST TUBES CLEANED?
TISSUE SAMPLES?
SOMEONE TO STEAL MONKEYS FROM THE ZOO?...
FRINK LABORATORIES
CALL FOR ALL OF YOUR PEST AND UNWANTED PET REMOVAL NEEDS!
FORTUNATELY, I HAVE ALL THE PRIMATES I NEED FOR THE TIME BEING, YOUNG BART! BUT I CAN ALWAYS USE SOME HELP CLEANING THE LAB--THOSE MONKEYS LIKE TO FLING THEIR GLAVIN! ALL OVER THE PLACE!
I'LL DO ANYTHING!
YOU'RE HIRED! NOW YOUR FIRST JOB WILL BE TO CLEAN UP MY OLD TIME MACHINE.
TIME MACHINE?! YOU MEAN LIKE TRAVELING TO THE FUTURE AND THE PAST AND ALL THAT?
PRECISELY. I BUILT IT WHEN I WAS A BOY NOT MUCH OLDER THAN YOU HOO-HEY!, BUT IT HASN'T BEEN USED IN A VERY LONG TIME. WHAT WITH THE CHANGING OF HISTORY AND CAUSING THE APOCALYPSE AND, OH GOD, THE CROCODILES RULE THE PLANET!
AFTER IT'S CLEAN, I'LL DONATE IT TO THE SPRINGFIELD MUSEUM OF SCIENCE. FLAVIN! THEY'RE GOING TO CONVERT IT INTO ONE OF THOSE JERKY, MOTORIZED, COIN-OPERATED RIDES FOR KIDS.
SO IT STILL WORKS?
THAT'S HIGHLY UNLIKELY, SEEING AS HOW I HAVEN'T TURNED THE MACHINE ON IN YEARS.
THEN YOU WON'T MIND IF I DO...
WELL, I GUESS IT WOULDN'T HURT...
...THIS!
CLICK!

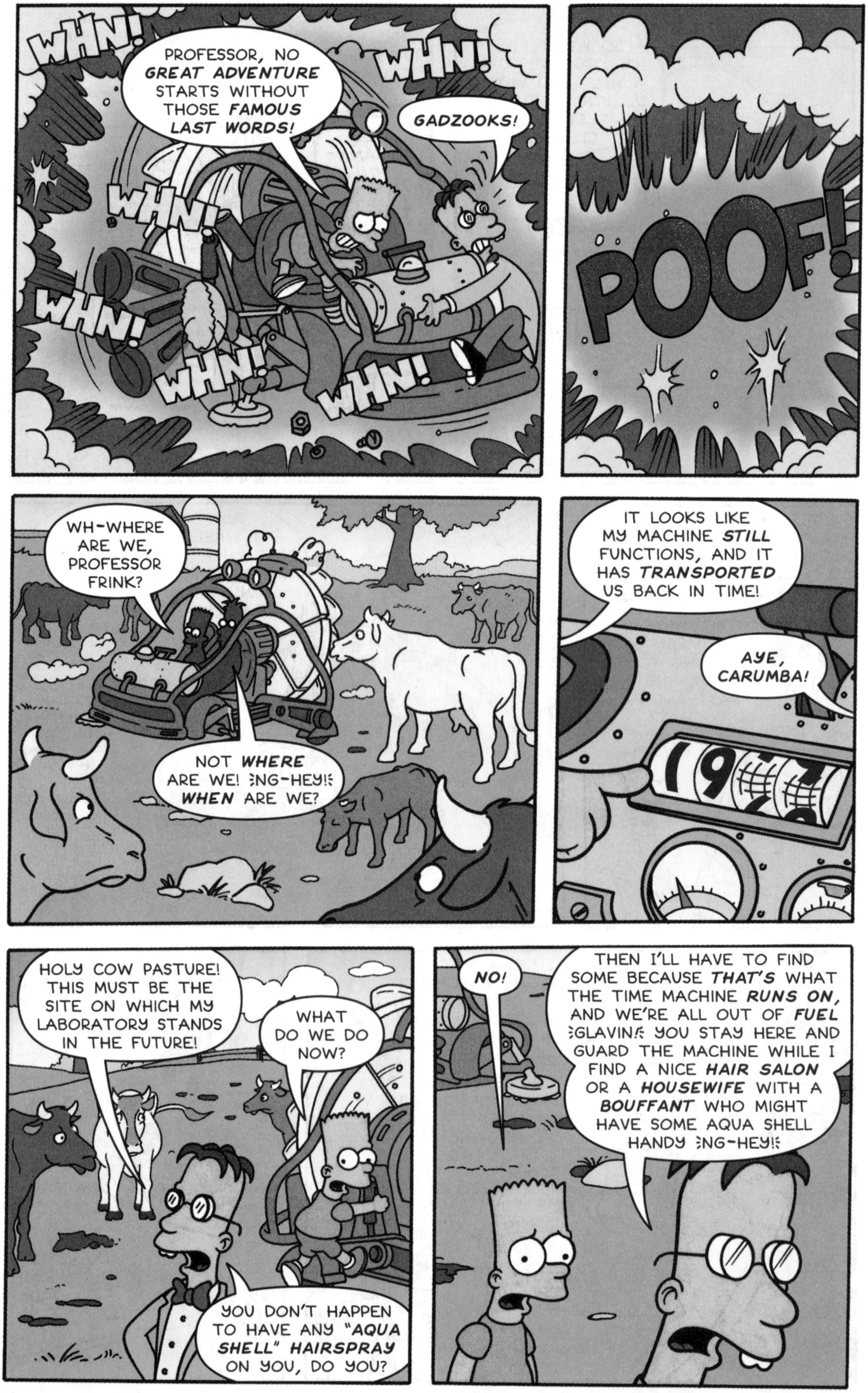
WHN!
PROFESSOR, NO GREAT ADVENTURE STARTS WITHOUT THOSE FAMOUS LAST WORDS!
WHN!
GADZOOKS!
WHN!
WHN!
WHN!
WHN!
POOF!
WH-WHERE ARE WE, PROFESSOR FRINK?
NOT WHERE ARE WE! ≋NG-HEY!≋ WHEN ARE WE?
IT LOOKS LIKE MY MACHINE STILL FUNCTIONS, AND IT HAS TRANSPORTED US BACK IN TIME!
AYE, CARUMBA!
HOLY COW PASTURE! THIS MUST BE THE SITE ON WHICH MY LABORATORY STANDS IN THE FUTURE!
WHAT DO WE DO NOW?
YOU DON'T HAPPEN TO HAVE ANY "AQUA SHELL" HAIRSPRAY ON YOU, DO YOU?
NO!
THEN I'LL HAVE TO FIND SOME BECAUSE THAT'S WHAT THE TIME MACHINE RUNS ON, AND WE'RE ALL OUT OF FUEL ≋GLAVIN!≋ YOU STAY HERE AND GUARD THE MACHINE WHILE I FIND A NICE HAIR SALON OR A HOUSEWIFE WITH A BOUFFANT WHO MIGHT HAVE SOME AQUA SHELL HANDY ≋NG-HEY!≋

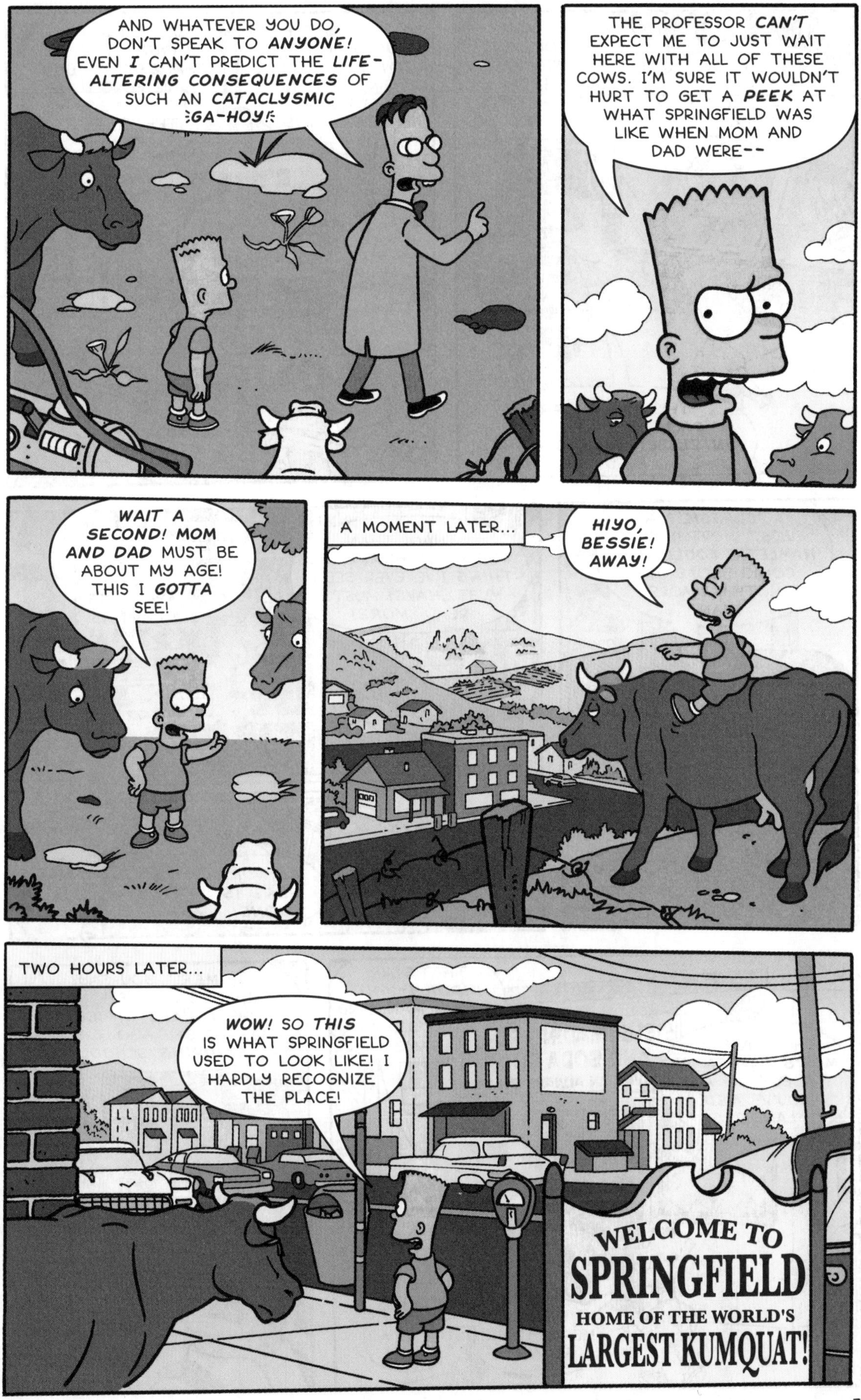
AND WHATEVER YOU DO, DON'T SPEAK TO ANYONE! EVEN I CAN'T PREDICT THE LIFE-ALTERING CONSEQUENCES OF SUCH AN CATACLYSMIC GA-HOY!
THE PROFESSOR CAN'T EXPECT ME TO JUST WAIT HERE WITH ALL OF THESE COWS. I'M SURE IT WOULDN'T HURT TO GET A PEEK AT WHAT SPRINGFIELD WAS LIKE WHEN MOM AND DAD WERE--
WAIT A SECOND! MOM AND DAD MUST BE ABOUT MY AGE! THIS I GOTTA SEE!
A MOMENT LATER...
HIYO, BESSIE! AWAY!
TWO HOURS LATER...
WOW! SO THIS IS WHAT SPRINGFIELD USED TO LOOK LIKE! I HARDLY RECOGNIZE THE PLACE!
WELCOME TO SPRINGFIELD HOME OF THE WORLD'S LARGEST KUMQUAT!

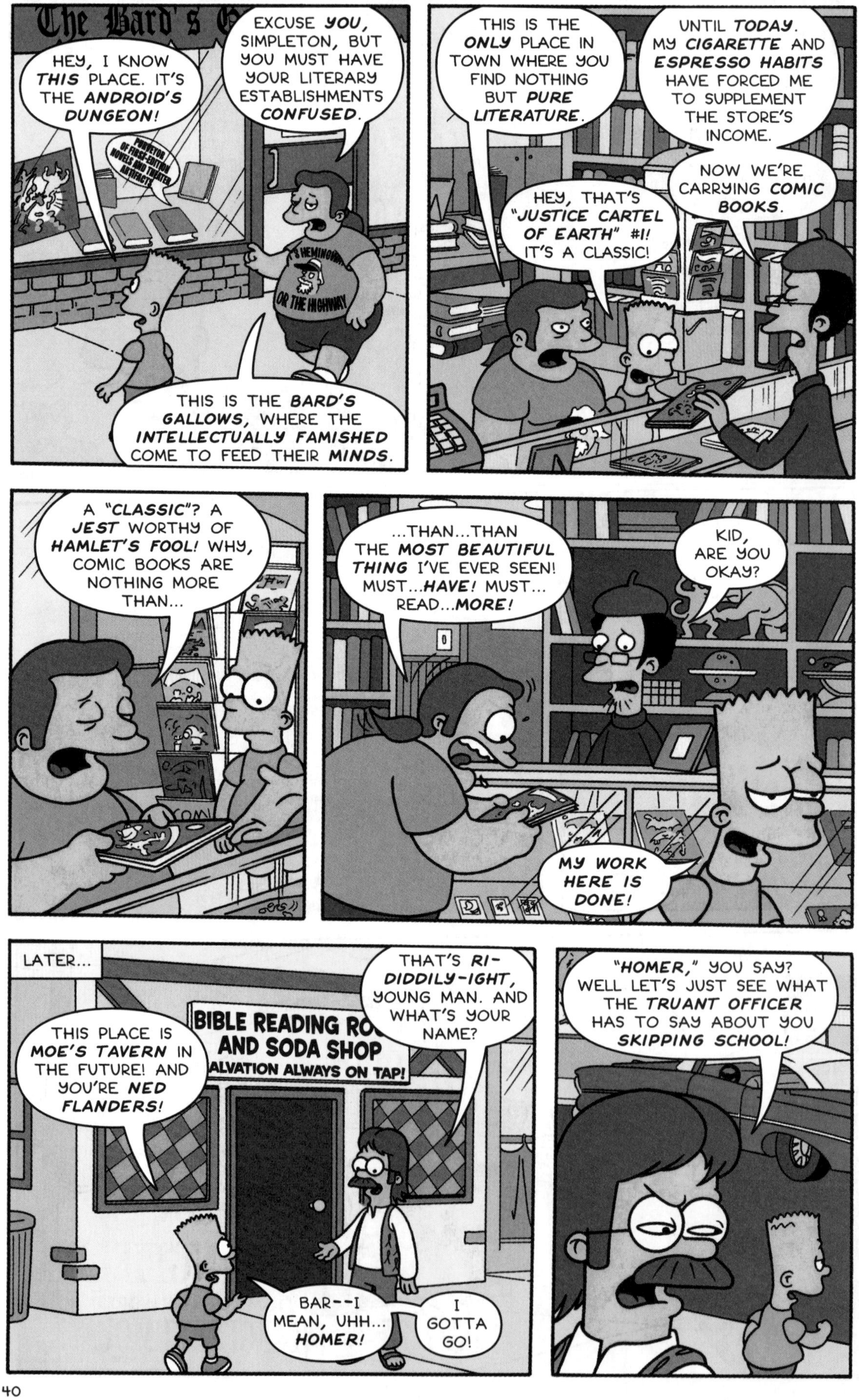

HEY, I KNOW THIS PLACE. IT'S THE ANDROID'S DUNGEON!
EXCUSE YOU, SIMPLETON, BUT YOU MUST HAVE YOUR LITERARY ESTABLISHMENTS CONFUSED.
PURVEYOR OF FIRST-EDITION NOVELS AND THEATER ARTIFACTS
THIS IS THE BARD'S GALLOWS, WHERE THE INTELLECTUALLY FAMISHED COME TO FEED THEIR MINDS.
THIS IS THE ONLY PLACE IN TOWN WHERE YOU FIND NOTHING BUT PURE LITERATURE.
UNTIL TODAY. MY CIGARETTE AND ESPRESSO HABITS HAVE FORCED ME TO SUPPLEMENT THE STORE'S INCOME.
NOW WE'RE CARRYING COMIC BOOKS.
HEY, THAT'S "JUSTICE CARTEL OF EARTH" #1! IT'S A CLASSIC!
A "CLASSIC"? A JEST WORTHY OF HAMLET'S FOOL! WHY, COMIC BOOKS ARE NOTHING MORE THAN...
...THAN...THAN THE MOST BEAUTIFUL THING I'VE EVER SEEN! MUST...HAVE! MUST... READ...MORE!
KID, ARE YOU OKAY?
MY WORK HERE IS DONE!
LATER...
BIBLE READING RO
AND SODA SHOP
ALVATION ALWAYS ON TAP!
THIS PLACE IS MOE'S TAVERN IN THE FUTURE! AND YOU'RE NED FLANDERS!
THAT'S RI-DIDDILY-IGHT, YOUNG MAN. AND WHAT'S YOUR NAME?
BAR--I MEAN, UHH... HOMER!
I GOTTA GO!
"HOMER," YOU SAY? WELL LET'S JUST SEE WHAT THE TRUANT OFFICER HAS TO SAY ABOUT YOU SKIPPING SCHOOL!

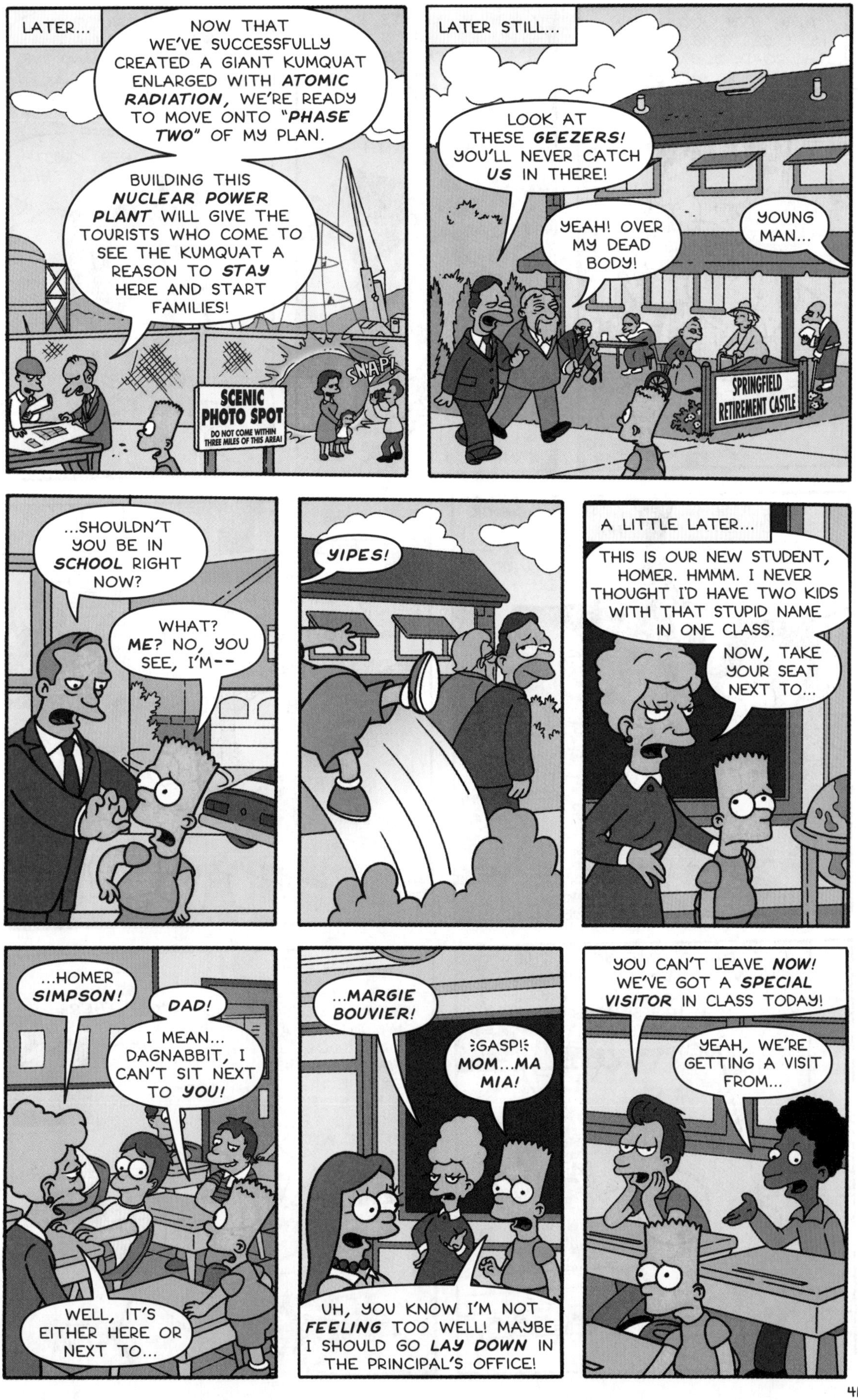
LATER...
NOW THAT WE'VE SUCCESSFULLY CREATED A GIANT KUMQUAT ENLARGED WITH ATOMIC RADIATION, WE'RE READY TO MOVE ONTO "PHASE TWO" OF MY PLAN.
BUILDING THIS NUCLEAR POWER PLANT WILL GIVE THE TOURISTS WHO COME TO SEE THE KUMQUAT A REASON TO STAY HERE AND START FAMILIES!
SCENIC PHOTO SPOT
DO NOT COME WITHIN THREE MILES OF THIS AREA!
SNAP!
LATER STILL...
LOOK AT THESE GEEZERS! YOU'LL NEVER CATCH US IN THERE!
YEAH! OVER MY DEAD BODY!
YOUNG MAN...
SPRINGFIELD RETIREMENT CASTLE
...SHOULDN'T YOU BE IN SCHOOL RIGHT NOW?
WHAT? ME? NO, YOU SEE, I'M--
YIPES!
A LITTLE LATER...
THIS IS OUR NEW STUDENT, HOMER. HMMM. I NEVER THOUGHT I'D HAVE TWO KIDS WITH THAT STUPID NAME IN ONE CLASS.
NOW, TAKE YOUR SEAT NEXT TO...
...HOMER SIMPSON!
DAD!
I MEAN... DAGNABBIT, I CAN'T SIT NEXT TO YOU!
WELL, IT'S EITHER HERE OR NEXT TO...
...MARGIE BOUVIER!
GASP! MOM...MA MIA!
UH, YOU KNOW I'M NOT FEELING TOO WELL! MAYBE I SHOULD GO LAY DOWN IN THE PRINCIPAL'S OFFICE!
YOU CAN'T LEAVE NOW! WE'VE GOT A SPECIAL VISITOR IN CLASS TODAY!
YEAH, WE'RE GETTING A VISIT FROM...

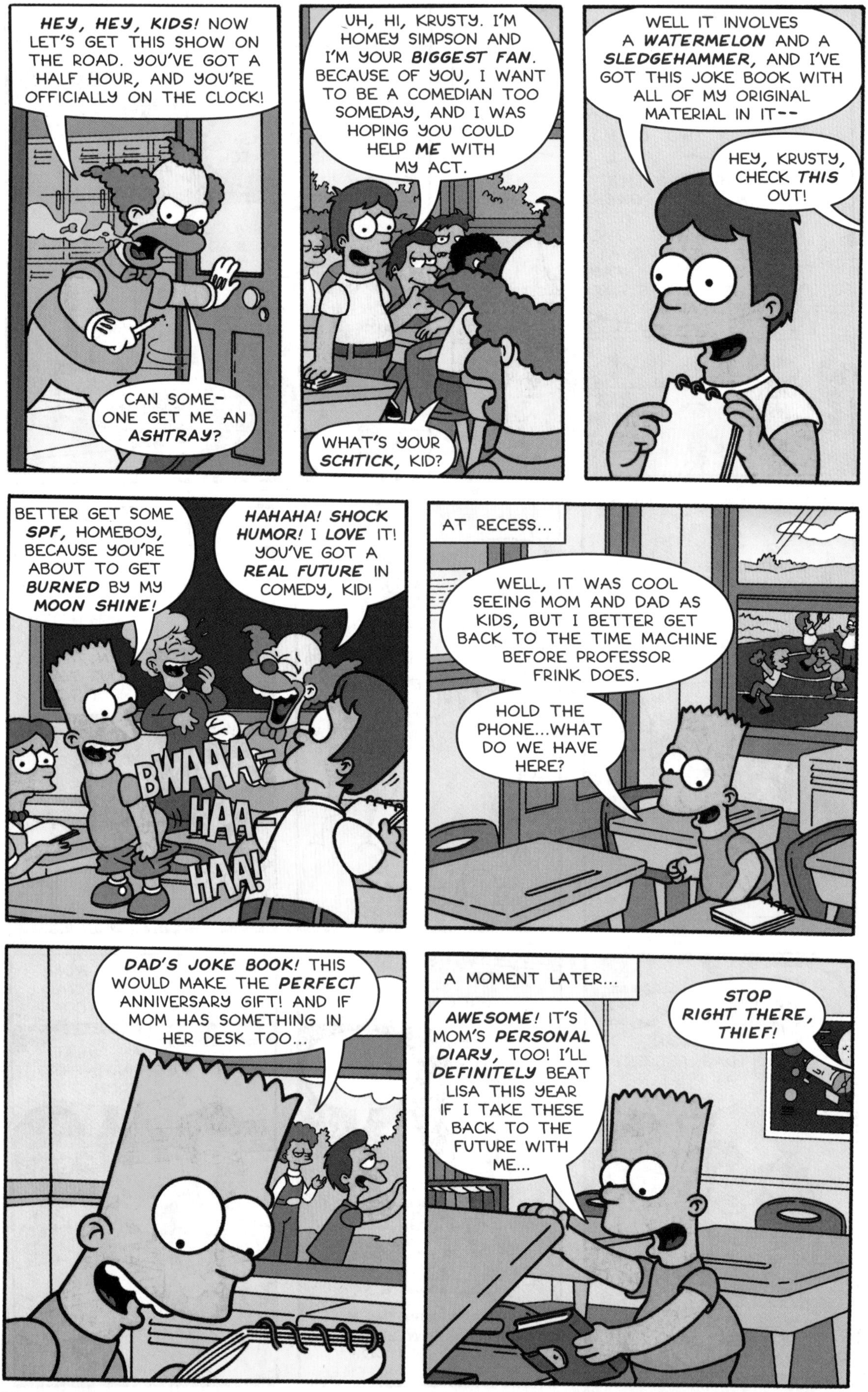
HEY, HEY, KIDS! NOW LET'S GET THIS SHOW ON THE ROAD. YOU'VE GOT A HALF HOUR, AND YOU'RE OFFICIALLY ON THE CLOCK!
CAN SOME-ONE GET ME AN ASHTRAY?
UH, HI, KRUSTY. I'M HOMEY SIMPSON AND I'M YOUR BIGGEST FAN. BECAUSE OF YOU, I WANT TO BE A COMEDIAN TOO SOMEDAY, AND I WAS HOPING YOU COULD HELP ME WITH MY ACT.
WHAT'S YOUR SCHTICK, KID?
WELL IT INVOLVES A WATERMELON AND A SLEDGEHAMMER, AND I'VE GOT THIS JOKE BOOK WITH ALL OF MY ORIGINAL MATERIAL IN IT--
HEY, KRUSTY, CHECK THIS OUT!
BETTER GET SOME SPF, HOMEBOY, BECAUSE YOU'RE ABOUT TO GET BURNED BY MY MOON SHINE!
HAHAHA! SHOCK HUMOR! I LOVE IT! YOU'VE GOT A REAL FUTURE IN COMEDY, KID!
BWAAA-HAA-HAA!
AT RECESS...
WELL, IT WAS COOL SEEING MOM AND DAD AS KIDS, BUT I BETTER GET BACK TO THE TIME MACHINE BEFORE PROFESSOR FRINK DOES.
HOLD THE PHONE...WHAT DO WE HAVE HERE?
DAD'S JOKE BOOK! THIS WOULD MAKE THE PERFECT ANNIVERSARY GIFT! AND IF MOM HAS SOMETHING IN HER DESK TOO...
A MOMENT LATER...
AWESOME! IT'S MOM'S PERSONAL DIARY, TOO! I'LL DEFINITELY BEAT LISA THIS YEAR IF I TAKE THESE BACK TO THE FUTURE WITH ME...
STOP RIGHT THERE, THIEF!

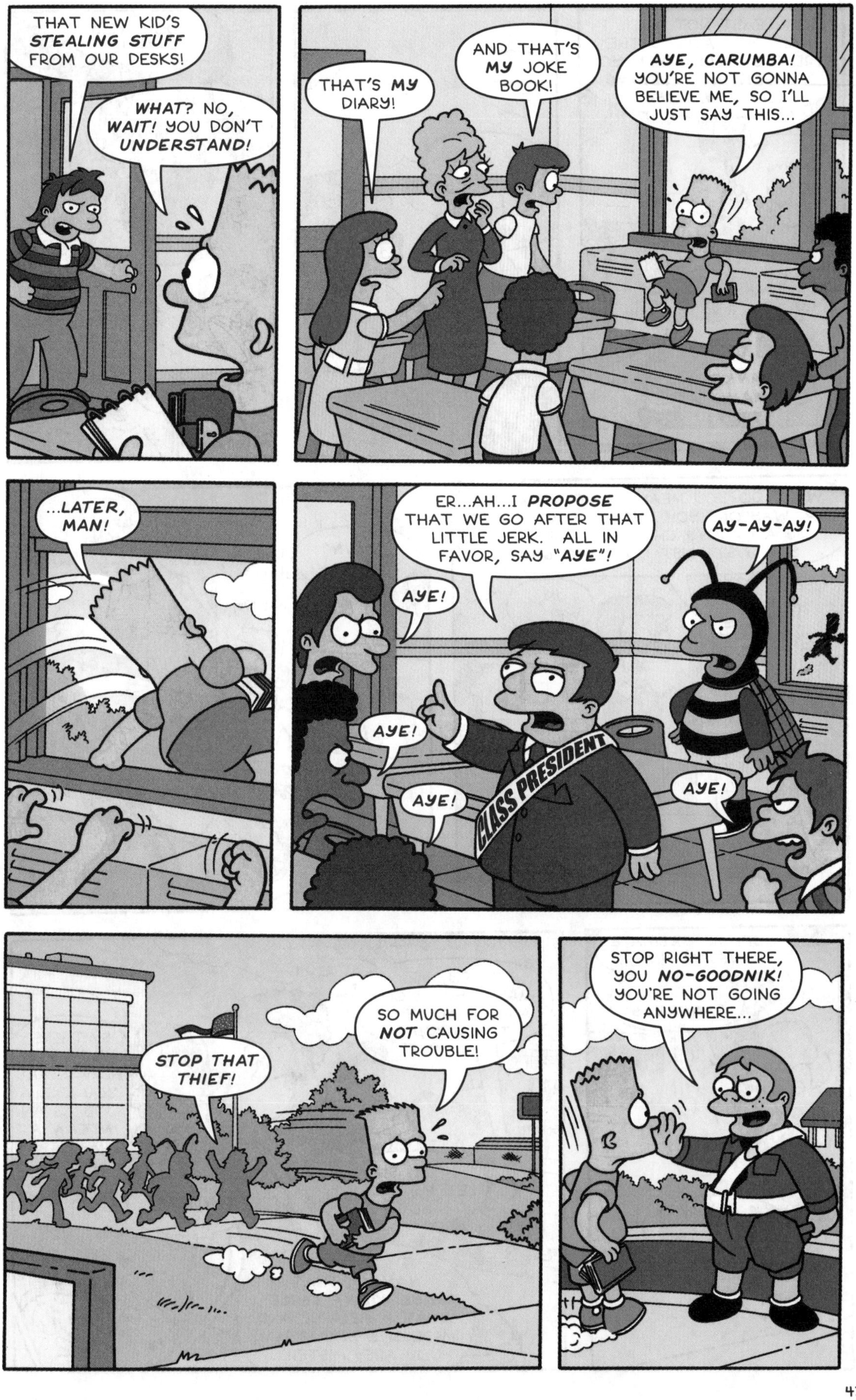
THAT NEW KID'S STEALING STUFF FROM OUR DESKS!
WHAT? NO, WAIT! YOU DON'T UNDERSTAND!
THAT'S MY DIARY!
AND THAT'S MY JOKE BOOK!
AYE, CARUMBA! YOU'RE NOT GONNA BELIEVE ME, SO I'LL JUST SAY THIS...
...LATER, MAN!
ER...AH...I PROPOSE THAT WE GO AFTER THAT LITTLE JERK. ALL IN FAVOR, SAY "AYE"!
AY-AY-AY!
AYE!
AYE!
AYE!
AYE!
CLASS PRESIDENT
STOP THAT THIEF!
SO MUCH FOR NOT CAUSING TROUBLE!
STOP RIGHT THERE, YOU NO-GOODNIK! YOU'RE NOT GOING ANYWHERE...

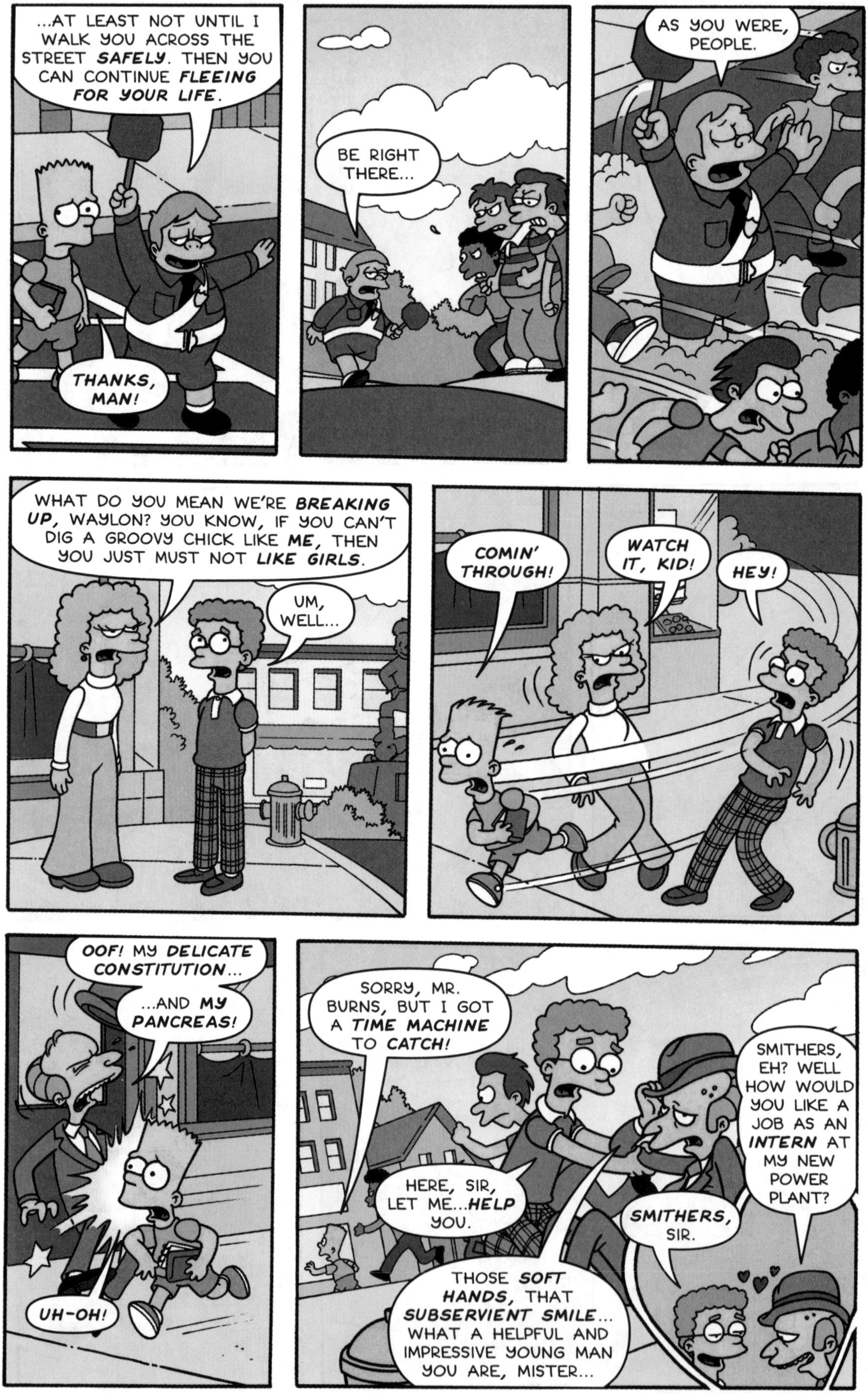
...AT LEAST NOT UNTIL I WALK YOU ACROSS THE STREET SAFELY. THEN YOU CAN CONTINUE FLEEING FOR YOUR LIFE.
THANKS, MAN!
BE RIGHT THERE...
AS YOU WERE, PEOPLE.
WHAT DO YOU MEAN WE'RE BREAKING UP, WAYLON? YOU KNOW, IF YOU CAN'T DIG A GROOVY CHICK LIKE ME, THEN YOU JUST MUST NOT LIKE GIRLS.
UM, WELL...
COMIN' THROUGH!
WATCH IT, KID!
HEY!
OOF! MY DELICATE CONSTITUTION...
...AND MY PANCREAS!
UH-OH!
SORRY, MR. BURNS, BUT I GOT A TIME MACHINE TO CATCH!
HERE, SIR, LET ME...HELP YOU.
THOSE SOFT HANDS, THAT SUBSERVIENT SMILE... WHAT A HELPFUL AND IMPRESSIVE YOUNG MAN YOU ARE, MISTER...
SMITHERS, SIR.
SMITHERS, EH? WELL HOW WOULD YOU LIKE A JOB AS AN INTERN AT MY NEW POWER PLANT?

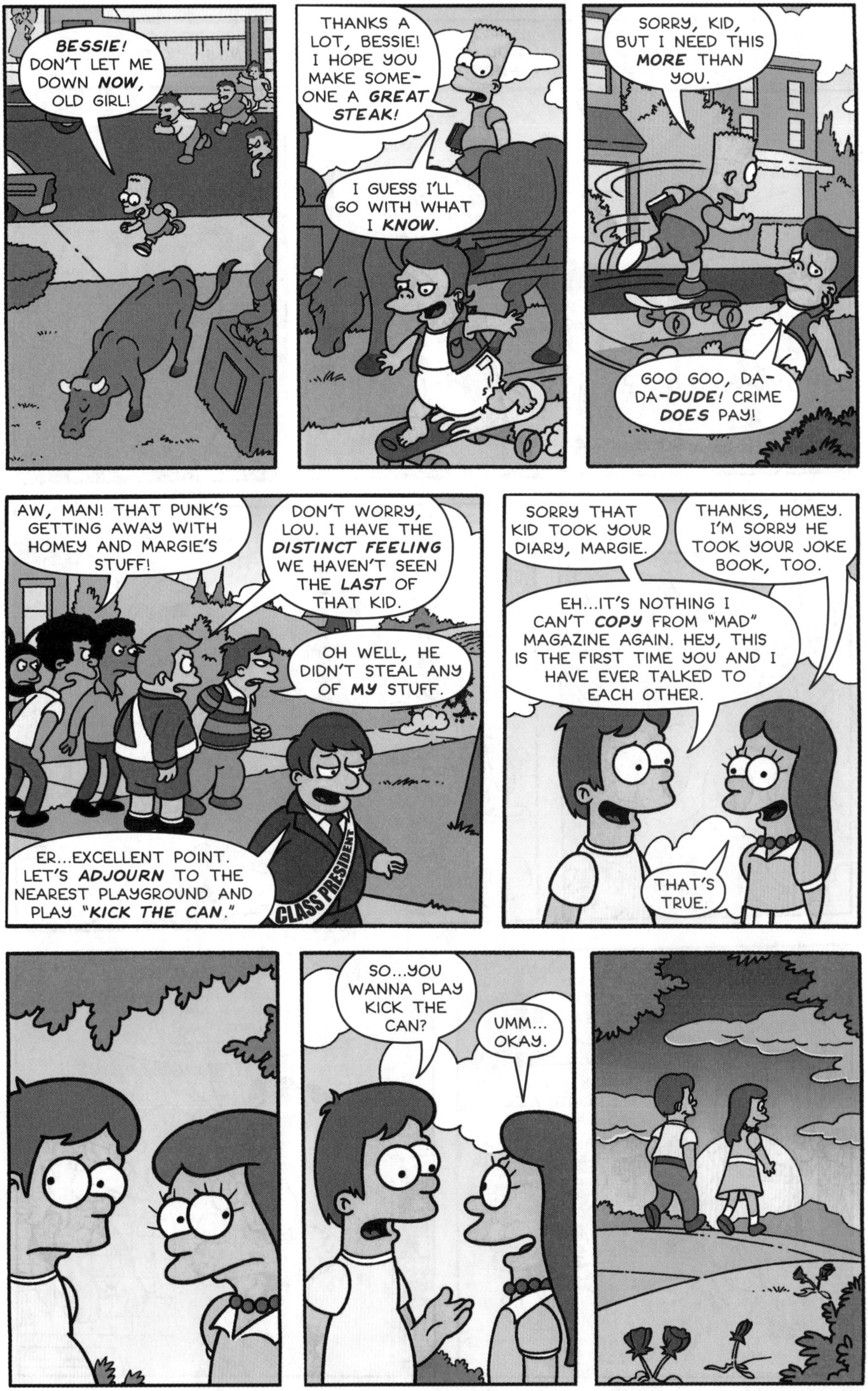
BESSIE! DON'T LET ME DOWN NOW, OLD GIRL!
THANKS A LOT, BESSIE! I HOPE YOU MAKE SOME-ONE A GREAT STEAK!
I GUESS I'LL GO WITH WHAT I KNOW.
SORRY, KID, BUT I NEED THIS MORE THAN YOU.
GOO GOO, DA-DA-DUDE! CRIME DOES PAY!
AW, MAN! THAT PUNK'S GETTING AWAY WITH HOMEY AND MARGIE'S STUFF!
DON'T WORRY, LOU. I HAVE THE DISTINCT FEELING WE HAVEN'T SEEN THE LAST OF THAT KID.
OH WELL, HE DIDN'T STEAL ANY OF MY STUFF.
ER...EXCELLENT POINT. LET'S ADJOURN TO THE NEAREST PLAYGROUND AND PLAY "KICK THE CAN."
CLASS PRESIDENT
SORRY THAT KID TOOK YOUR DIARY, MARGIE.
THANKS, HOMEY. I'M SORRY HE TOOK YOUR JOKE BOOK, TOO.
EH...IT'S NOTHING I CAN'T COPY FROM "MAD" MAGAZINE AGAIN. HEY, THIS IS THE FIRST TIME YOU AND I HAVE EVER TALKED TO EACH OTHER.
THAT'S TRUE.
SO...YOU WANNA PLAY KICK THE CAN?
UMM... OKAY.

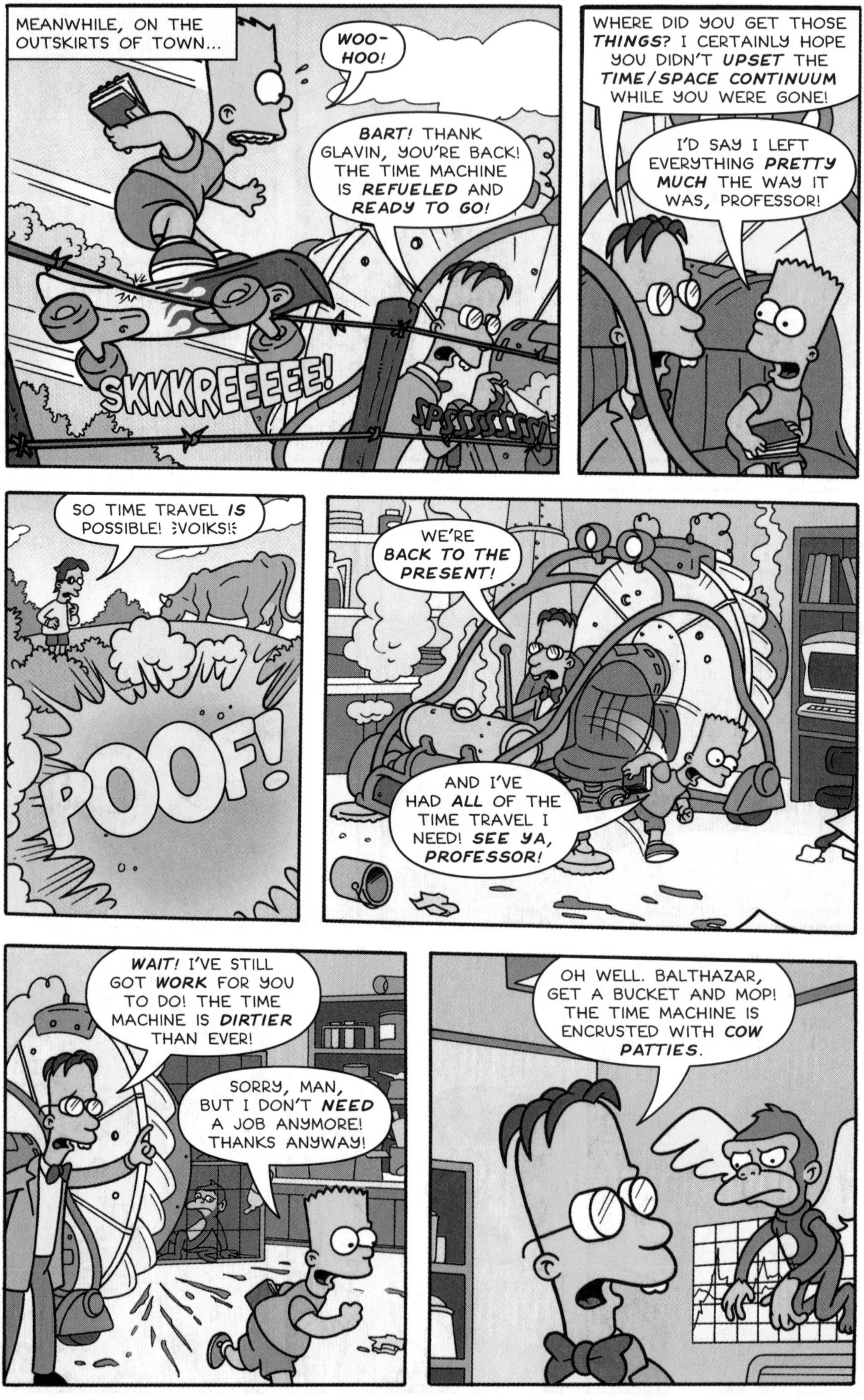
MEANWHILE, ON THE OUTSKIRTS OF TOWN...
WOO-HOO!
BART! THANK GLAVIN, YOU'RE BACK! THE TIME MACHINE IS REFUELED AND READY TO GO!
SKKKREEEEEE!
SPSSSSSSSS!
WHERE DID YOU GET THOSE THINGS? I CERTAINLY HOPE YOU DIDN'T UPSET THE TIME/SPACE CONTINUUM WHILE YOU WERE GONE!
I'D SAY I LEFT EVERYTHING PRETTY MUCH THE WAY IT WAS, PROFESSOR!
SO TIME TRAVEL IS POSSIBLE! VOIKS!
POOF!
WE'RE BACK TO THE PRESENT!
AND I'VE HAD ALL OF THE TIME TRAVEL I NEED! SEE YA, PROFESSOR!
WAIT! I'VE STILL GOT WORK FOR YOU TO DO! THE TIME MACHINE IS DIRTIER THAN EVER!
SORRY, MAN, BUT I DON'T NEED A JOB ANYMORE! THANKS ANYWAY!
OH WELL. BALTHAZAR, GET A BUCKET AND MOP! THE TIME MACHINE IS ENCRUSTED WITH COW PATTIES.

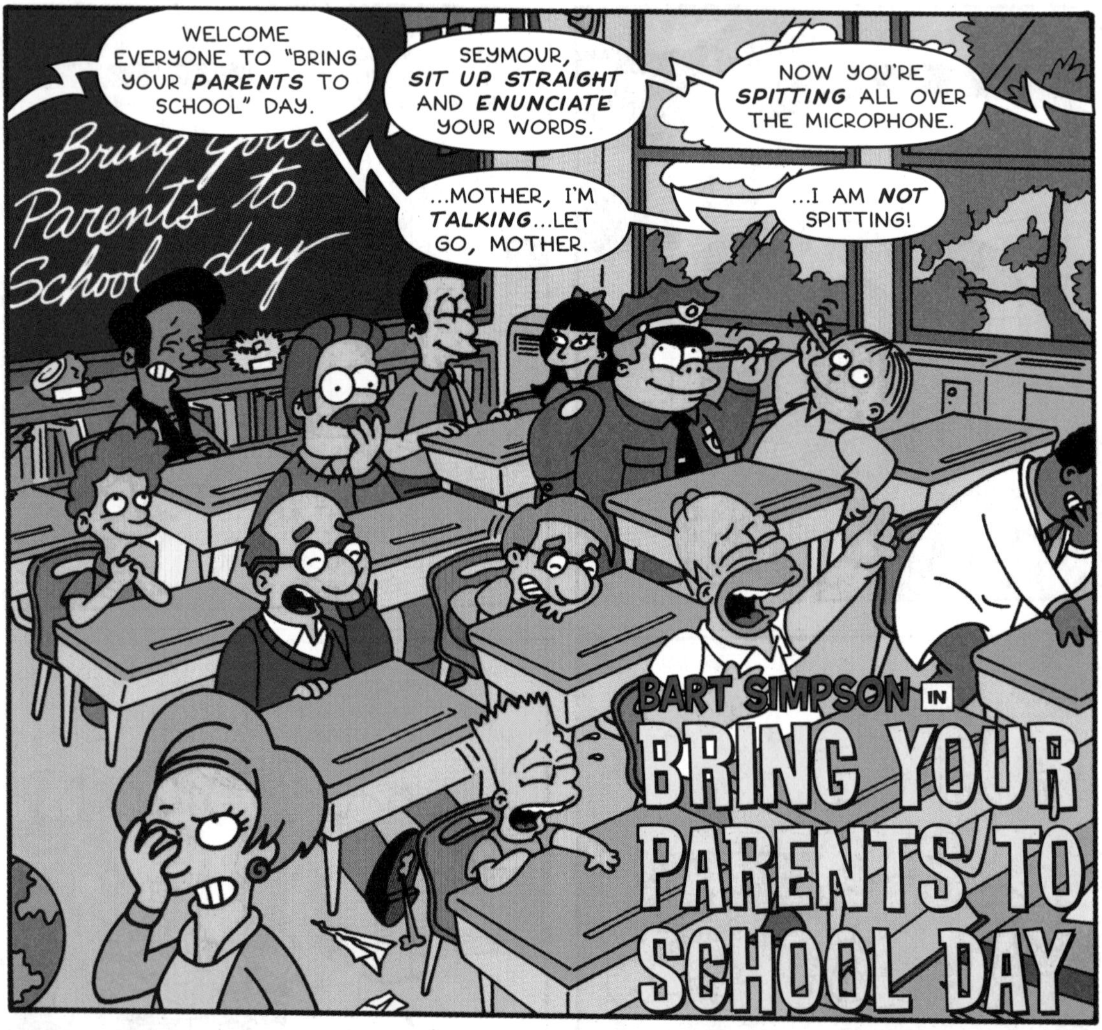
WELCOME EVERYONE TO "BRING YOUR **PARENTS** TO SCHOOL" DAY.
SEYMOUR, ***SIT UP STRAIGHT*** AND ***ENUNCIATE*** YOUR WORDS.
NOW YOU'RE ***SPITTING*** ALL OVER THE MICROPHONE.
...MOTHER, I'M ***TALKING***...LET GO, MOTHER.
...I AM ***NOT*** SPITTING!
Bring your Parents to School day
BART SIMPSON IN
BRING YOUR PARENTS TO SCHOOL DAY

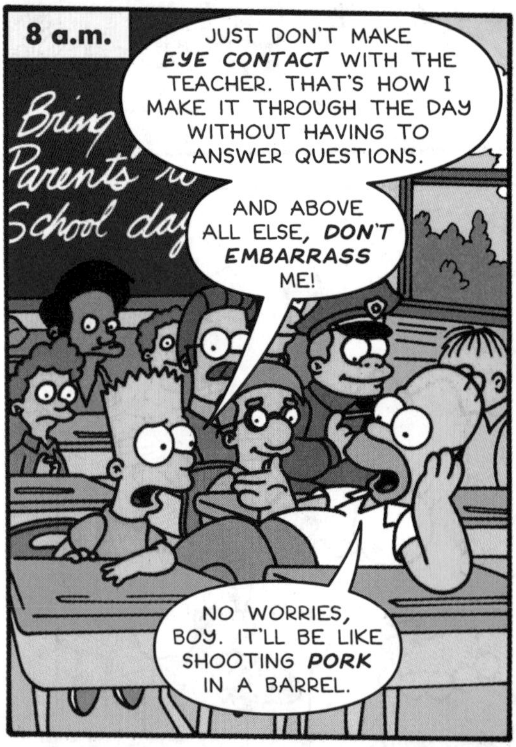
8 a.m.
JUST DON'T MAKE ***EYE CONTACT*** WITH THE TEACHER. THAT'S HOW I MAKE IT THROUGH THE DAY WITHOUT HAVING TO ANSWER QUESTIONS.
AND ABOVE ALL ELSE, ***DON'T EMBARRASS*** ME!
NO WORRIES, BOY. IT'LL BE LIKE SHOOTING ***PORK*** IN A BARREL.

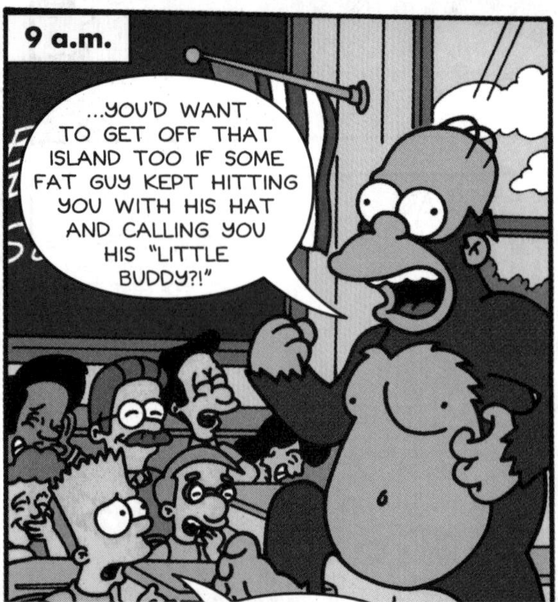
9 a.m.
...YOU'D WANT TO GET OFF THAT ISLAND TOO IF SOME FAT GUY KEPT HITTING YOU WITH HIS HAT AND CALLING YOU HIS "LITTLE BUDDY?!"
DAD! WE'RE TALKING ABOUT THE ***WAR OF 1812***.

JESSE LEON MCCANN
ABBY DENSON
STORY

JOHN COSTANZA
PENCILS

PATRICK OWSLEY
INKS

ART VILLANUEVA
COLORS

KAREN BATES
LETTERS

BILL MORRISON
EDITOR

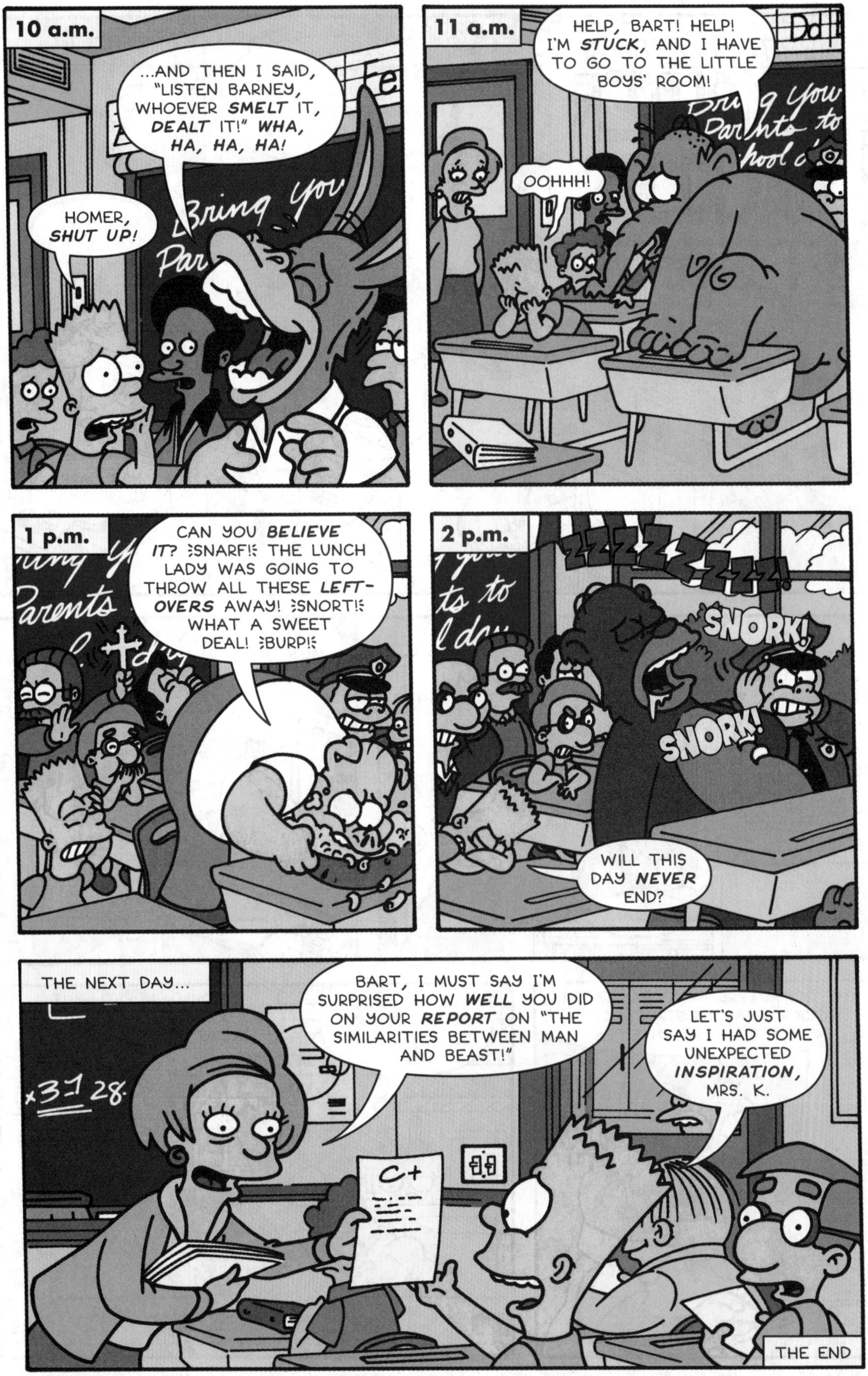
10 a.m.
...AND THEN I SAID, "LISTEN BARNEY, WHOEVER SMELT IT, DEALT IT!" WHA, HA, HA, HA!
HOMER, SHUT UP!
11 a.m.
HELP, BART! HELP! I'M STUCK, AND I HAVE TO GO TO THE LITTLE BOYS' ROOM!
OOHHH!
1 p.m.
CAN YOU BELIEVE IT? SNARF! THE LUNCH LADY WAS GOING TO THROW ALL THESE LEFT-OVERS AWAY! SNORT! WHAT A SWEET DEAL! BURP!
2 p.m.
ZZZZZZZZZ!
SNORK!
SNORK!
WILL THIS DAY NEVER END?
THE NEXT DAY...
BART, I MUST SAY I'M SURPRISED HOW WELL YOU DID ON YOUR REPORT ON "THE SIMILARITIES BETWEEN MAN AND BEAST!"
LET'S JUST SAY I HAD SOME UNEXPECTED INSPIRATION, MRS. K.
C+
THE END

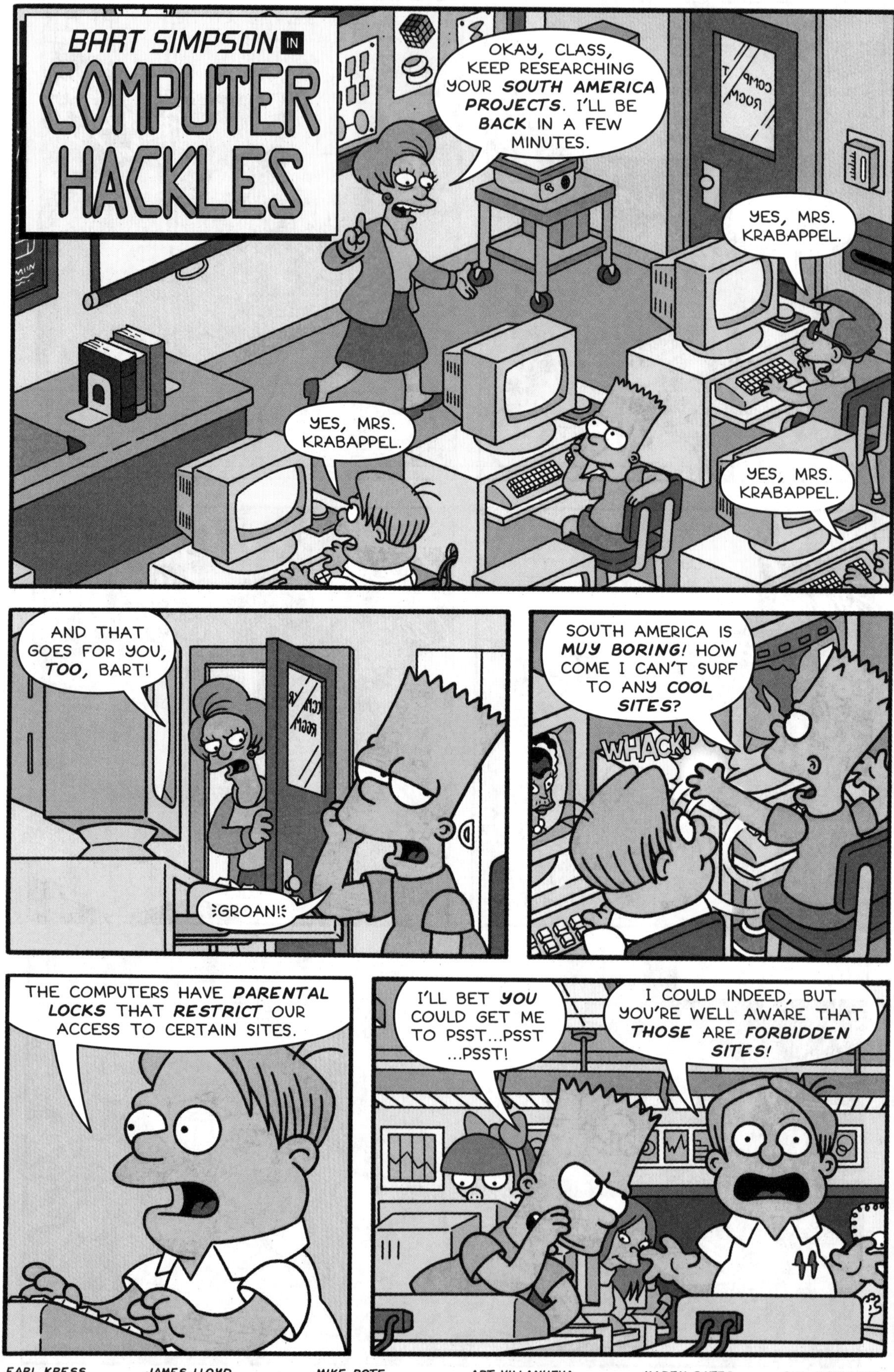
BART SIMPSON IN
COMPUTER HACKLES
OKAY, CLASS, KEEP RESEARCHING YOUR SOUTH AMERICA PROJECTS. I'LL BE BACK IN A FEW MINUTES.
YES, MRS. KRABAPPEL.
YES, MRS. KRABAPPEL.
YES, MRS. KRABAPPEL.
COMP ROOM
AND THAT GOES FOR YOU, TOO, BART!
GROAN!
SOUTH AMERICA IS MUY BORING! HOW COME I CAN'T SURF TO ANY COOL SITES?
WHACK!
THE COMPUTERS HAVE PARENTAL LOCKS THAT RESTRICT OUR ACCESS TO CERTAIN SITES.
I'LL BET YOU COULD GET ME TO PSST...PSST ...PSST!
I COULD INDEED, BUT YOU'RE WELL AWARE THAT THOSE ARE FORBIDDEN SITES!

EARL KRESS STORY | **JAMES LLOYD** PENCILS | **MIKE ROTE** INKS | **ART VILLANUEVA** COLORS | **KAREN BATES** LETTERS | **BILL MORRISON** EDITOR

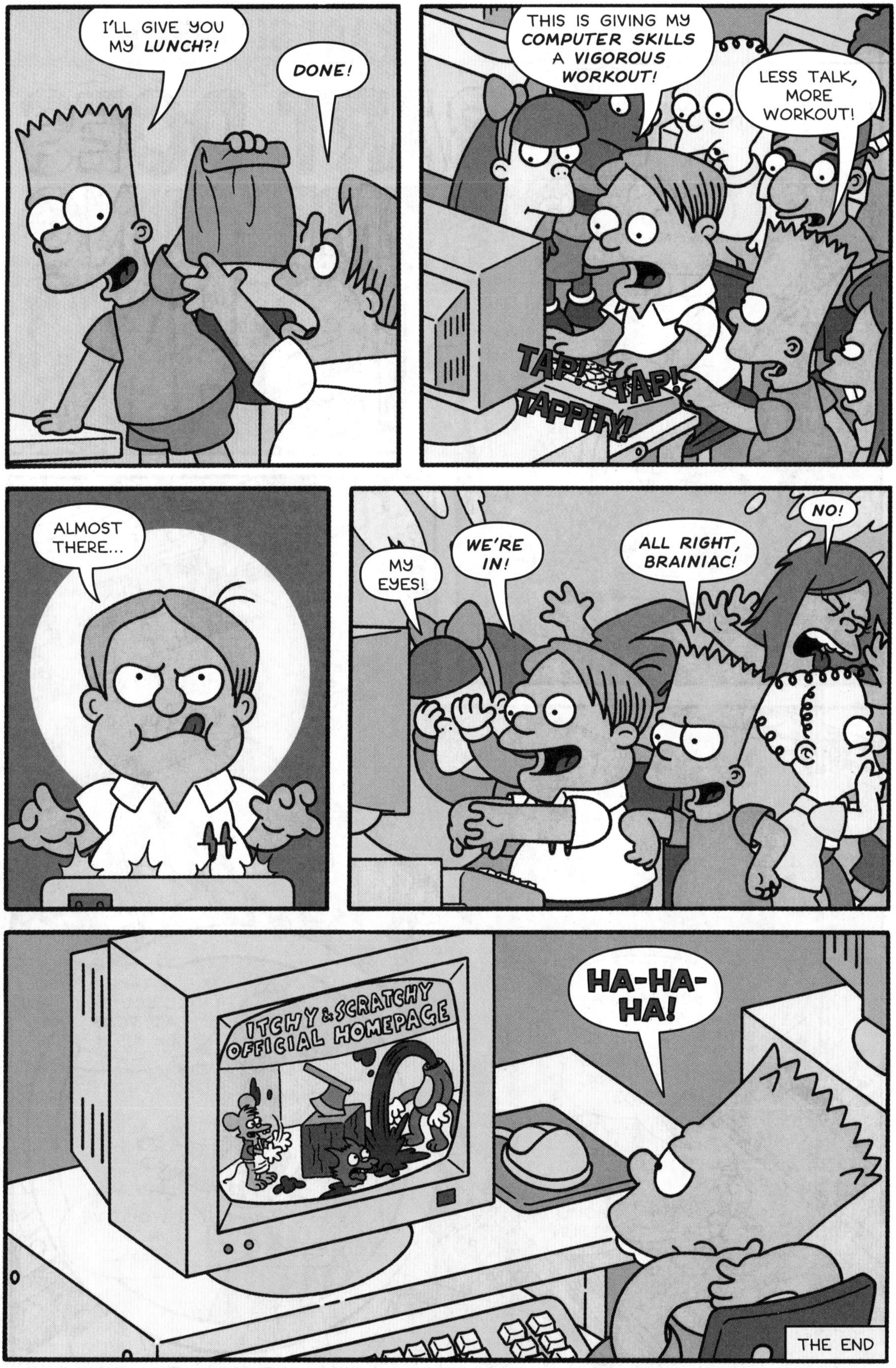
I'LL GIVE YOU MY LUNCH?!
DONE!
THIS IS GIVING MY COMPUTER SKILLS A VIGOROUS WORKOUT!
LESS TALK, MORE WORKOUT!
TAP! TAP! TAPPITY!
ALMOST THERE...
MY EYES!
WE'RE IN!
ALL RIGHT, BRAINIAC!
NO!
ITCHY & SCRATCHY OFFICIAL HOMEPAGE
HA-HA-HA!
THE END

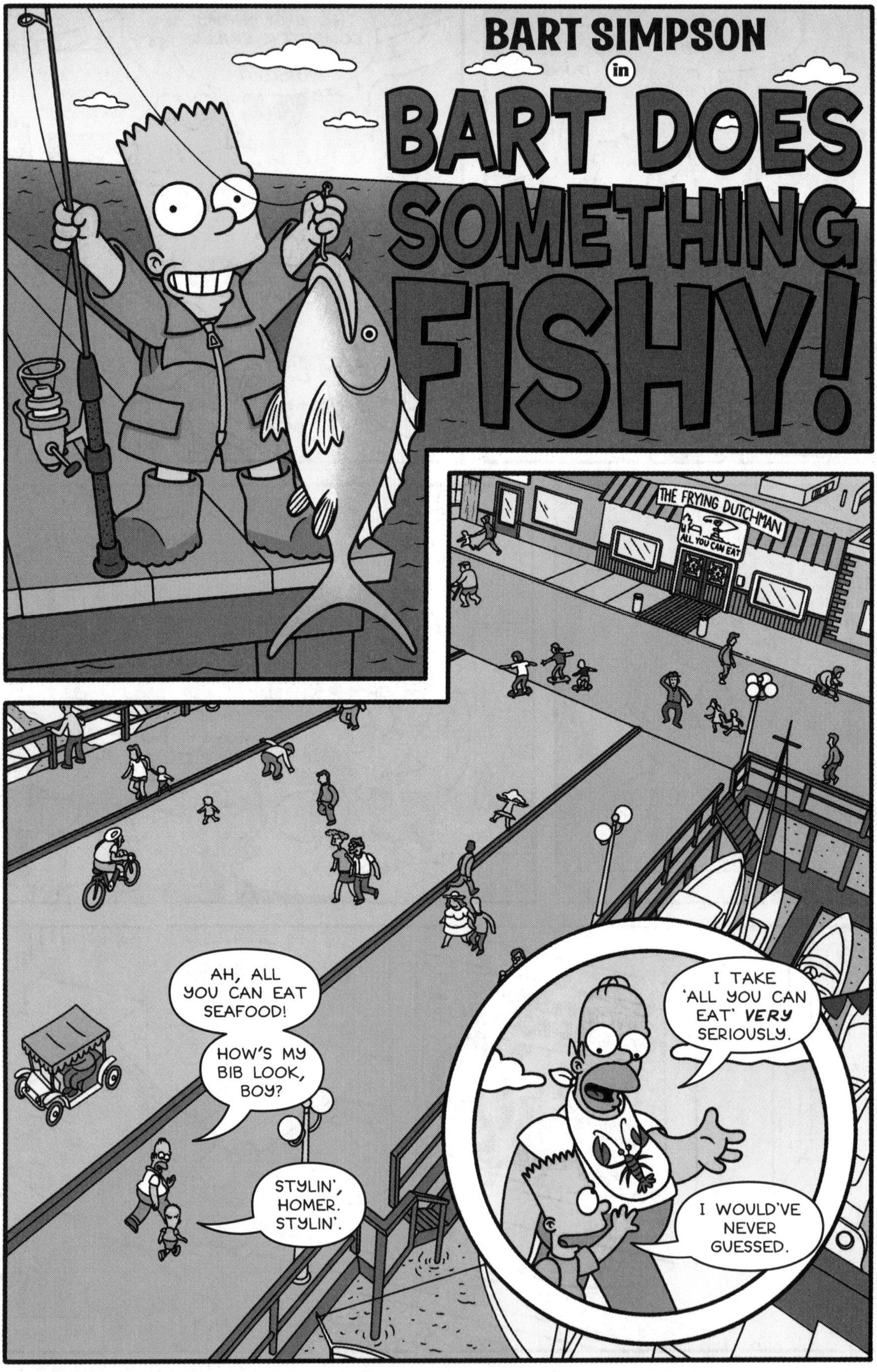
BART SIMPSON
in
BART DOES SOMETHING FISHY!
THE FRYING DUTCHMAN
ALL YOU CAN EAT
AH, ALL YOU CAN EAT SEAFOOD!
HOW'S MY BIB LOOK, BOY?
STYLIN', HOMER. STYLIN'.
I TAKE 'ALL YOU CAN EAT' *VERY* SERIOUSLY.
I WOULD'VE NEVER GUESSED.

JAMES BATES STORY | *ISTVAN MAJOROS* PENCILS | *MIKE ROTE* INKS | *ART VILLANUEVA* COLORS | *KAREN BATES* LETTERS | *BILL MORRISON* EDITOR

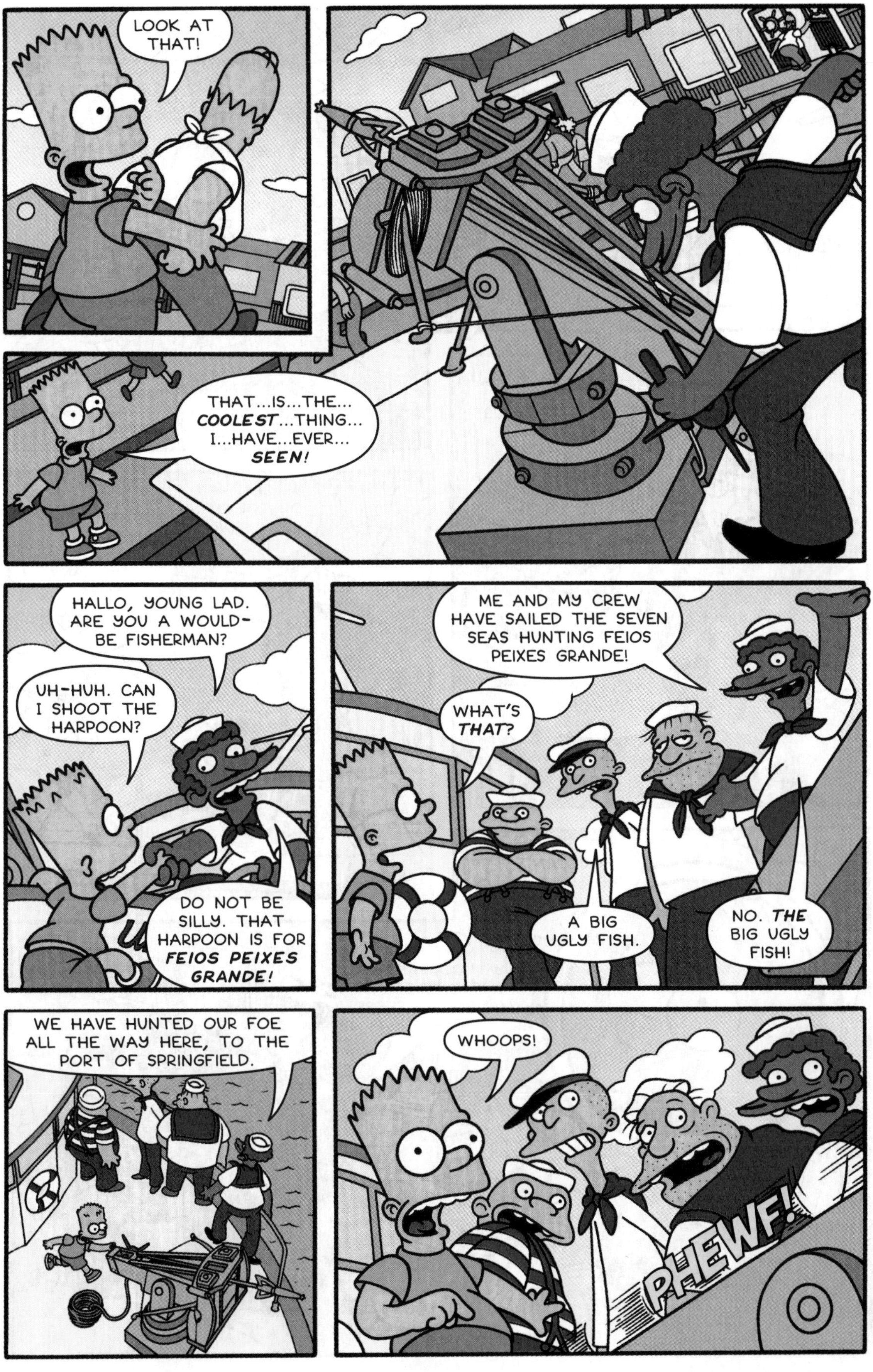
LOOK AT THAT!
THAT...IS...THE... COOLEST...THING... I...HAVE...EVER... SEEN!
HALLO, YOUNG LAD. ARE YOU A WOULD-BE FISHERMAN?
UH-HUH. CAN I SHOOT THE HARPOON?
DO NOT BE SILLY. THAT HARPOON IS FOR FEIOS PEIXES GRANDE!
ME AND MY CREW HAVE SAILED THE SEVEN SEAS HUNTING FEIOS PEIXES GRANDE!
WHAT'S THAT?
A BIG UGLY FISH.
NO. THE BIG UGLY FISH!
WE HAVE HUNTED OUR FOE ALL THE WAY HERE, TO THE PORT OF SPRINGFIELD.
WHOOPS!
PHEWF!

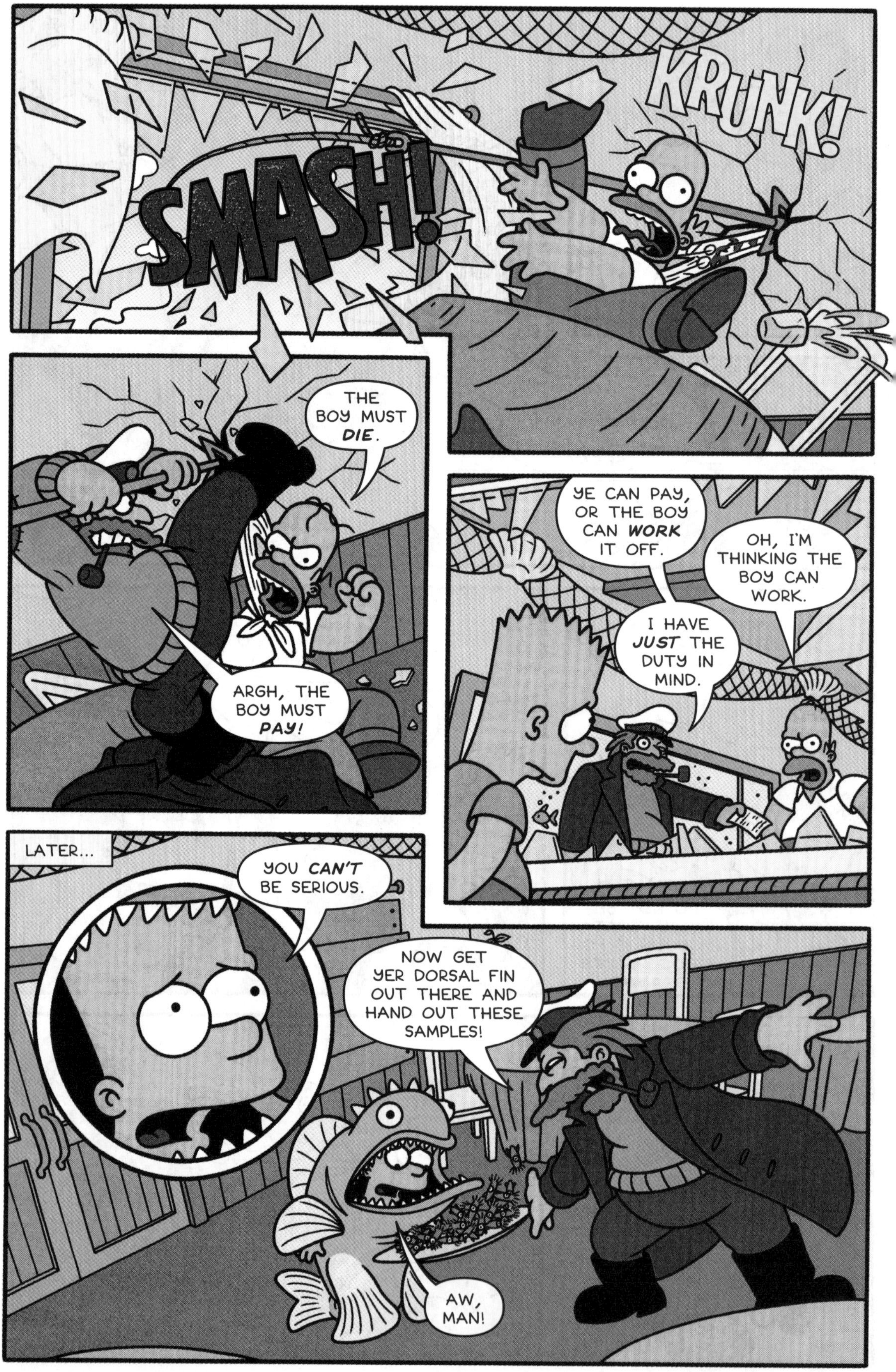
KRUNK!
SMASH!
THE BOY MUST DIE.
ARGH, THE BOY MUST PAY!
YE CAN PAY, OR THE BOY CAN WORK IT OFF.
OH, I'M THINKING THE BOY CAN WORK.
I HAVE JUST THE DUTY IN MIND.
LATER...
YOU CAN'T BE SERIOUS.
NOW GET YER DORSAL FIN OUT THERE AND HAND OUT THESE SAMPLES!
AW, MAN!

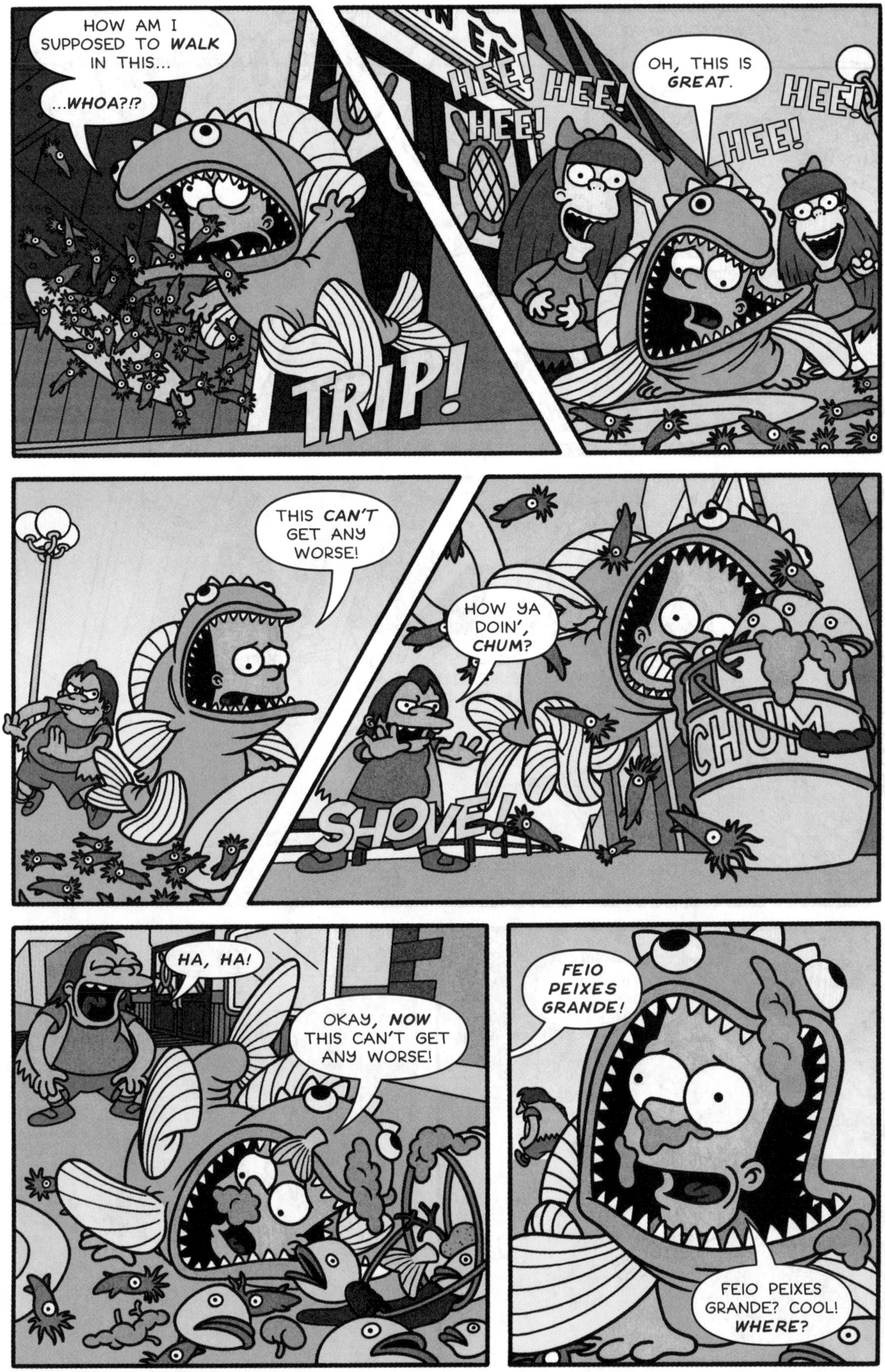
HOW AM I SUPPOSED TO WALK IN THIS...
...WHOA?!?
TRIP!
HEE! HEE! HEE!
OH, THIS IS GREAT.
HEE! HEE!
THIS CAN'T GET ANY WORSE!
HOW YA DOIN', CHUM?
CHUM
SHOVE!
HA, HA!
OKAY, NOW THIS CAN'T GET ANY WORSE!
FEIO PEIXES GRANDE!
FEIO PEIXES GRANDE? COOL! WHERE?

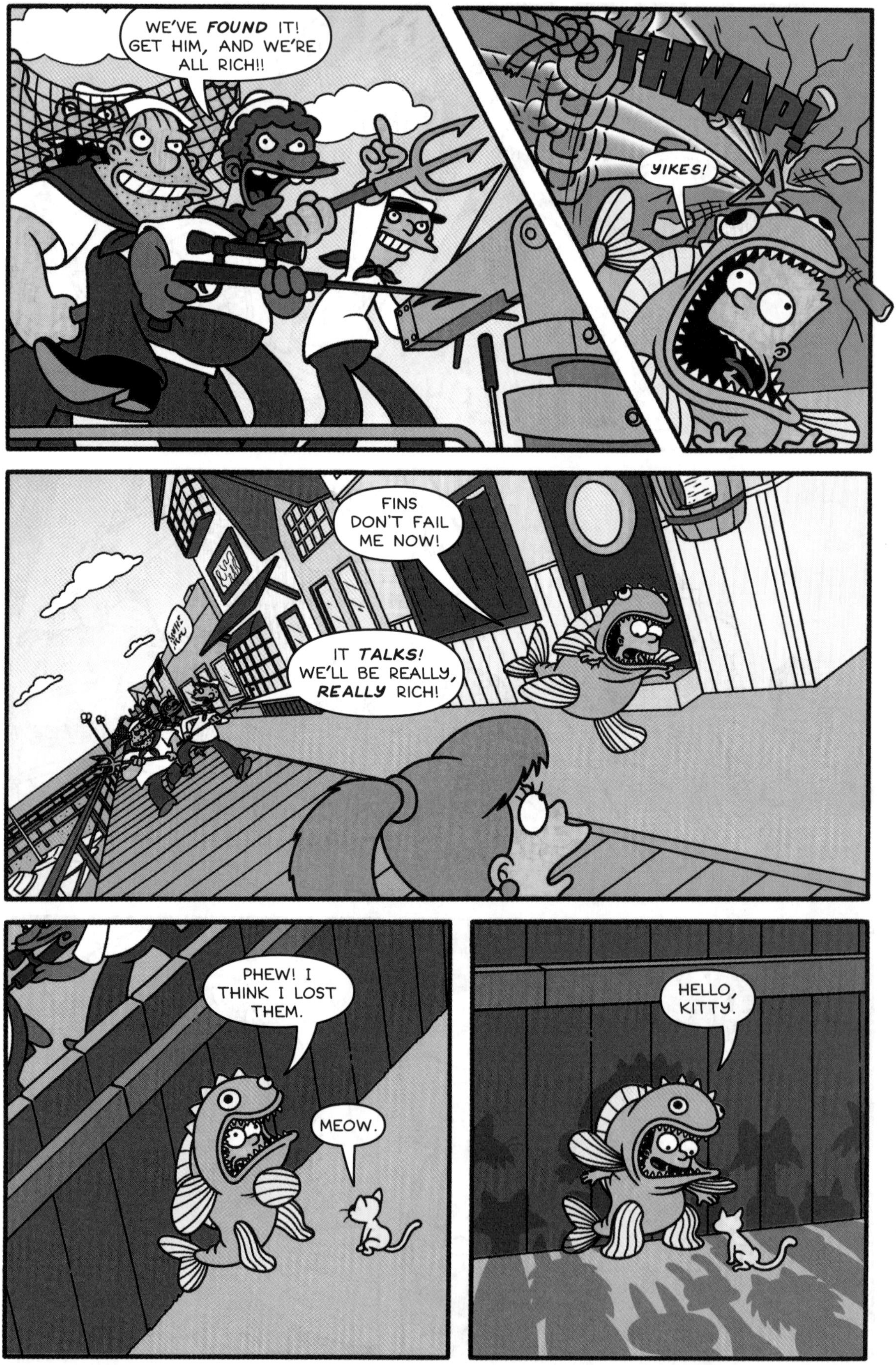
WE'VE **FOUND** IT! GET HIM, AND WE'RE ALL RICH!!
THWAP!
YIKES!
FINS DON'T FAIL ME NOW!
IT **TALKS!** WE'LL BE REALLY, **REALLY** RICH!
PHEW! I THINK I LOST THEM.
MEOW.
HELLO, KITTY.

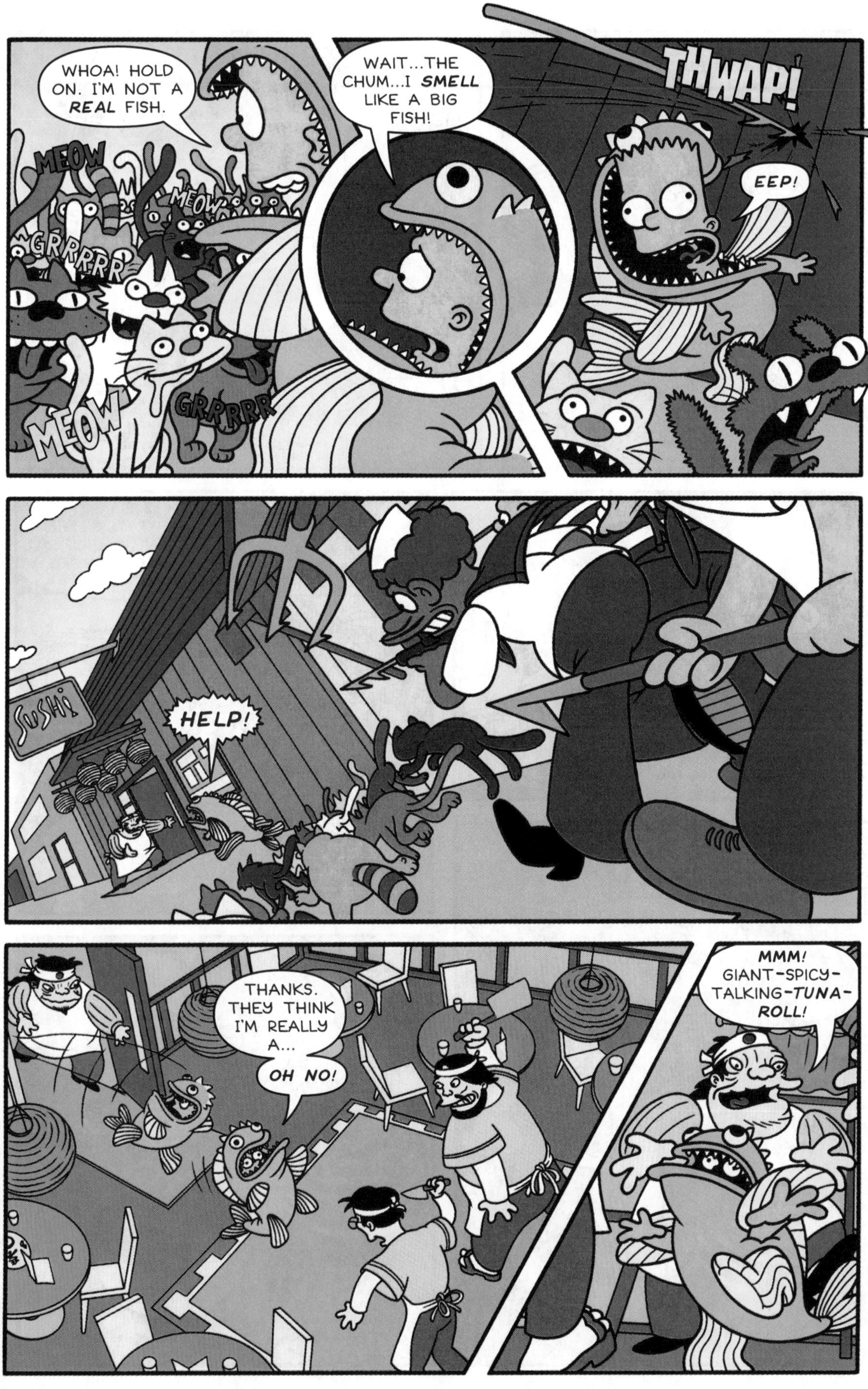

WHOA! HOLD ON. I'M NOT A REAL FISH.
MEOW
MEOW
GRRRRRR
MEOW
GRRRRR
WAIT...THE CHUM...I SMELL LIKE A BIG FISH!
THWAP!
EEP!
SUSHI
HELP!
THANKS. THEY THINK I'M REALLY A...
OH NO!
MMM! GIANT-SPICY-TALKING-TUNA-ROLL!

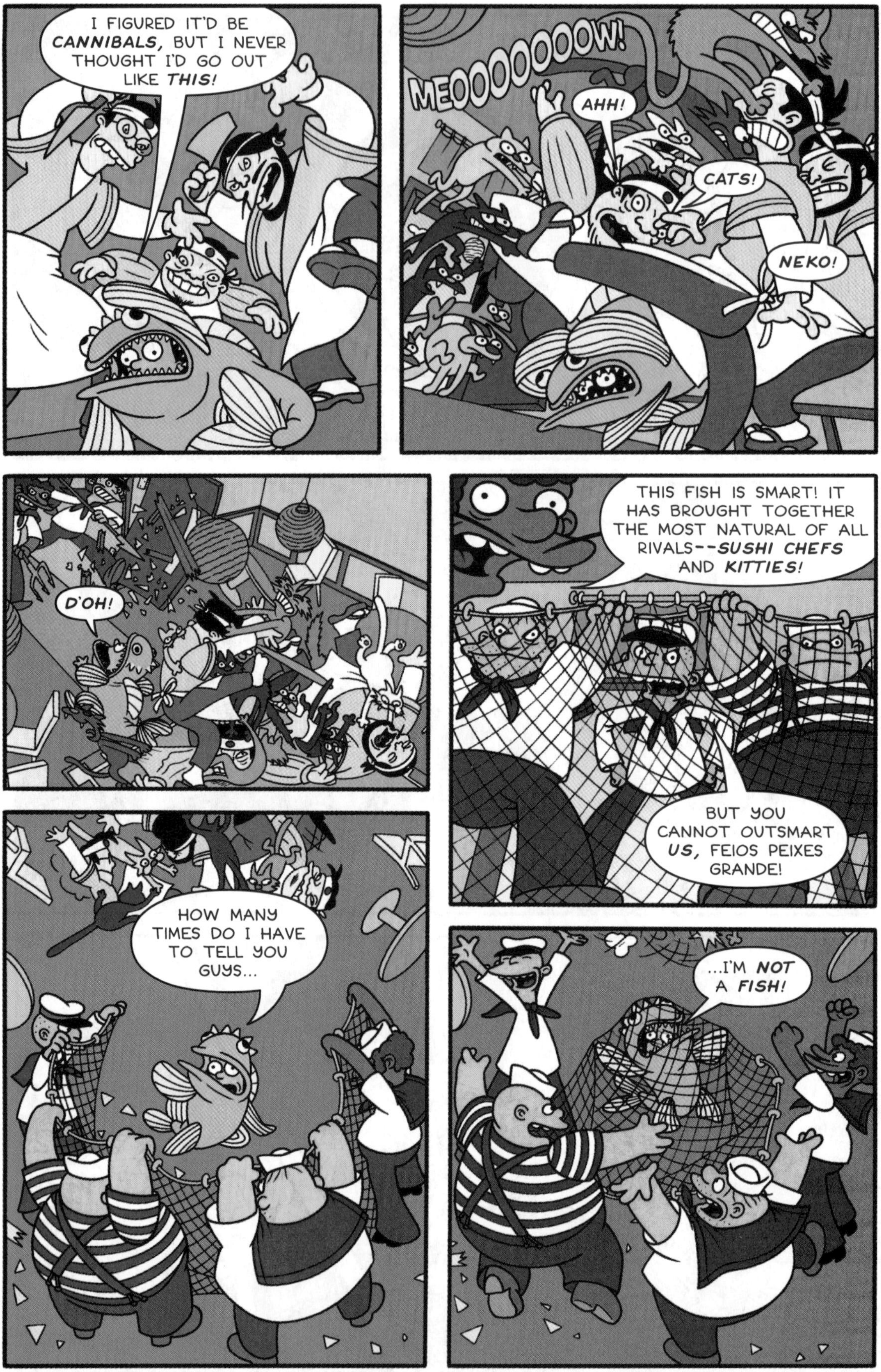
I FIGURED IT'D BE CANNIBALS, BUT I NEVER THOUGHT I'D GO OUT LIKE THIS!
MEOOOOOOOW!
AHH!
CATS!
NEKO!
D'OH!
THIS FISH IS SMART! IT HAS BROUGHT TOGETHER THE MOST NATURAL OF ALL RIVALS--SUSHI CHEFS AND KITTIES!
BUT YOU CANNOT OUTSMART US, FEIOS PEIXES GRANDE!
HOW MANY TIMES DO I HAVE TO TELL YOU GUYS...
...I'M NOT A FISH!

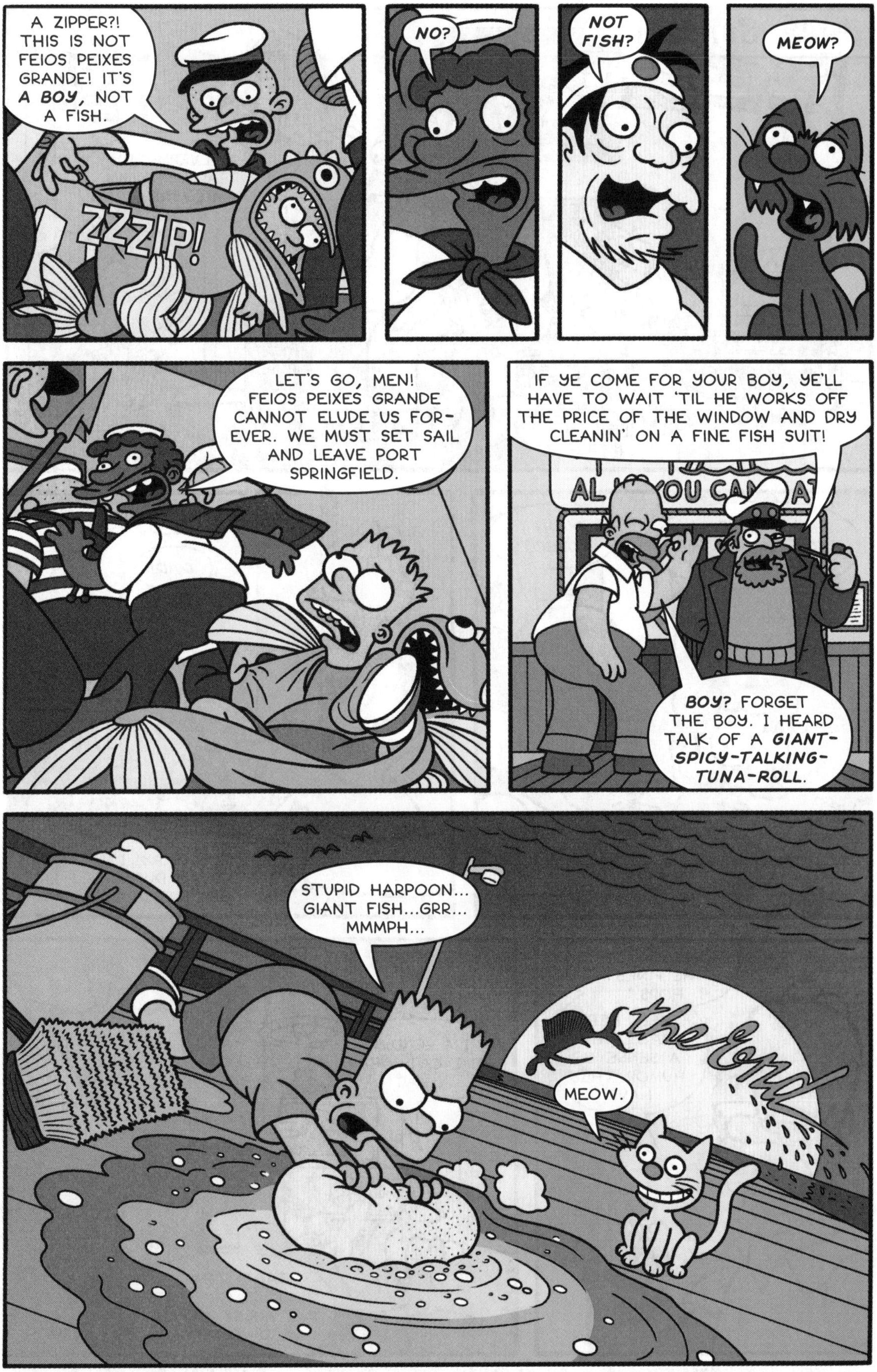

A ZIPPER?! THIS IS NOT FEIOS PEIXES GRANDE! IT'S A *BOY*, NOT A FISH.
ZZZIP!
NO?
NOT FISH?
MEOW?
LET'S GO, MEN! FEIOS PEIXES GRANDE CANNOT ELUDE US FOR-EVER. WE MUST SET SAIL AND LEAVE PORT SPRINGFIELD.
IF YE COME FOR YOUR BOY, YE'LL HAVE TO WAIT 'TIL HE WORKS OFF THE PRICE OF THE WINDOW AND DRY CLEANIN' ON A FINE FISH SUIT!
BOY? FORGET THE BOY. I HEARD TALK OF A *GIANT-SPICY-TALKING-TUNA-ROLL*.
STUPID HARPOON... GIANT FISH...GRR... MMMPH...
the end
MEOW.

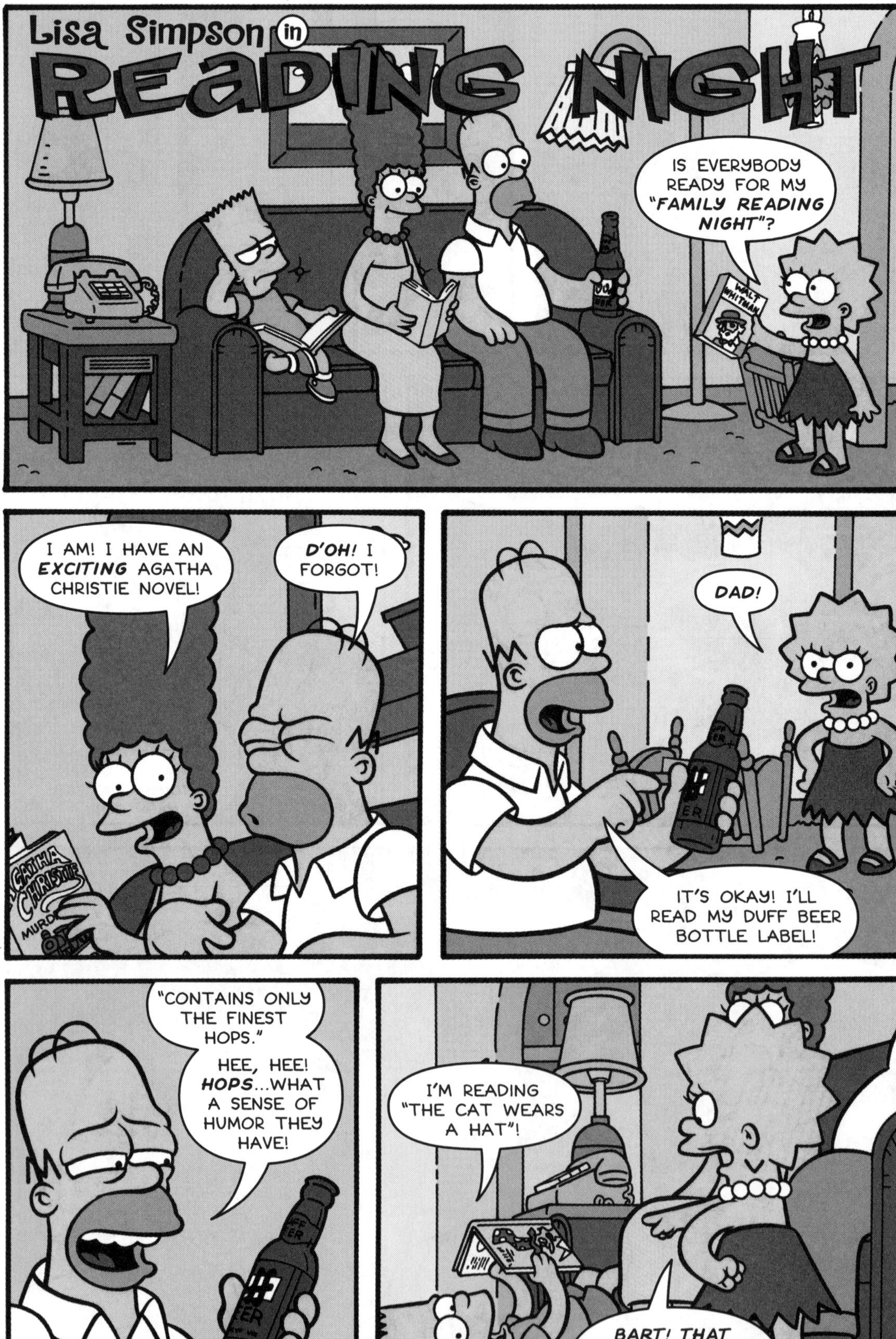
Lisa Simpson in
READING NIGHT
IS EVERYBODY READY FOR MY "FAMILY READING NIGHT"?
WALT WHITMAN
I AM! I HAVE AN EXCITING AGATHA CHRISTIE NOVEL!
D'OH! I FORGOT!
AGATHA CHRISTIE
DAD!
IT'S OKAY! I'LL READ MY DUFF BEER BOTTLE LABEL!
"CONTAINS ONLY THE FINEST HOPS."
HEE, HEE! HOPS...WHAT A SENSE OF HUMOR THEY HAVE!
I'M READING "THE CAT WEARS A HAT"!
BART! THAT BOOK IS ONLY AT THE FIRST GRADE READING LEVEL!

EARL KRESS STORY | **JAMES LLOYD** PENCILS | **PATRICK OWSLEY** INKS | **ART VILLANUEVA** COLORS | **KAREN BATES** LETTERS | **BILL MORRISON** EDITOR

:GROAN: I DIDN'T THINK IT HAD *ANY* WORDS IN IT! I WAS JUST GONNA LOOK AT THE *PICTURES!*

GRRR!! WOULD YOU ALL RATHER *WATCH TV?*

YES!!

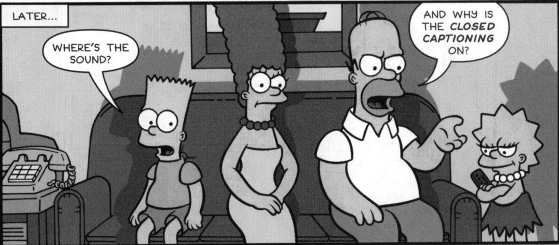

LATER...

WHERE'S THE SOUND?

AND WHY IS THE *CLOSED CAPTIONING* ON?

HEY! YOU'RE MAKING US *READ TV!* WHAT A GYP!

GIVE ME THAT REMOTE!

THE VIEWS OF LISA SIMPSON ARE HER OWN, AND DO NOT NECESSARILY REFLECT THOSE OF KRUSTILU STUDIOS, WHO WOULD LIKE TO REMIND YOU THAT THERE'S STILL *PLENTY* TO WATCH ON TELEVISION!

GIVE A HOOT! WATCH MY SHOW!

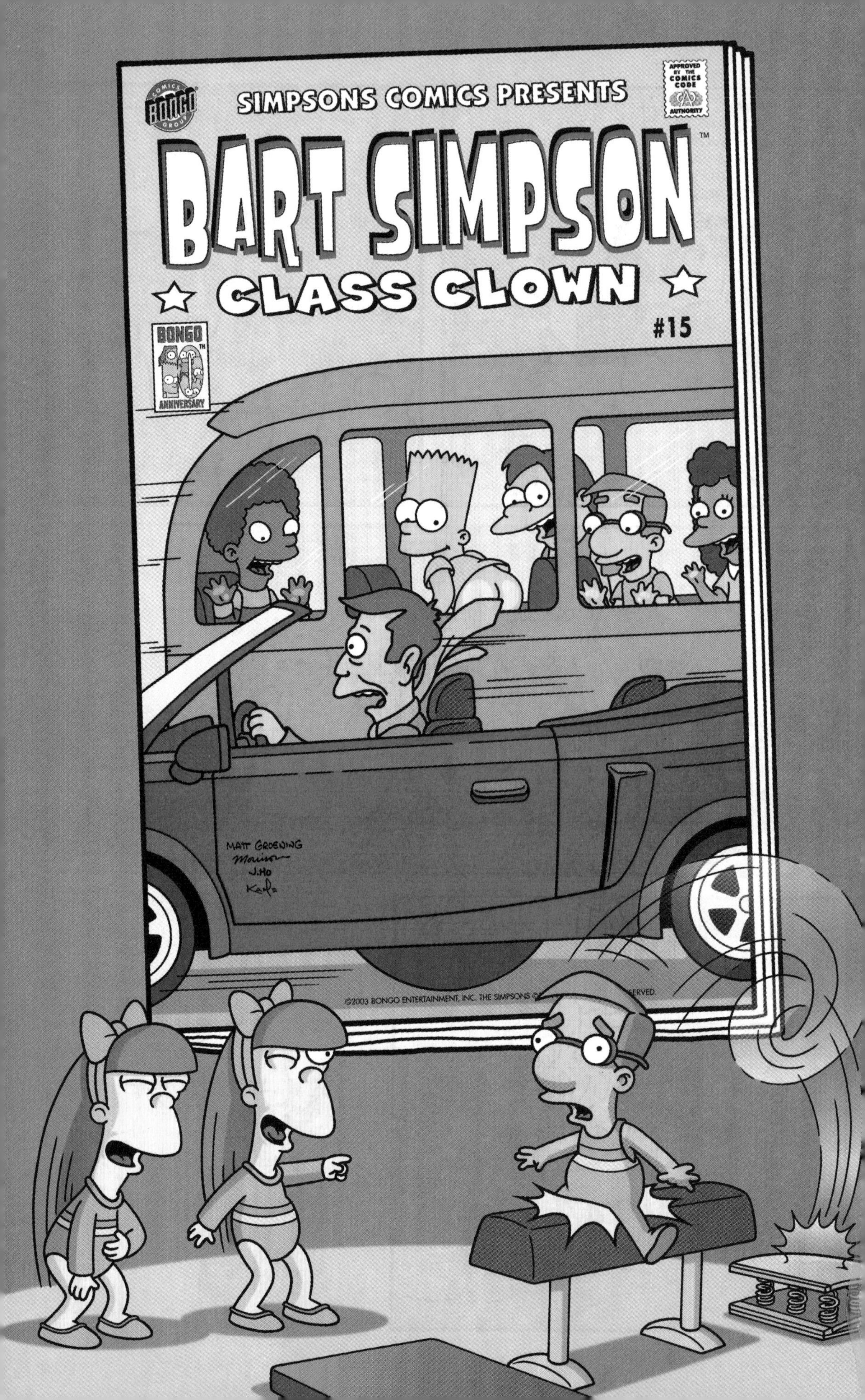
SIMPSONS COMICS PRESENTS
APPROVED BY THE COMICS CODE AUTHORITY
BART SIMPSON
CLASS CLOWN
#15
BONGO
ANNIVERSARY
MATT GROENING
J.HO
©2003 BONGO ENTERTAINMENT, INC. THE SIMPSONS

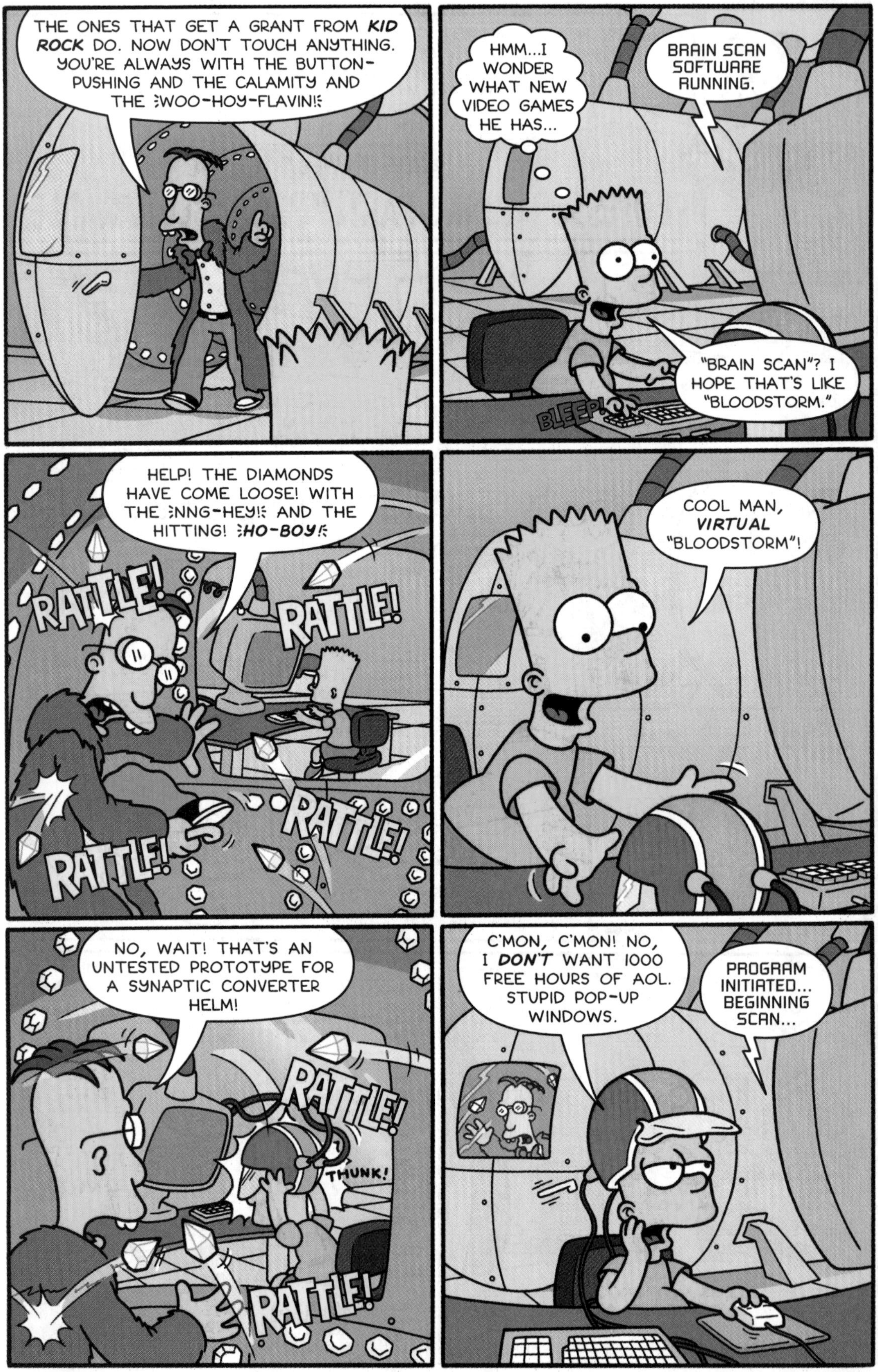

THE ONES THAT GET A GRANT FROM KID ROCK DO. NOW DON'T TOUCH ANYTHING. YOU'RE ALWAYS WITH THE BUTTON-PUSHING AND THE CALAMITY AND THE WOO-HOY-FLAVIN!
HMM...I WONDER WHAT NEW VIDEO GAMES HE HAS...
BRAIN SCAN SOFTWARE RUNNING.
"BRAIN SCAN"? I HOPE THAT'S LIKE "BLOODSTORM."
BLEEP!
HELP! THE DIAMONDS HAVE COME LOOSE! WITH THE NNG-HEY! AND THE HITTING! HO-BOY!
RATTLE!
RATTLE!
RATTLE!
RATTLE!
COOL MAN, VIRTUAL "BLOODSTORM"!
NO, WAIT! THAT'S AN UNTESTED PROTOTYPE FOR A SYNAPTIC CONVERTER HELM!
RATTLE!
THUNK!
RATTLE!
C'MON, C'MON! NO, I DON'T WANT 1000 FREE HOURS OF AOL. STUPID POP-UP WINDOWS.
PROGRAM INITIATED... BEGINNING SCAN...

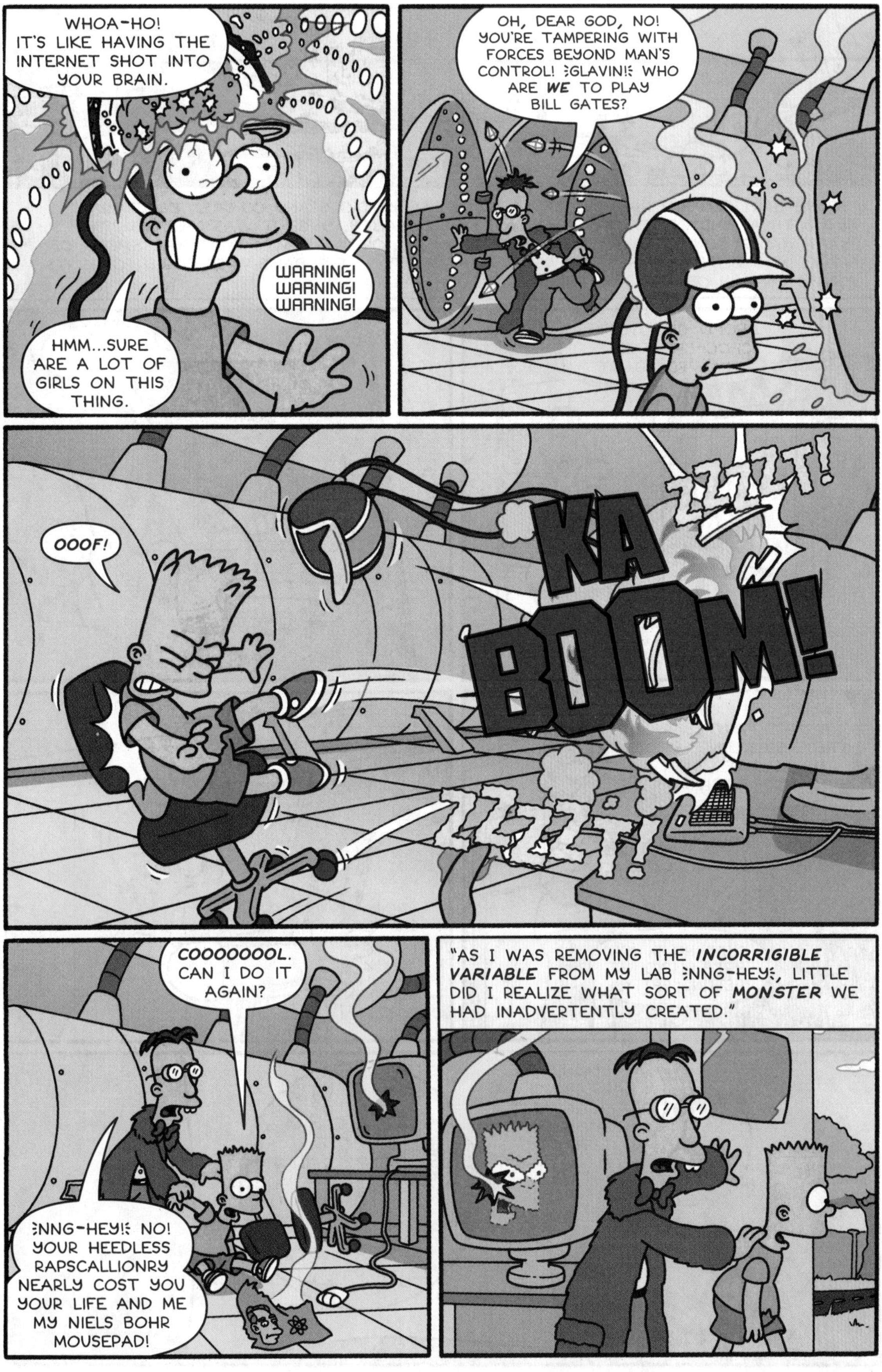
WHOA-HO! IT'S LIKE HAVING THE INTERNET SHOT INTO YOUR BRAIN.
WARNING! WARNING! WARNING!
HMM...SURE ARE A LOT OF GIRLS ON THIS THING.
OH, DEAR GOD, NO! YOU'RE TAMPERING WITH FORCES BEYOND MAN'S CONTROL! GLAVIN! WHO ARE *WE* TO PLAY BILL GATES?
OOOF!
KA BOOM!
ZZZZT!
ZZZZT!
COOOOOOOL. CAN I DO IT AGAIN?
NNG-HEY! NO! YOUR HEEDLESS RAPSCALLIONRY NEARLY COST YOU YOUR LIFE AND ME MY NIELS BOHR MOUSEPAD!
"AS I WAS REMOVING THE *INCORRIGIBLE VARIABLE* FROM MY LAB NNG-HEY, LITTLE DID I REALIZE WHAT SORT OF *MONSTER* WE HAD INADVERTENTLY CREATED."

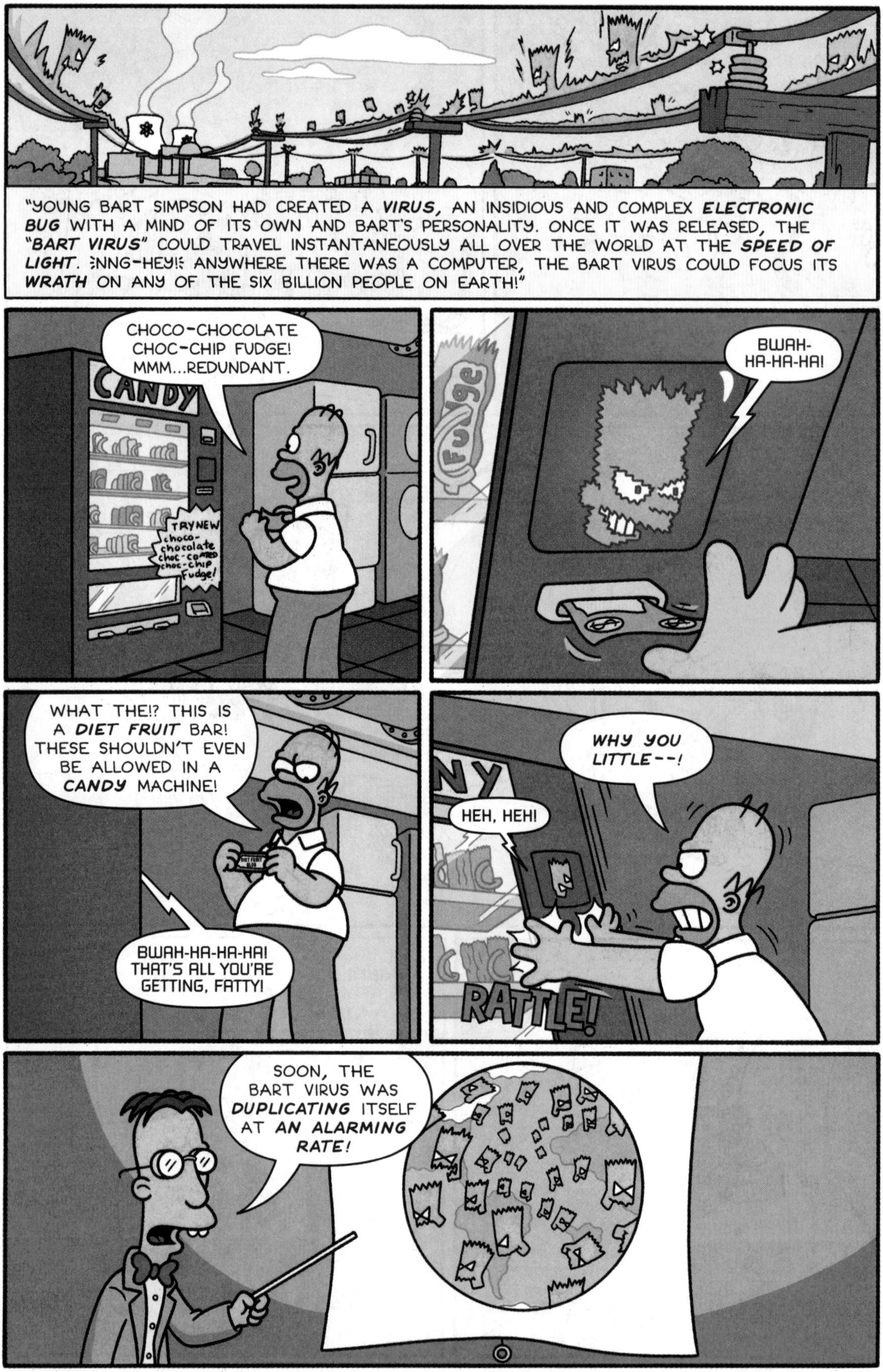
"YOUNG BART SIMPSON HAD CREATED A VIRUS, AN INSIDIOUS AND COMPLEX ELECTRONIC BUG WITH A MIND OF ITS OWN AND BART'S PERSONALITY. ONCE IT WAS RELEASED, THE "BART VIRUS" COULD TRAVEL INSTANTANEOUSLY ALL OVER THE WORLD AT THE SPEED OF LIGHT. ⁝NNG-HEY!⁝ ANYWHERE THERE WAS A COMPUTER, THE BART VIRUS COULD FOCUS ITS WRATH ON ANY OF THE SIX BILLION PEOPLE ON EARTH!"
CANDY
CHOCO-CHOCOLATE CHOC-CHIP FUDGE! MMM...REDUNDANT.
TRY NEW choco-chocolate choc-coated choc-chip Fudge!
Fudge
BWAH-HA-HA-HA!
WHAT THE!? THIS IS A DIET FRUIT BAR! THESE SHOULDN'T EVEN BE ALLOWED IN A CANDY MACHINE!
BWAH-HA-HA-HA! THAT'S ALL YOU'RE GETTING, FATTY!
WHY YOU LITTLE--!
HEH, HEH!
RATTLE!
SOON, THE BART VIRUS WAS DUPLICATING ITSELF AT AN ALARMING RATE!

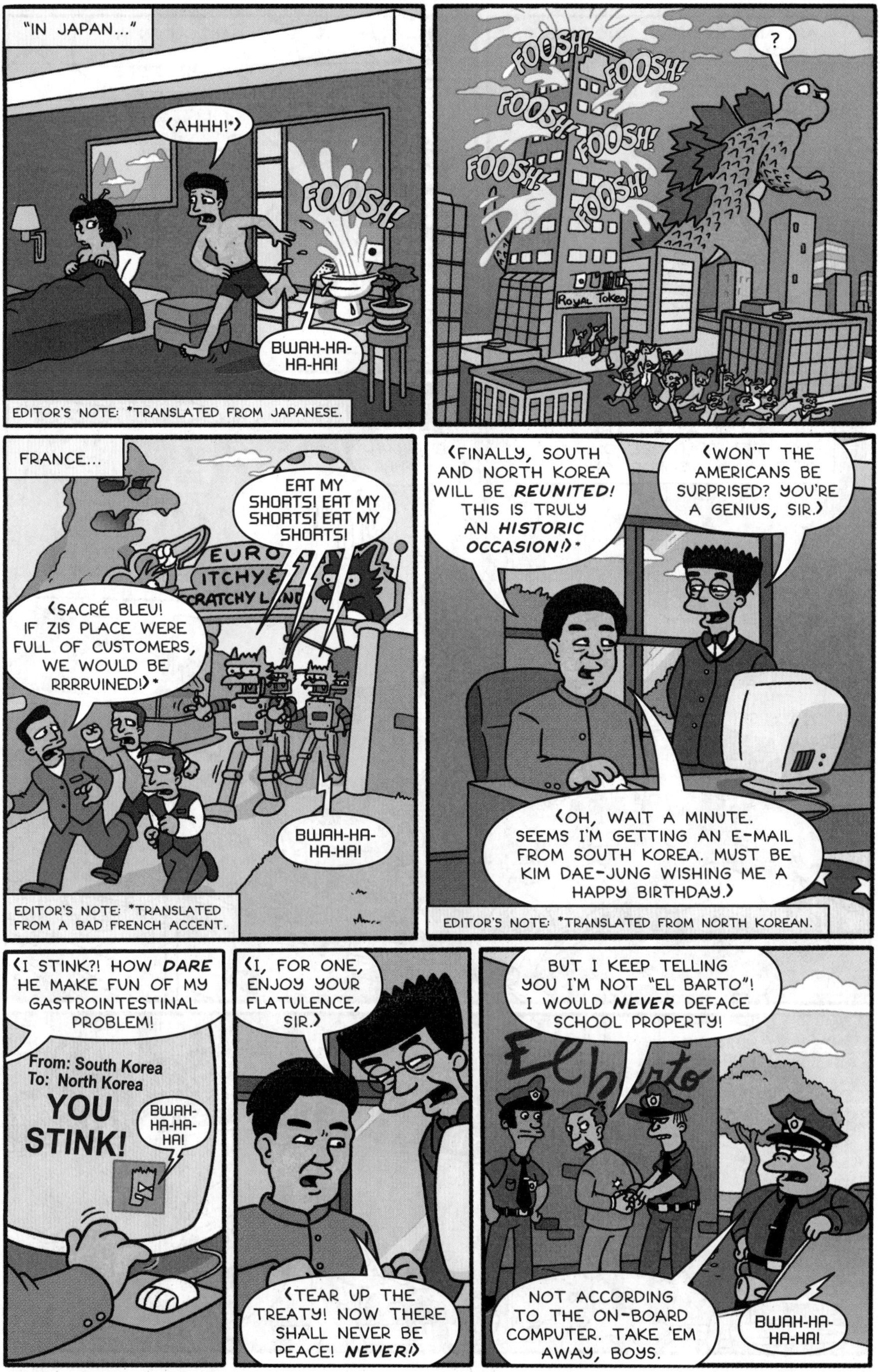
"IN JAPAN..."
‹AHHH!*›
FOOSH!
BWAH-HA-HA-HA!
EDITOR'S NOTE: *TRANSLATED FROM JAPANESE.
FOOSH! FOOSH! FOOSH! FOOSH! FOOSH! FOOSH!
?
Royal Tokeo
FRANCE...
EAT MY SHORTS! EAT MY SHORTS! EAT MY SHORTS!
EURO ITCHY & SCRATCHY LAND
‹SACRÉ BLEU! IF ZIS PLACE WERE FULL OF CUSTOMERS, WE WOULD BE RRRRUINED!›*
BWAH-HA-HA-HA!
EDITOR'S NOTE: *TRANSLATED FROM A BAD FRENCH ACCENT.
‹FINALLY, SOUTH AND NORTH KOREA WILL BE ***REUNITED***! THIS IS TRULY AN ***HISTORIC OCCASION***!›*
‹WON'T THE AMERICANS BE SURPRISED? YOU'RE A GENIUS, SIR.›
‹OH, WAIT A MINUTE. SEEMS I'M GETTING AN E-MAIL FROM SOUTH KOREA. MUST BE KIM DAE-JUNG WISHING ME A HAPPY BIRTHDAY.›
EDITOR'S NOTE: *TRANSLATED FROM NORTH KOREAN.
‹I STINK?! HOW ***DARE*** HE MAKE FUN OF MY GASTROINTESTINAL PROBLEM!
From: South Korea
To: North Korea
YOU STINK!
BWAH-HA-HA-HA!
‹I, FOR ONE, ENJOY YOUR FLATULENCE, SIR.›
‹TEAR UP THE TREATY! NOW THERE SHALL NEVER BE PEACE! ***NEVER!***›
BUT I KEEP TELLING YOU I'M NOT "EL BARTO"! I WOULD ***NEVER*** DEFACE SCHOOL PROPERTY!
El Barto
NOT ACCORDING TO THE ON-BOARD COMPUTER. TAKE 'EM AWAY, BOYS.
BWAH-HA-HA-HA!

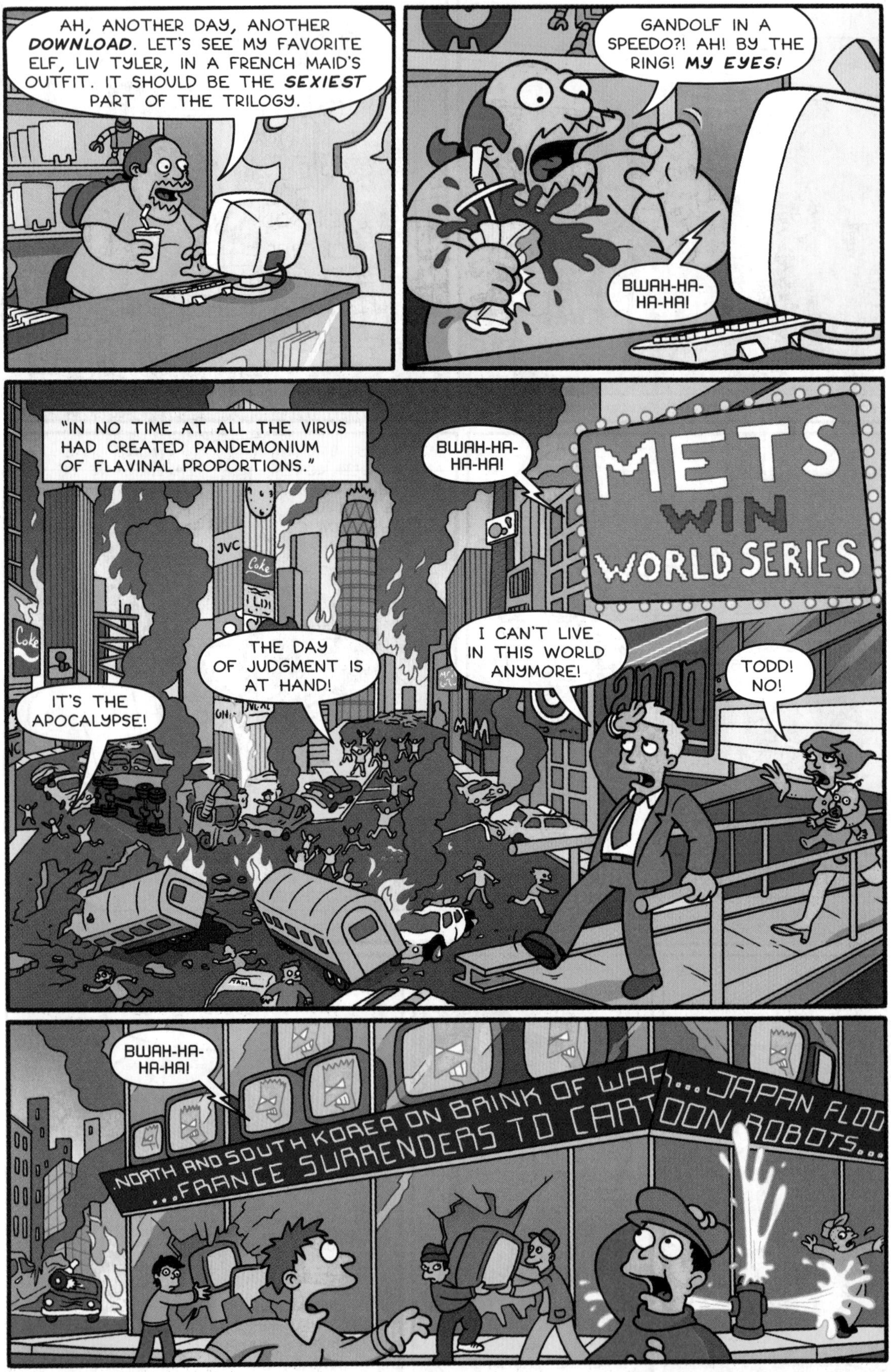
AH, ANOTHER DAY, ANOTHER **DOWNLOAD**. LET'S SEE MY FAVORITE ELF, LIV TYLER, IN A FRENCH MAID'S OUTFIT. IT SHOULD BE THE ***SEXIEST*** PART OF THE TRILOGY.
GANDOLF IN A SPEEDO?! AH! BY THE RING! ***MY EYES!***
BWAH-HA-HA-HA!
"IN NO TIME AT ALL THE VIRUS HAD CREATED PANDEMONIUM OF FLAVINAL PROPORTIONS."
BWAH-HA-HA-HA!
METS WIN WORLD SERIES
JVC
Coke
THE DAY OF JUDGMENT IS AT HAND!
I CAN'T LIVE IN THIS WORLD ANYMORE!
TODD! NO!
IT'S THE APOCALYPSE!
BWAH-HA-HA-HA!
NORTH AND SOUTH KOREA ON BRINK OF WAR...JAPAN FLOO
...FRANCE SURRENDERS TO CARTOON ROBOTS...

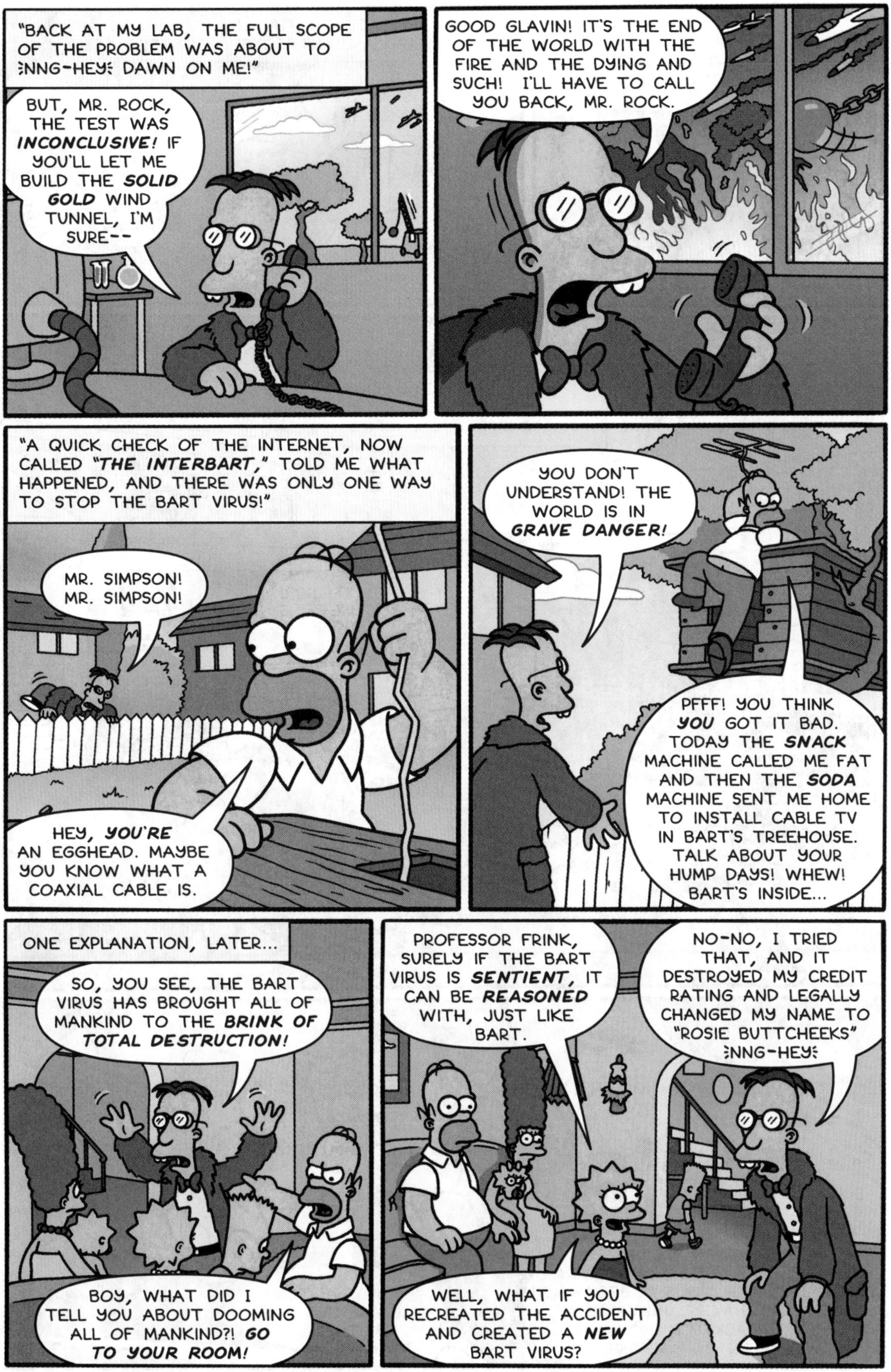
"BACK AT MY LAB, THE FULL SCOPE OF THE PROBLEM WAS ABOUT TO ⁝NNG-HEY⁝ DAWN ON ME!"
BUT, MR. ROCK, THE TEST WAS INCONCLUSIVE! IF YOU'LL LET ME BUILD THE SOLID GOLD WIND TUNNEL, I'M SURE--
GOOD GLAVIN! IT'S THE END OF THE WORLD WITH THE FIRE AND THE DYING AND SUCH! I'LL HAVE TO CALL YOU BACK, MR. ROCK.
"A QUICK CHECK OF THE INTERNET, NOW CALLED "THE INTERBART," TOLD ME WHAT HAPPENED, AND THERE WAS ONLY ONE WAY TO STOP THE BART VIRUS!"
MR. SIMPSON! MR. SIMPSON!
HEY, YOU'RE AN EGGHEAD. MAYBE YOU KNOW WHAT A COAXIAL CABLE IS.
YOU DON'T UNDERSTAND! THE WORLD IS IN GRAVE DANGER!
PFFF! YOU THINK YOU GOT IT BAD. TODAY THE SNACK MACHINE CALLED ME FAT AND THEN THE SODA MACHINE SENT ME HOME TO INSTALL CABLE TV IN BART'S TREEHOUSE. TALK ABOUT YOUR HUMP DAYS! WHEW! BART'S INSIDE...
ONE EXPLANATION, LATER...
SO, YOU SEE, THE BART VIRUS HAS BROUGHT ALL OF MANKIND TO THE BRINK OF TOTAL DESTRUCTION!
BOY, WHAT DID I TELL YOU ABOUT DOOMING ALL OF MANKIND?! GO TO YOUR ROOM!
PROFESSOR FRINK, SURELY IF THE BART VIRUS IS SENTIENT, IT CAN BE REASONED WITH, JUST LIKE BART.
WELL, WHAT IF YOU RECREATED THE ACCIDENT AND CREATED A NEW BART VIRUS?
NO-NO, I TRIED THAT, AND IT DESTROYED MY CREDIT RATING AND LEGALLY CHANGED MY NAME TO "ROSIE BUTTCHEEKS" ⁝NNG-HEY⁝

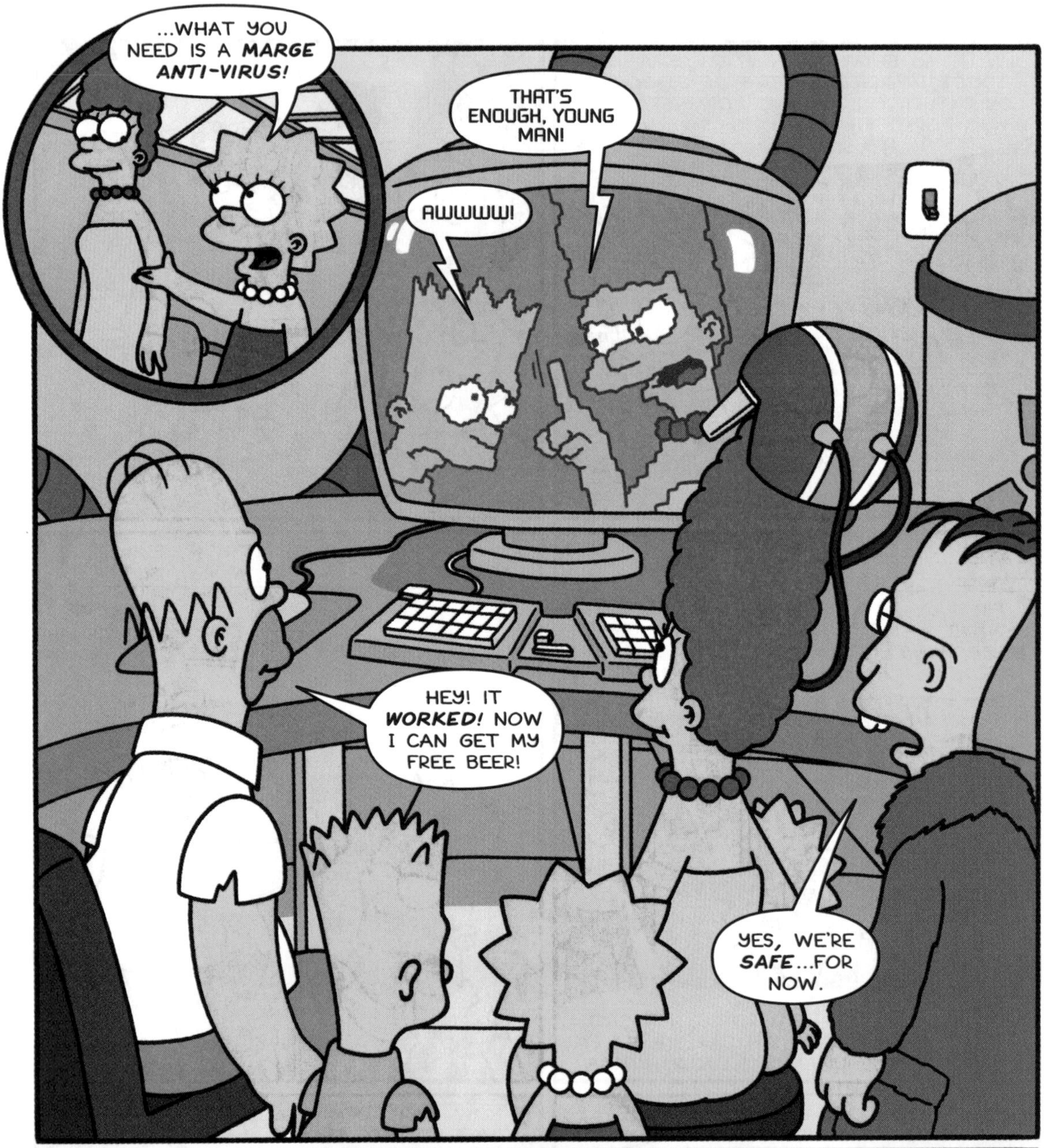
...WHAT YOU NEED IS A **MARGE ANTI-VIRUS!**
THAT'S ENOUGH, YOUNG MAN!
AWWWW!
HEY! IT **WORKED!** NOW I CAN GET MY FREE BEER!
YES, WE'RE **SAFE**...FOR NOW.

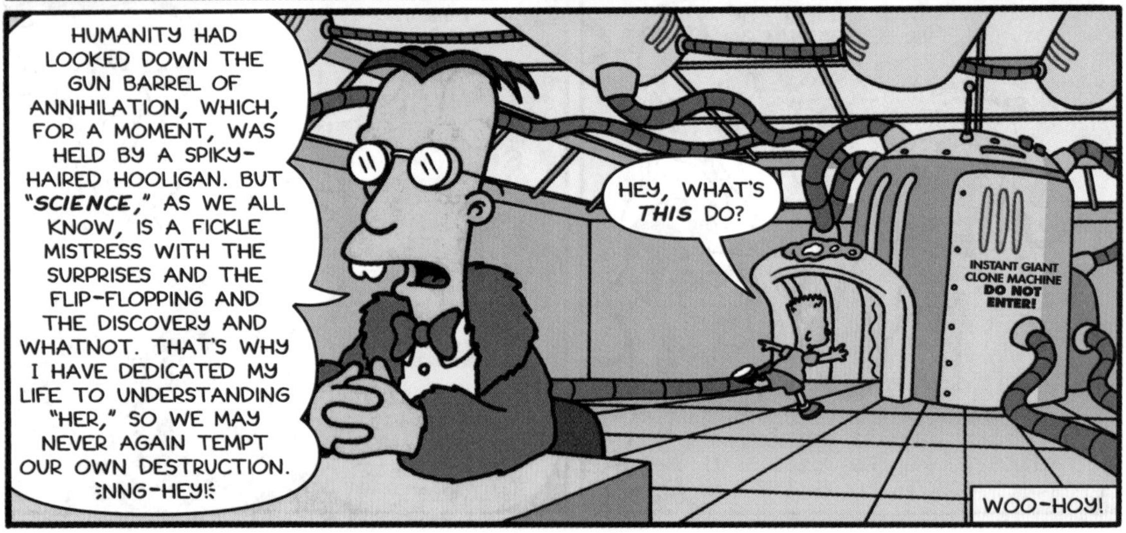
HUMANITY HAD LOOKED DOWN THE GUN BARREL OF ANNIHILATION, WHICH, FOR A MOMENT, WAS HELD BY A SPIKY-HAIRED HOOLIGAN. BUT "**SCIENCE,**" AS WE ALL KNOW, IS A FICKLE MISTRESS WITH THE SURPRISES AND THE FLIP-FLOPPING AND THE DISCOVERY AND WHATNOT. THAT'S WHY I HAVE DEDICATED MY LIFE TO UNDERSTANDING "HER," SO WE MAY NEVER AGAIN TEMPT OUR OWN DESTRUCTION. NNG-HEY!
HEY, WHAT'S **THIS** DO?
INSTANT GIANT CLONE MACHINE DO NOT ENTER!
WOO-HOY!

JESSE McCANN & SERAN WILLIAMS
STORY

BRIAN ILES
PENCILS

MIKE ROTE
INKS

CHRIS UNGAR
COLORS

KAREN BATES
LETTERS

BILL MORRISON
EDITOR

GEORGE GLADIR & ERIC ROGERS
STORY

MIKE WORLEY
PENCILS

MIKE ROTE
INKS

CHRIS UNGAR
COLORS

KAREN BATES
LETTERS

BILL MORRISON
EDITOR

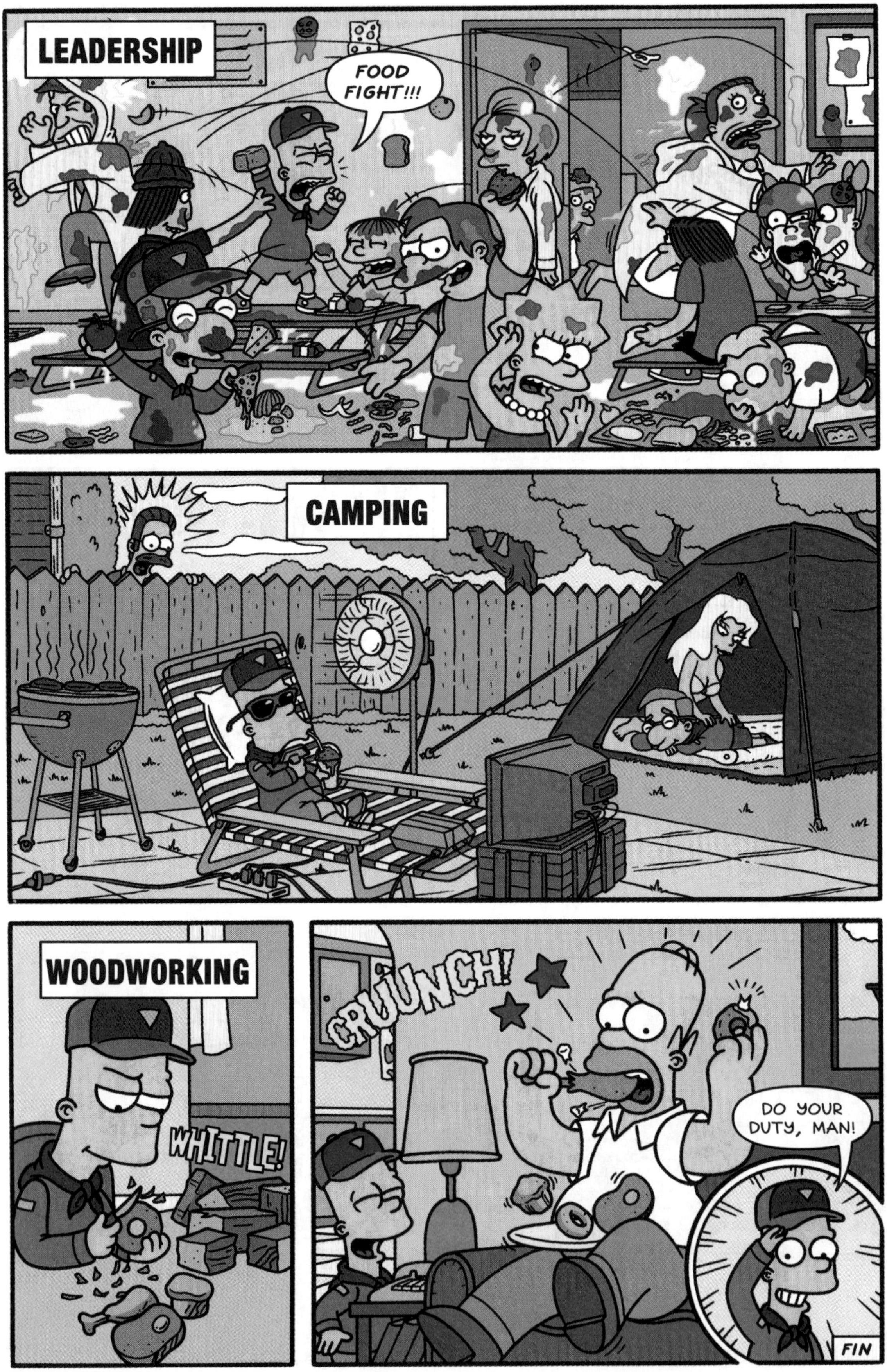
LEADERSHIP
FOOD FIGHT!!!
CAMPING
WOODWORKING
WHITTLE!
CRUUNCH!
DO YOUR DUTY, MAN!
FIN

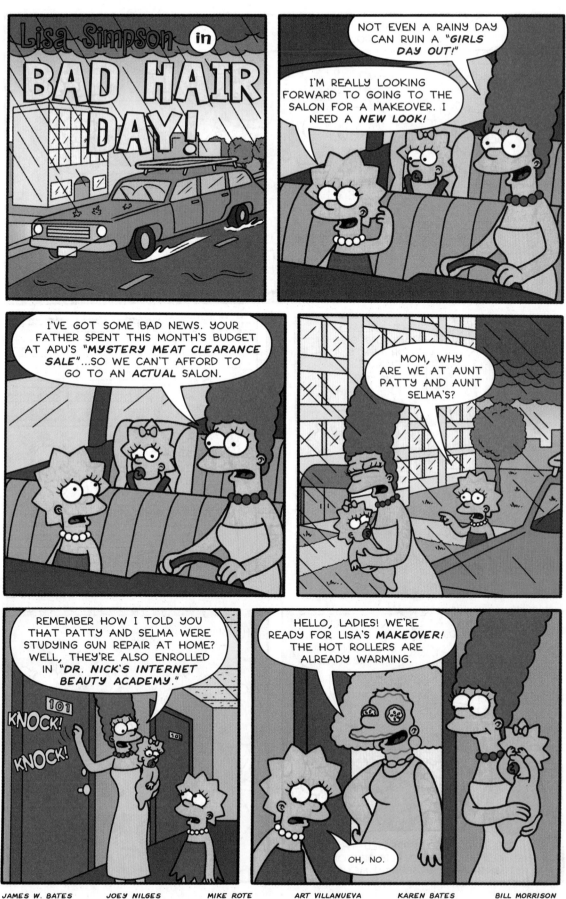

JAMES W. BATES
STORY

JOEY NILGES
PENCILS

MIKE ROTE
INKS

ART VILLANUEVA
COLORS

KAREN BATES
LETTERS

BILL MORRISON
EDITOR

JAMES W. BATES
STORY

JOEY NILGES
PENCILS

MIKE ROTE
INKS

ART VILLANUEVA
COLORS

KAREN BATES
LETTERS

BILL MORRISON
EDITOR

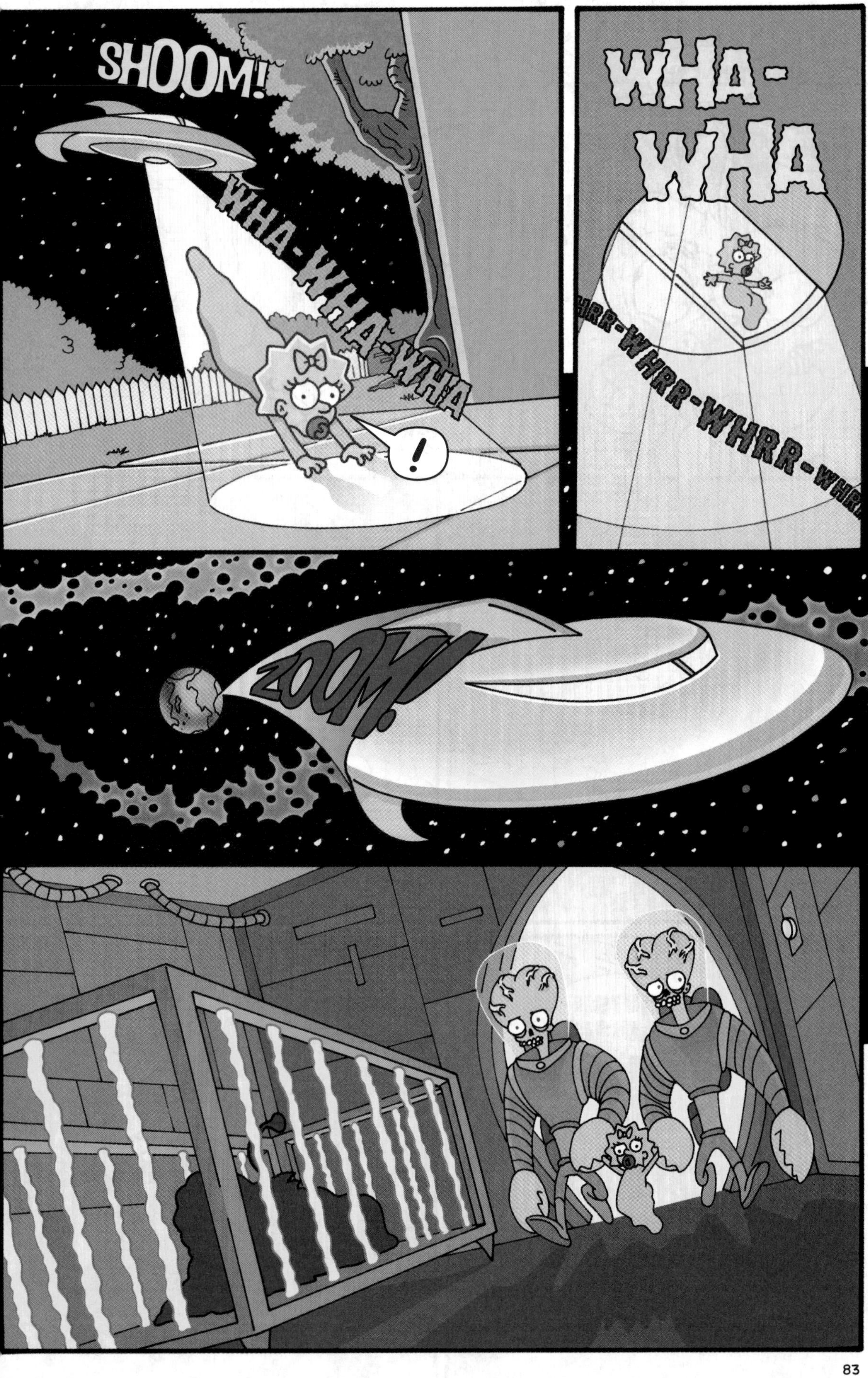
SHOOM!
WHA-WHA-WHA-WHA
!
WHA-WHA
HRR-WHRR-WHRR-WHR
ZOOM!

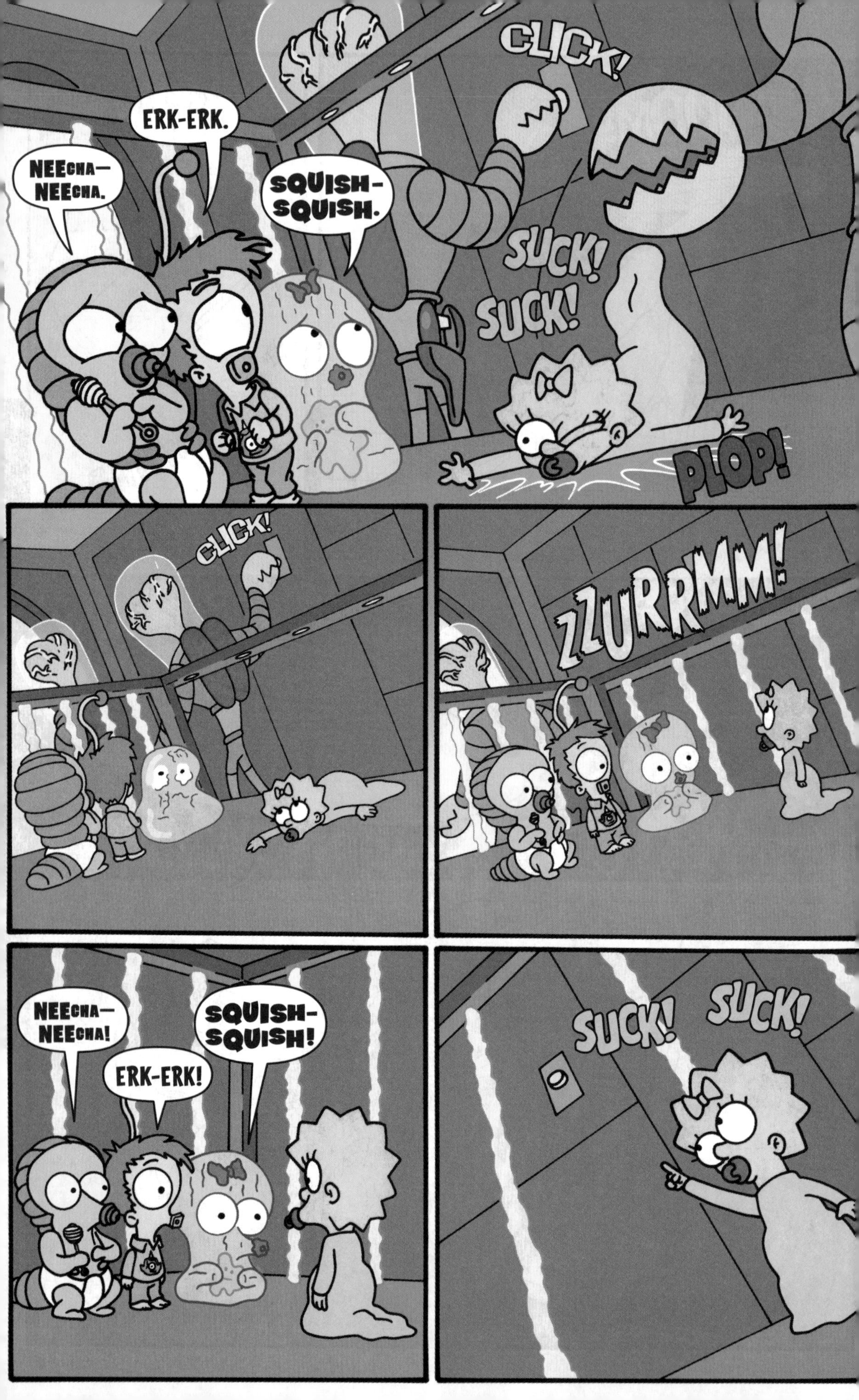

CLICK!
NEECHA—NEECHA.
ERK-ERK.
SQUISH-SQUISH.
SUCK!
SUCK!
PLOP!
CLICK!
ZZURRMM!
NEECHA—NEECHA!
ERK-ERK!
SQUISH-SQUISH!
SUCK!
SUCK!

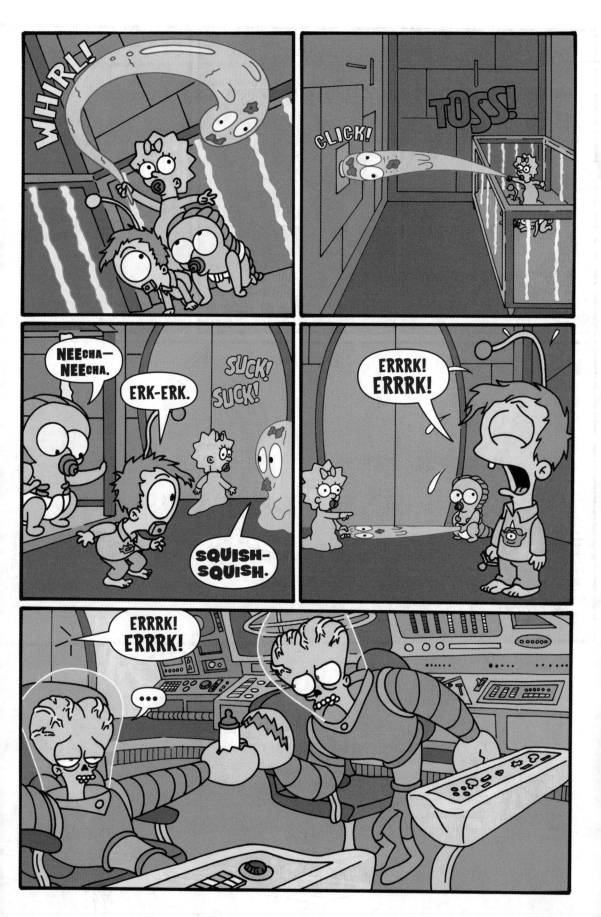

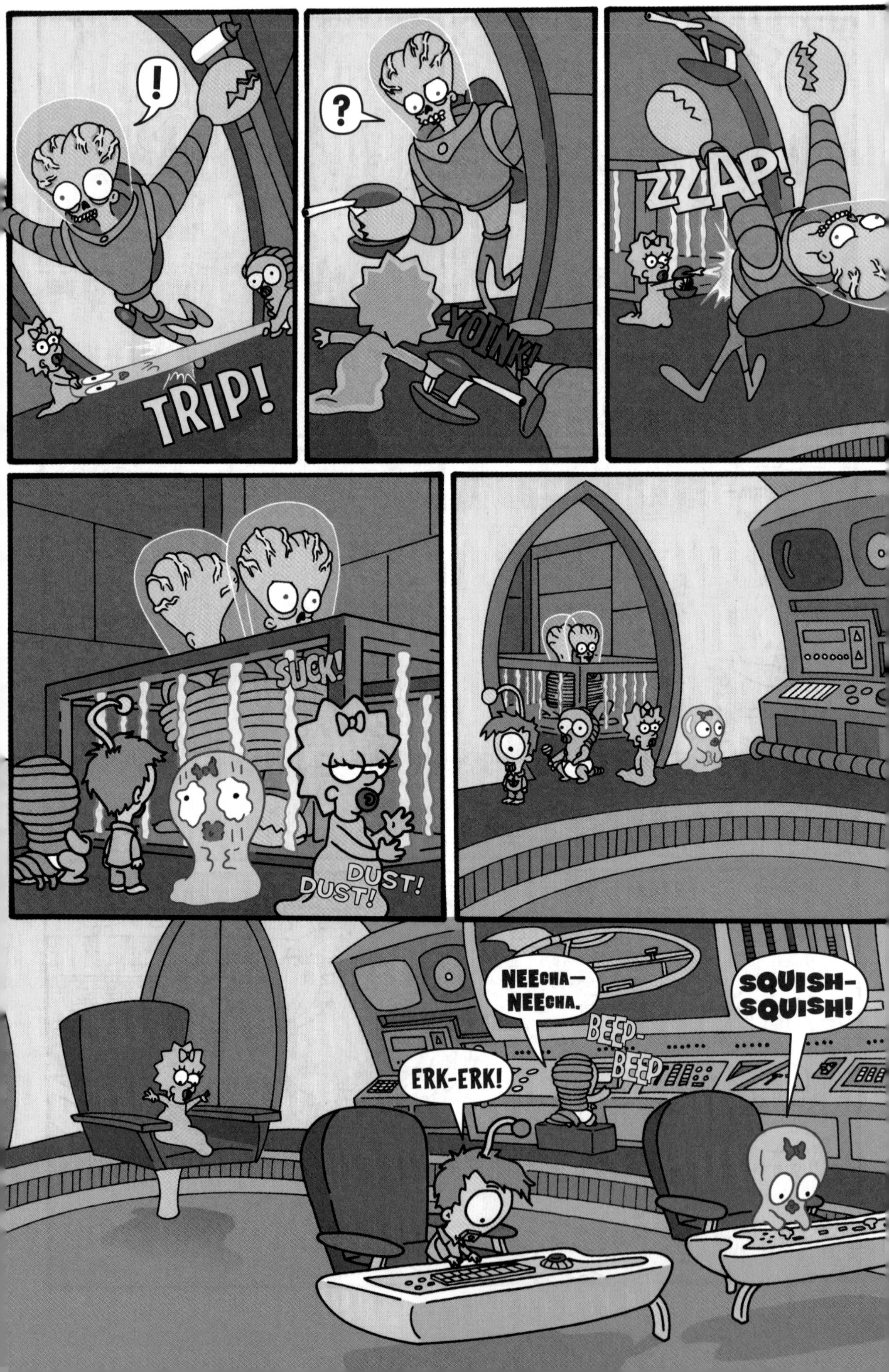
!
TRIP!
?
YOINK!
ZZAP!
SUCK!
DUST!
DUST!
NEECHA—
NEECHA.
SQUISH-
SQUISH!
BEEP-
BEEP
ERK-ERK!

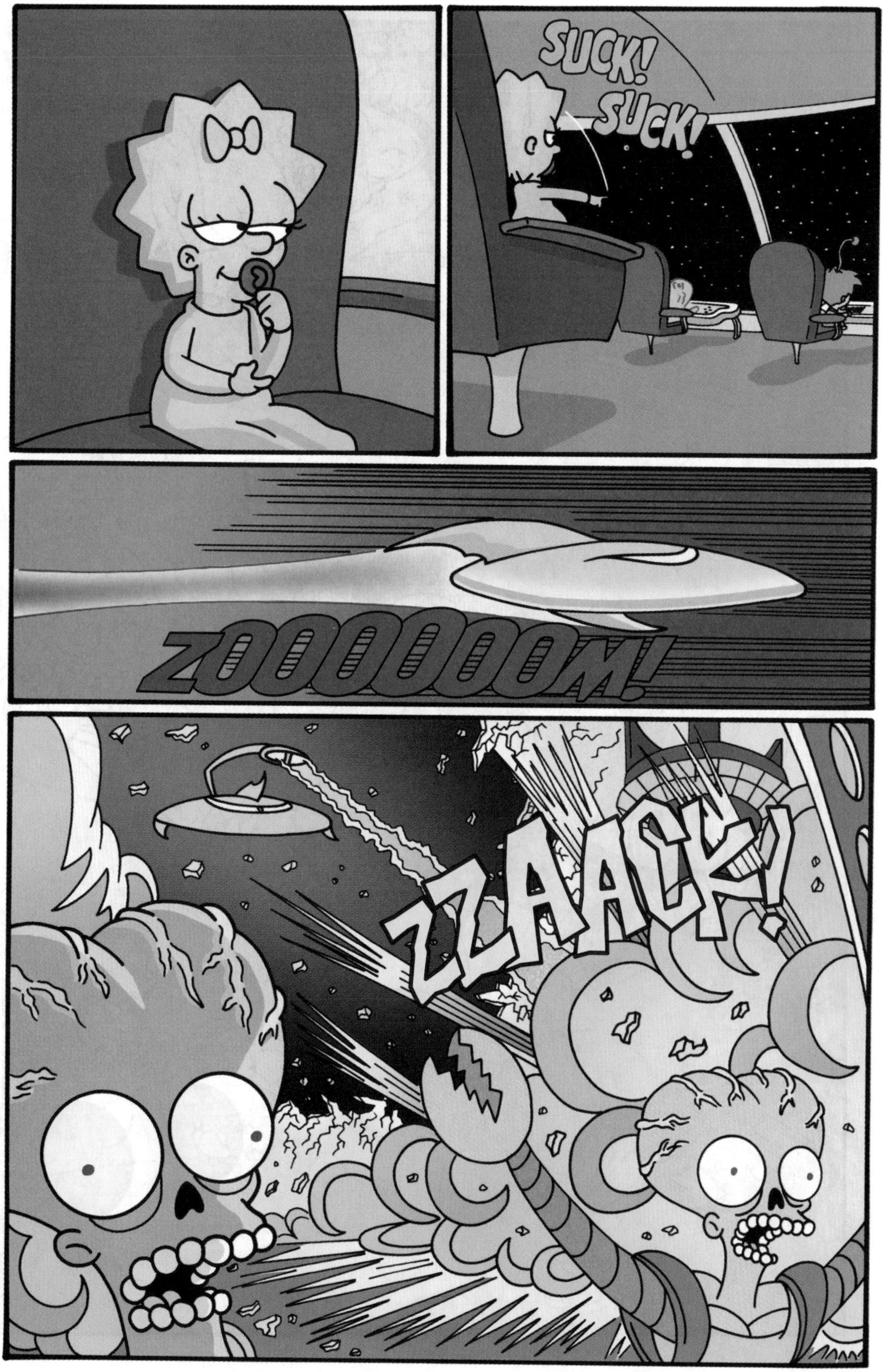
SUCK!
SUCK!
ZOOOOOOOM!
ZZAACK!

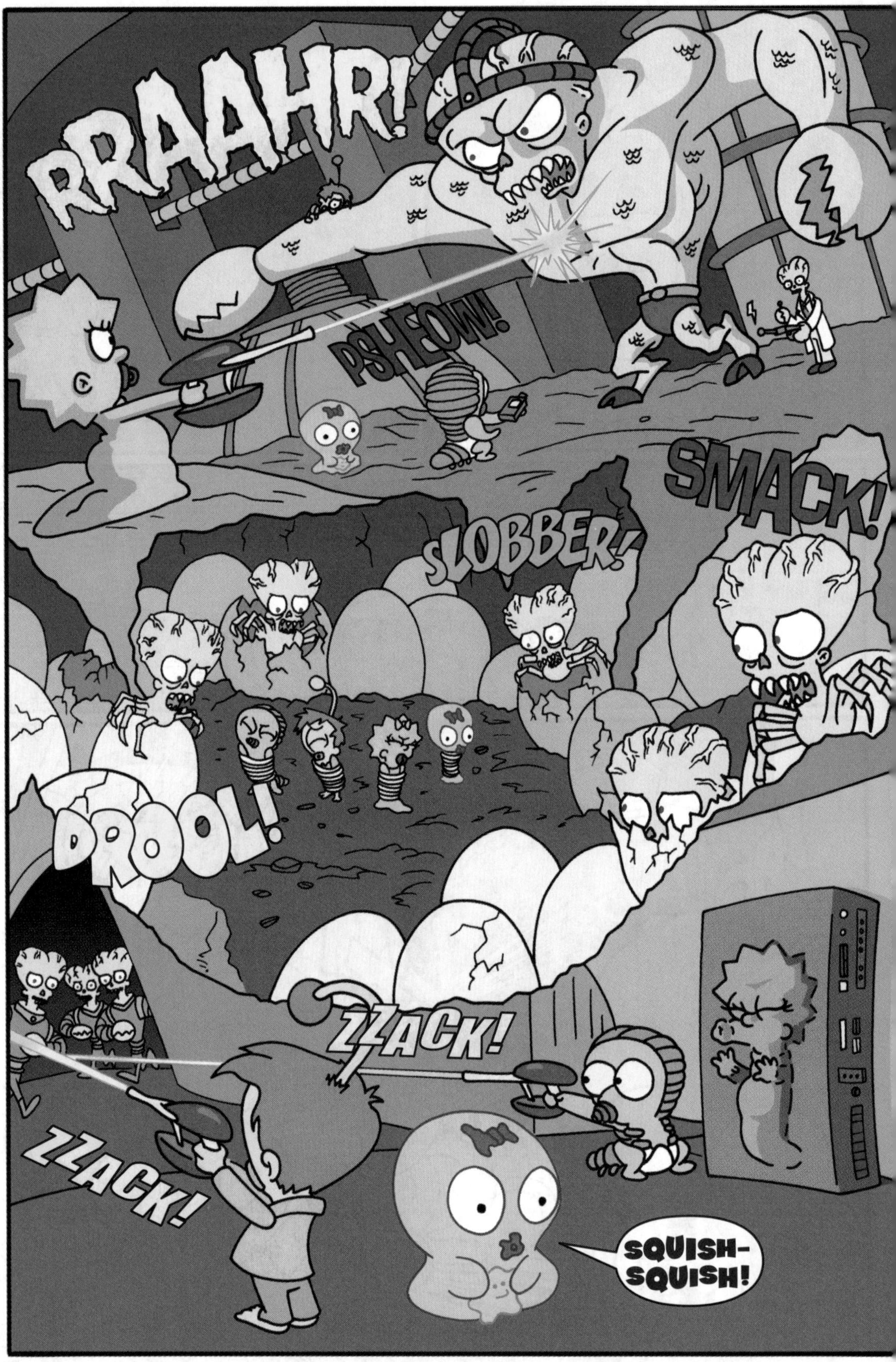
RRAAHR!
PSHEOW!
SMACK!
SLOBBER!
DROOL!
ZZACK!
ZZACK!
SQUISH-SQUISH!

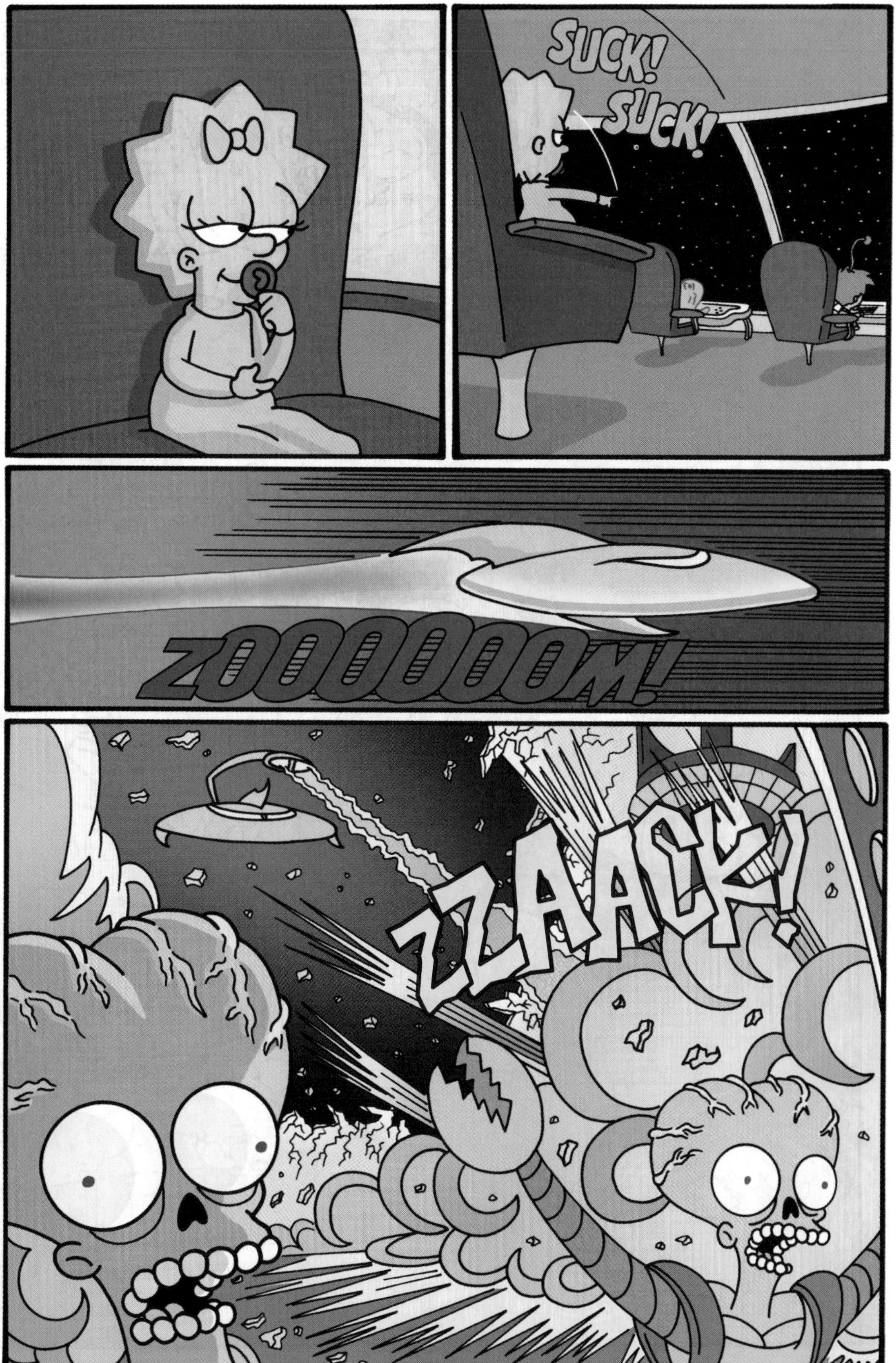
SUCK!
SUCK!
ZOOOOOOOM!
ZZAACK!

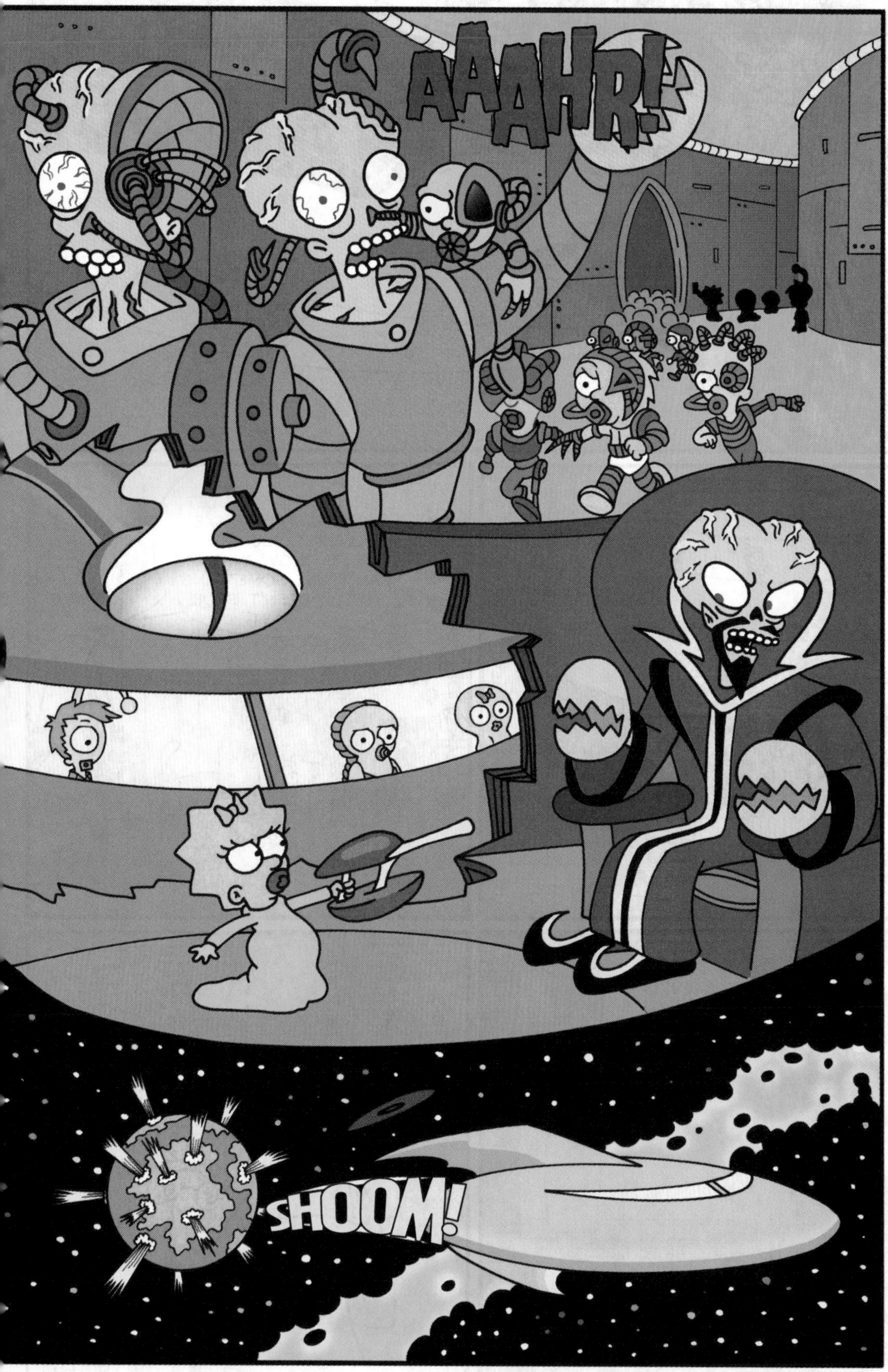
AAAHR!
SHOOM!

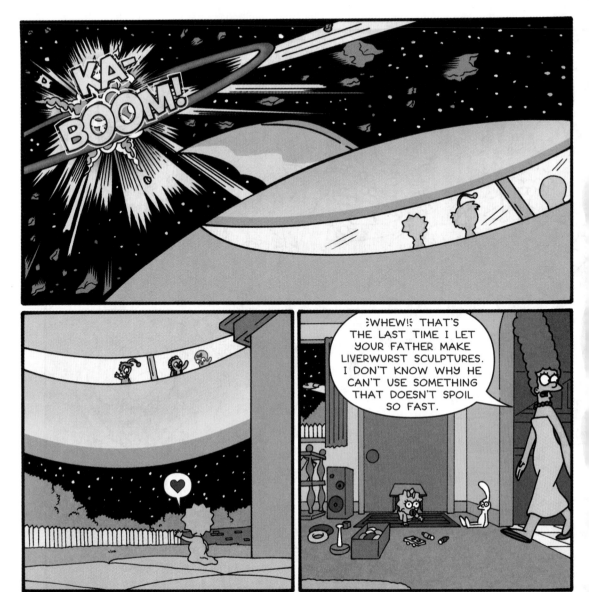

:WHEW!: THAT'S THE LAST TIME I LET YOUR FATHER MAKE LIVERWURST SCULPTURES. I DON'T KNOW WHY HE CAN'T USE SOMETHING THAT DOESN'T SPOIL SO FAST.

AW, ISN'T THAT CUTE? ALL TUCKERED OUT FROM PLAYING.

I SURE WISH *I* HAD AN EVENING THAT EASY!

THE END

93

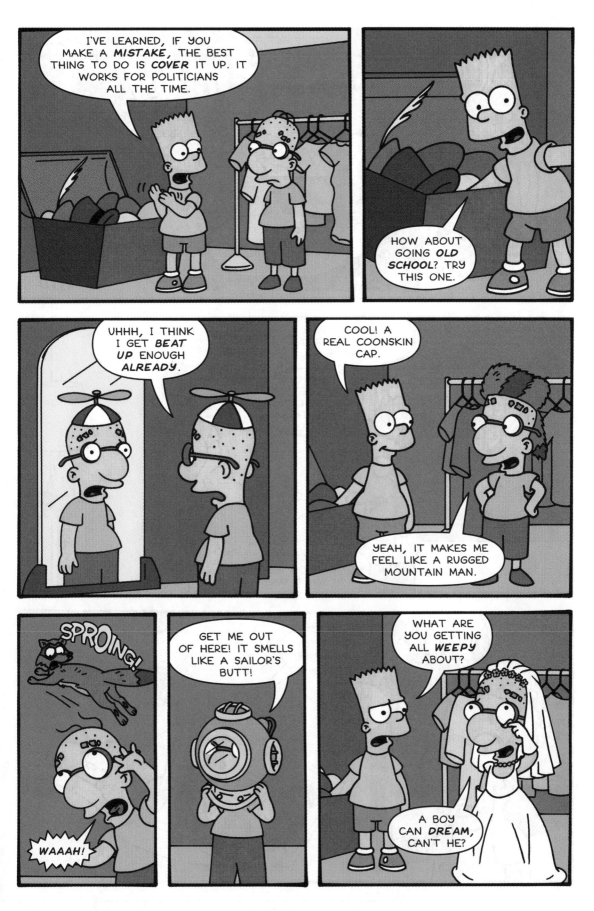

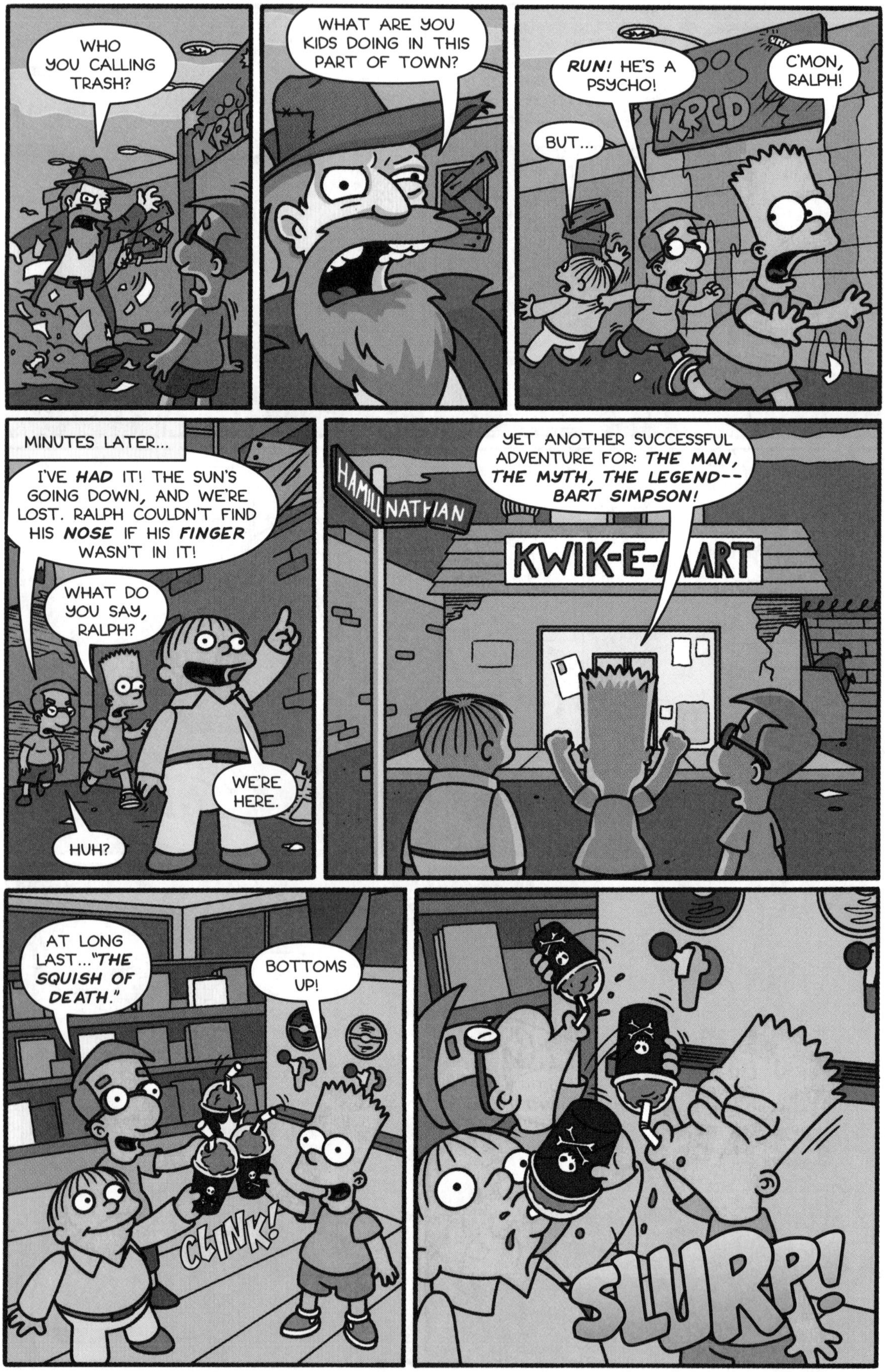
WHO YOU CALLING TRASH?
WHAT ARE YOU KIDS DOING IN THIS PART OF TOWN?
RUN! HE'S A PSYCHO!
BUT...
C'MON, RALPH!
KPLD
MINUTES LATER...
I'VE HAD IT! THE SUN'S GOING DOWN, AND WE'RE LOST. RALPH COULDN'T FIND HIS NOSE IF HIS FINGER WASN'T IN IT!
WHAT DO YOU SAY, RALPH?
WE'RE HERE.
HUH?
HAMILL
NATHAN
KWIK-E-MART
YET ANOTHER SUCCESSFUL ADVENTURE FOR: THE MAN, THE MYTH, THE LEGEND--BART SIMPSON!
AT LONG LAST..."THE SQUISH OF DEATH."
BOTTOMS UP!
CLINK!
SLURP!

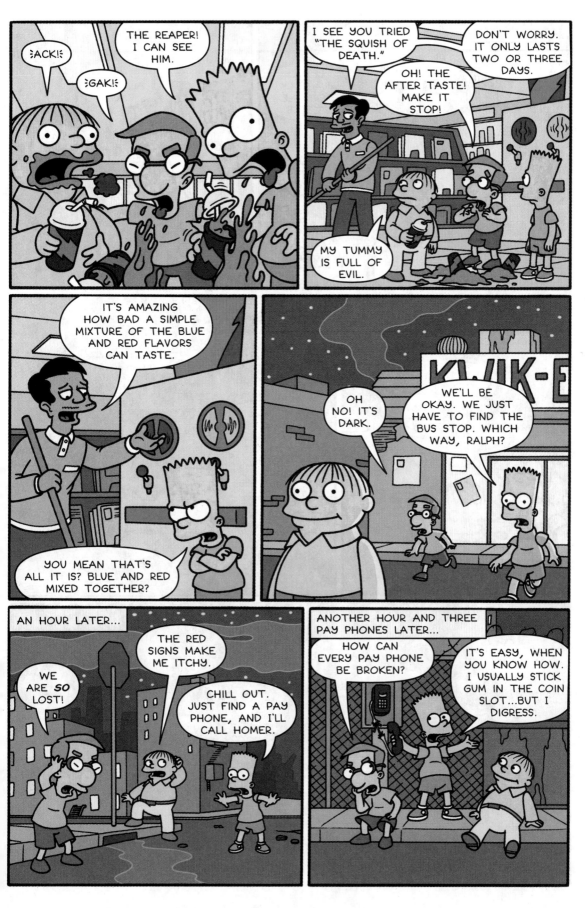

EARL KRESS
TERRY DELEGEANE
SCRIPT

PHIL ORTIZ
PENCILS

PATRICK OWSLEY
INKS

ART VILLANUEVA
COLORS

KAREN BATES
LETTERS

BILL MORRISON
EDITOR

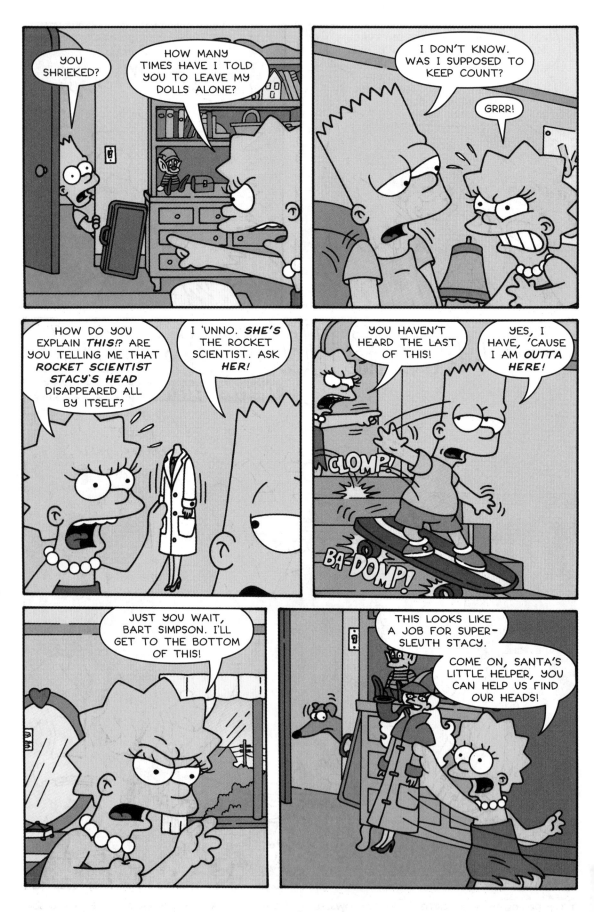

BRYAN UHLENBROCK
SCRIPT

JOEY NILGES
PENCILS

PHYLLIS NOVIN
INKS

ART VILLANUEVA
COLORS

KAREN BATES
LETTERS

BILL MORRISON
EDITOR